Ghosts of the Black Rose

MAGIC PROSE Publishing
http://magicprose.com/publisher
publisher@magicprose.com

ISBN: 1-4820-3393-3
ISBN-13: 9781482033939
Library of Congress Control Number: 2013901414
CreateSpace, North Charleston SC

Ghosts of the Black Rose

Land of Enchantment # 2

Belinda Vasquez Garcia

Other books by Belinda Vasquez Garcia

The Witch Narratives Reincarnation (Land of Enchantment # 1)

Return of the Bones

For Robin, Luther, and Margit with all my love

Part One

Aftermath

One spark can change the world forever.

1

June 20, 1934
Madrid, New Mexico

What the beautician Marcelina left off her sign was that she was a witch, dispensing white magic. From the roof of her coal mining shack her ambitious sign dangled:

Eternal Beauty & Out of This World Health
Marcelina Martinez, Owner—kitchen beauty shop & spa

Marcelina was peasant-like with large hands, thick neck and face puffed even more by pregnancy. She rubbed her aching back and lay on the bed for her daily nap, staring as she always did at a picture hanging on the wall of three witches. She had helped herself to the piece of artwork from the master bedroom of the house at the bottom of Witch Hill. Her best friend, Salia, looked out of the painting with haunted eyes—half-breed, third-generation witch and outcast. Salia had been her best friend since they were both twelve years old, and Marcelina loved her like the sister she never had.

In the picture, Salia held a doll that had just one arm. Salia appeared as helpless as her doll though she was a grown woman in the portrait. She was very pale because her mother, Felicita, was pinching her arm. Felicita's chin was up, defiant. Regal. With menacing eyes. But it was Salia's grandmother in the picture who arrested Marcelina as she stared, hypnotized, at the ordinary looking rock the Native American witch proudly held out in her hand—a piedra imán, a rare shapeshifting stone, allowing her to transform to a permanent teenager, while others around her age. Indeed, Felicita looking decades older, glared at her mother-in-law, her eyes green with envy. She seemed to pinch Salia harder as if it was her daughter's fault she looked her age and not eighteen years old, like La India. Salia's "teenage grandmother" was 130 years old when the picture was painted.

Marcelina would be twenty-two years of age come October. *But I look thirty-two. With the piedra imán I would never age. And I could be thin and lovely. Where did Salia hide her grandmother's magic rock?*

Marcelina drifted off to sleep, hugging her unborn child and dreaming of swimming in cream. She rose, holding an ugly rock, clenching the piedra imán and spinning until a lean and long-legged Marcelina emerged, clothed in a skinny, silky, red dress with a slim waist. Her coarse hair was smoothly bobbed and dyed silky, whitish-blonde. She no longer toiled in her kitchen beauty parlor because she was famous across America for perfecting the invention of hair dye. Cameras flashed, and handsome men begged for her autograph...

A noise wakened Marcelina. She cursed at having her dream disturbed and swung her feet over the edge of the bed.

The front door was slightly open—she had locked the door handle!

Marcelina clenched her waist, gasping for courage. She couldn't sit here like a fool all day with her mouth hanging open, her double chin trembling with fear. She caressed her unborn infant kicking furiously because of her fear. She would protect her unborn child with her life, if need be. She grabbed the poker from the fireplace and tiptoed from the room.

Marcelina slammed a hand to her lips when the beauty chair spun. *Salia,* she thought.

But no. It was only a U.S. Marshal hunched low in the chair with his hands folded on his stomach and his boots tapping out a tune on the wooden floor.

"You made my heart stop," she said.

"Joseph Quill. I could use a haircut, ma'am," he said.

Her shop only had one second-hand beauty parlor chair, imported from Santa Fe, along with two electric hair-dryers which she wielded like pistolas. "There is a barber shop just up the street with two chairs," she said, eying his badge.

"I prefer a lady. Your kind's gentler with the scissors," he said.

She removed his hat and wrapped an apron around his chest.

He dipped his head and she snipped at his hair.

"So what do you know about what happened to Salia Stuwart? Ouch! Damn it. Be careful with those scissors, Lady," he said with a steely eye.

"I'm sorry." She looked at him with hooded eyes, cocking her head at his jugular vein where he would bleed to death if she cut him. She had been Salia's secret best friend, the forbidden friendship of a strict Catholic girl and a third-generation witch. Her sixth sense screamed that this stranger nosing around knew about their relationship.

"I figured being the beautician, you know all the gossip," he added.

She shrugged her shoulders. "The villagers have always gossiped about Salia. They're claiming Samuel Stuwart, on his way home from a meeting the night before his accident, saw a light coming from the Engine House Melodrama Theatre. There were no actors in town, except for her. He looked in through the window and saw a party of witches dancing, like at a masquerade ball. He recognized Salia from her last performance at the theatre. She was draped in red velvet with a feathery mask and ruby-red lips with masses of reddish hair swept up, just so," she said, dramatically pushing her hand behind his head.

"Then Salia's mask floated from the stage. The theatre grew quiet and dark, except for that mask in the window. A strange feeling came over him when he looked at her eyes staring at him. But then he was himself again and he started yelling at her that, 'witch or no, you'll never have my son. I'll see you dead first,' he roared. Samuel was murdering mad. 'This is my theatre! How dare you pollute it with your witchery.' He ran around to the front and tried the door handle, but it was locked. He pulled out his key, but when he placed it in the knob, the keyhole melted closed. He yanked out his jack from the trunk of his car, but none of the windows would break. He finally drove away with a heavy foot. In his rear-view mirror, the lights flashed on in the theatre and the music blared out once more."

"But the funny thing is, Marshal, Big Sam didn't believe in witches so I suggest you swallow the gossip like a spoiled tamale. I didn't know Salia well," she lied. "Nobody knew her. She was a chameleon, an opera singer who could change into any character she pleased."

"And what about her being beautiful?" he said in a voice sounding wistful, like most men.

"If you wish to see her beauty, Salia's painting hangs at the *Engine House Melodrama Theatre and Opera*," she snapped more impatient than she intended, but Marcelina was sick of hearing about Salia's exquisiteness.

"Yeah. I hear she was a great actress," he said sarcastically.

The marshal acted as if he held something against Salia, yet there was both yearning and sadness in his eyes. Perhaps, he had seen her perform in an opera. But...he was a stranger to Madrid. As far as Anglos went he wasn't bad looking. A bit too lanky. Hair too golden. His brown lashes full and long for a man. His lips wide and sensuous. His cheekbones prominent. His coloring was nice though. At least he wasn't white like a ghost. And his eyes were golden brown in color. He looked like a golden god. Indeed, he had the same greedy look like all Anglos. The same hunger on their faces for all that isn't theirs.

"Tilt your head to the right so I can trim your sideburn," she said.

Marcelina slammed the scissors on the counter and placed her hands across his head.

He grasped her wrists, twisting until she cried out.

"What are you doing?" he said.

"Putting Wildroot on your hair."

"Don't ever touch my hair with your bare hands, understand me?"

She wiped the hair tonic on her apron and nodded.

"Maybe you've heard that all the boy babies under the age of one have died at four of the pueblos. They stopped breathing in their sleep. Small claw marks were left on their lips and noses," he said.

She swooned, her legs wobbling, the floor rising to meet her head.

He jumped from his seat and caught her. "Damn! I'm sorry. I forgot you're pregnant."

He sat her down, fetched a glass of water and fanned her face with a sex adventure magazine with a story entitled, *Indolent Kisses*.

"Breathe slowly. Don't faint on me, Lady."

She clutched his arms. "La Llorona," she said with an anxious face. A desperate face. A crazed face. "It was La Llorona." [pronounced Lah yoh roh nah]

"La Yah who?"

"The Weeping Ghost. For centuries she has been trying to get her own children back by kidnapping others."

He looked at her like she was crazy.

"You're obviously not from around these parts. I...I'll finish your cut," she said.

He plopped back down in the chair, keeping a watchful eye on the scissors. "No corpses were found after the witch burning," he added.

"The Penitentes did their job well," she said, referring to the fanatical Catholic society that had Madrid in its clutches and brought back the Spanish Inquisition for just one night.

She reached around him, removing the apron and lifting his money clip. She removed a few bills and then replaced the clip. Marcelina wasn't stupid enough to steal all of his money. He was a marshal after all. Nor had the Great Depression affected his paycheck, so he wouldn't miss the money.

He took out his wallet to pay her.

She swept up his hair with a broom.

"Uh-uh," he said, grabbing her hand.

He held his palm out.

She swayed, feeling faint. She would go to jail for stealing the marshal's money.

"My hair," he said, snapping his fingers.

She breathed a sigh of relief and handed the cuttings to him.

He lit a match, burning his hair cuttings.

Ah, so he knew about witchcraft. How dare he insult her! She only practiced white magic. "Next time, you will be more comfortable at the barber shop with the rest of the men," she snapped. How dare he think her a witch who would use his hair against him!

He tipped his hat to her. "Good morning to you, lady," he said in a voice with a bite to it.

She stuck out her tongue at his back. The bastard didn't even leave a tip. She furrowed her brow, trying to remember if she had ever seen him in Madrid before.

She searched her pocket for his money she had stolen but her pockets were empty. What the...?

A fly buzzed at the window. "Leave me alone, Lord Tez," she mumbled sleepily, resting her head on the desk.

Tezcatlipoca, Aztec Lord of the Night and Patron of the Witches, flew through a hole in the screen, buzzing around her head. He landed on her scalp, hopping about her itching follicles. She previously thought of her benefactor as simply *the voice*, since she had never actually seen Lord Tez in the flesh before a month ago when he manifested himself as a pesky fly. He had slid across a buttery tortilla and mated with another fly on the salt shaker. Since then, he always visited as a fly instead of just a bodiless voice. He appeared like any ordinary, tan and black house fly with huge buggy eyes on the sides of his face. The only differences were: a yellow stripe painted across his face, and he walked on his two back fly legs, his front legs open like he was about to give her a hug. A miniature, smoking mirror was on his hairy chest.

Lord Tez hovered, and it was as if she was looking at the fly through a magnifying glass. His transparent wings were like a pool of water, and she could see her reflection in the wings. She reached out a finger and petted the fleshy-fly, avoiding its sensitive antennae.

His compound eyes took in every aspect of her beauty shop at once.

"Ah, so you finally notice that I have remodeled a bit. And yes, you may help yourself to some milk, but after you tell me your news," she said.

Lord Tez buzzed in her ear, *you are about to give birth.*

Her womb cramped. "Ay!"

She waddled towards the door, warm liquid seeping between her thighs. "Yi!"

She fell to her knees.

"Help me," she whispered, clinging to her womb, fearful that once more she was losing a baby.

———— ◆ ————

2

A sparkling light blinded her. She squinted at the four tips of a marshal's badge. Marshal Quill bent over her, stuffing some herbs in her mouth. "Just swallow," he said.

She did and blissfully, the pain went away. "My baby," she sobbed.

"Just push."

Her unborn child kicked furiously. At least the right side of her womb kicked in protest. Her left side purred.

"You're doing good," the marshal muttered.

An ache rocked her pelvic bones, making her cry out. She tried to sit up and pain rippled across her womb like a bolt of lightning. *I must get out of here. Now! I can't give birth in front of a man,* she thought.

Her body crumpled and everything went black.

When she came to, she lay on the narrow kitchen table with her ankles elevated on two pillows. She hurt so between her legs. In her hip bones. Her tail bone and pelvic bones. She never felt such painful cramping between her legs, all the way up to her womb, pulsing as if a life beat there still.

How odd that her now empty womb seemed to have a memory, refusing to let go of life. The pulsing and cramping continued, as if she was still giving birth. She ran a hand over her flat stomach and tears filled her eyes. "My baby! Where's my baby?"

It took what little strength she had to pull herself up and look around. She sighed with relief. Marshal Quill rocked two infants in his arms, cooing at her babies.

Babies? Marcelina always yearned for a child and miscarried several times. She now had two babies kicking their strong legs and thrashing their arms. Juan would be so proud. He always wanted a son. Now he had two.

"They're girls," Quill said, placing the twins in her arms.

She nearly dropped them—on purpose. Two identical daughters? Not even one boy to call son?

A keen disappointment overwhelmed her, but then she came to her senses, realizing that even a daughter would bind Juan to her. And two daughters were an even greater insurance that Juan would never leave her for another woman.

Marcelina felt weak, and Quill pushed another bitter herb in her mouth before she blacked out.

She blinked her eyes and lay in the back of a car. Her exhaustion and weakness from giving birth was gone. She frowned at Quill's stiff head, his white knuckles clinging to the steering wheel, his jaw hard.

A hungry cry rattled her nerves. No. Make that two cries. Beside her lay two babies, one on each side.

She squeezed the vision of the twins closer to her heart, tears rolling down her cheeks. At last, motherhood, what she was meant to be.

"Why don't you feed your brats and shut them up?" he barked.

She must have earlier imagined him nuzzling her girls, kissing their tiny fingers.

The two brown, wrinkled babies had hair growing on their cheeks and a single eyebrow sweeping across their foreheads. These were the prettiest infants she had given birth to. "Isabella and Carlotta," she named them as she fed a breast to each girl who it turned out weren't exactly identical.

Carlotta, the bigger baby, sucked greedily on her nipple, pinching her breast. The baby's black eyes were wide open, and she stared as if she would like to devour her. If only Carlotta had teeth, she would probably bite off her nipple and spit it out. Then she could have more. And Carlotta sucked harder and pinched so Marcelina cried out in pain. She stretched out a tiny leg and jabbed her bony heel against Marcelina's ribs.

The runt of the litter, Isabella, suckled silently and gently on her other breast with her small fists clenched on each side of her face. Isabella kept one eye on Carlotta. These two survived in the womb together for nearly nine months. Perhaps this was why Isabella had her hands clenched so tightly in front of her bruised face, as if she was protecting herself from blows—she already knew her sister.

Quill deposited them at the Madrid hospital and tilted his hat to her.

"Thanks," she murmured, looking at the floor with great embarrassment.

He informed the nurse, "The runt was born a minute before midnight and the other a minute after."

"What did you give me for my pain?" Marcelina said, thinking she could sell it in her shop, something surely better than laudanum.

"I gave you nothing." Quill spun on his heels, walking quickly away before she could question him further about the strange herbs.

What an odd man, she thought.

"Where is your husband?" the nurse asked suspiciously.

"Juan is working the night shift at the mine."

"Shall I call him for you?"

"No," she said in a panicked voice. Miners were being laid off left and right due to the Great Depression and the coal mine only operating three days a week.

The nurse wheeled her into a room to spend the night. The nurse tried to shut the window but it was stuck. "Well, it's a nice summer night. Try and get some rest," she said, leaving her alone with the babies.

Her daughters were twins, but Isabella was born on Thursday and Carlotta on Friday, the high night for witches. Carlotta opened her mouth and laughed, exposing three teeth.

Marcelina reached back her hand and slapped the baby, her excuse being the old superstition that *When you see a child's first tooth, immediately slap her face, and she will teethe easier.*

She upset both babies, or so she thought, but perhaps it was a sweeping noise from the open window that disturbed them.

A hawk flew in and circled the bed. Marcelina recognized the damaged eye and ugly hawkish features of Jefe, Salia's half-brother, a Native American witch from the Santo Domingo Pueblo.

The hawk swooped with talons drawn like it was going to snatch the babies.

"No!" she screeched, hugging her girls. Marcelina feared that because she refused to join the *Enchanting Black Rose* coven, as La Llorona wished, the witch was claiming one of her babies as her own, like in those dark fairytales.

The hawk lifted the receiving blankets, cocked its head at the girls' privates and then soared out the window.

Carlotta glared at Marcelina, punching her in the stomach.

"Stop!" she cried out in pain, which caused both babies to scream and scream and...

Marcelina cuffed her hands to her ears and yelled at both babies to, "shut up!"

She laid both girls in dresser drawers, slammed the drawers shut and then climbed back in bed.

Marcelina yanked the covers over her head, muffling their crying which now sounded like two mewing kittens flung down a well. Motherhood was not turning out to be the joy she had reverently believed it would be. Perhaps, if she'd given birth to only one child.

She lay on the bed, still a mound of a woman, looking as if she was pregnant. It felt like two boulders were yet wedged in her womb, just like a stone lodged in her heart at the thought of having mothered two girls.

Juan will leave me for a skinny woman who can make him a boy.

A nurse marched into the room. "What did you do with your babies?"

Marcelina pointed her chin at the dresser.

"For shame, Mrs. Rodríguez. You must feed your children, and let the babies have some light."

"I have no milk," she whined, truthfully, having whispered a health spell to dry up her milk, so her breasts shrunk to the size of two eggs.

The nurse swept her daughters from the dresser and offered them to her.

Marcelina turned her back to them.

"It will get easier," the nurse said, carrying the babies from the room.

Marcelina breathed a sigh of relief—blessed silence and so happy to be alone.

She cried until her sobs turned to hiccups.

I'm going to hell for being a bad mother.

———

3

Jefe flew out the hospital window, flapping his wings towards the San Felipe Pueblo.

He swooped from the sky and hopped into the apartments at San Felipe. With his hawk beak, he lifted the blankets serving as doors of the apartments. He silently entered and if there was a baby sleeping of the proper age, Jefe climbed in the cradle, grasped a clawed foot over the tiny mouth, and held the nose shut with his beak.

He happily bounced in and out of the apartments, searching for baby boys.

Jefe exited the last apartment, feeling giddy from never once ruffling his feathers when a father turned in his sleep.

He did not notice a mountain lion observing him.

Jefe lifted his wings and flew towards home—to the Santo Domingo Pueblo some fifteen miles northwest of Madrid.

Witch Hill inclined above the village. Jefe winked his good eye at the burnt-out remains of a once grand Victorian house. *Slut*, he thought, referring to his half-sister Salia, who was born twenty-one years after him.

In true bird form he crapped from the air, circling the damaged house in triumph. His grandmother and half-sister deserved it, considering that they hid the family shape-shifting stone from him.

Jefe couldn't dismiss the feeling someone was watching him. He twisted his head to look behind him. He swore he could hear someone flying behind him but each time, no one was there.

At the Santo Domingo Pueblo, he bounced on the soft earth.

He folded his wings, bowing his head, and transforming back into a hunchbacked man wearing just a belt and knife sheath, solidly built in his forties, well hung, with hair combed into a single, graying braid, snaking across his humped back.

Jefe was contrary to the rest of the Puebloans and chose not to live in boxed apartment buildings. There is power in a circle and other than tipis, hogans are the closest Native American architecture resembling a circle—

although with five walls. Jefe's hogan was constructed from sod and leaned crookedly by the relentless wind shoving his home, banishing him to the far ends of Santo Domingo. No one, not even his father-in-law, his enemy, the powerful shaman Storm-Chaser could have chased him away. His banishment was self-imposed, though welcomed with relief by the Pueblo. The people dwelling at Santo Domingo slept more soundly because he was no longer their close neighbor. Jefe was expelled as a member, shunned behind his back, respected face-to-face, and sucked up to out of necessity. It was because of Jefe that the people felt cursed.

He was not cast out alone. Three other hogans leaned towards his hogan, surrounding him like bees buzzing around their queen. The hogans were inhabited by his disciples.

The Pueblo was so quiet; he could hear smoke puffing from the kiva fireplaces. The Pueblo was isolated from the outside world, the desolation welcomed by Jefe.

He did not notice the mountain lion, stretched out on a large branch of a tree with its head hanging down, licking its chops.

Jefe's face was cloaked in darkness, even the full moon shying away from his ugliness. A jagged knife scar ran diagonally all the way from his temple to his pock-marked chin, cutting his lips into four pieces. He appeared to be blind in his damaged eye but could see all of his peripheral vision to his left. Thus, there was always a black hole in front of that eye, a little to the left of a nose that had been broken in several places.

He adjusted his head to counterbalance the black hole of his sight as he studied the odd cloud in the sky that returned every night since the house burned at Witch Hill. The cloud draped the mountain top in the shape of a tipi.

A full silver moon moved across the dark sky, tucking inside the tipi cloud and teetering at the mountain tip.

Jefe stiffened, glaring at the tipi-moon, his body taut with tension. All the people knew what this omen meant. A tipi-moon had been seen only once before in New Mexico, on the night of Montezuma's birth centuries ago. The great witch Montezuma was famous among the Indian people. There is a legend that Montezuma created the New Mexico Pueblos. He then transformed into an eagle and flew southward, founding the mighty Mexico City and all civilization there. Montezuma promised to one day return and lead the Pueblo people once more. Jefe always laughed at this fairy tale, believing it would not come to pass. He never accepted that the great witch Montezuma would return...

Until now.

"The great one has returned to the people," he whispered. All he worked for was threatened. There was still work to be done, other pueblos to visit, to neutralize this tipi-moon omen.

Jefe was still unaware he had company, and the mountain lion cocked its head at the tipi-moon.

Jefe's legs gave out and he crawled to his hogan, reeling with fatigue. If he had his grandmother's piedra imán instead of just magic powder, his shape-shifting could last indefinitely. His transformation would not be tiring and cause him to sleep like the dead afterwards. Without La India's magic stone, his transformation could only last four hours, limiting his visits to one pueblo a night. Some of the further pueblos would take him a round trip of eight nights. But each night he had to recover, making his ordeal last even longer. This was risky because once his shape-shifting ability wore off; he was zapped of all powers, making him vulnerable. Another witch could sneak up on him while he slept, and he would not be able to defend himself. It was a trade-off. He could get killed, but his transformation into a hawk was the best way to accomplish his mission—the only way, given the danger, unless he could get his hands on the piedra imán, their grandmother's shapeshifting stone that Salia had.

Jefe snorted at the three hogans surrounding his, anger engulfing him. He would deal later with Big-Belly, the Bat, and Dead-Man-Walking. None of his disciples were awakened by the prophetic moon. Big-Belly was a lazy witch and Jefe still hadn't forgiven the Bat for speaking up for Salia. As for Dead-Man-Walking, his best disciple would make a good companion in this deed but he did not want Dead-Man-Walking to be the one to kill Montezuma's reincarnation, else the power would all go into him when the spirit of life left the great witch.

Jefe was unaware the mountain lion still lay on a branch with its chin on its paws, watching him.

He grabbed the hogan wall for support, holding the blanket open, wheezing. He couldn't last much longer and would pass out soon. Faintness was coming on him, the accursed weakness that made him so damned helpless. Even his wife, Weeping-Woman, could kill him in his sleep. He scoffed, as if she would ever find the courage. More likely his love-starved wife might mount him while he was passed out from the effects of animal transformation. His hogan stunk so much of women, he was choking on vagina. Jefe was born cursed by women, for women and of women. From his grandmother La India, to Felicita his stepmother. And Salia, his half-sister. From his wife. His mistress. His daughters. Women would surely be the death of him.

He weakly called out, "Weeping-Woman. Bitch."

His long suffering wife shuffled over with her head bowed obediently, the moonlight illuminating her hips wide from childbirth. She limped, the result of being crippled by polio, a disease even her father was unable to cure. However, Storm-Chaser used his powers so Weeping-Woman did not end up in a wheelchair or with braces on her legs.

Jefe had no patience with tears. "Quit crying, woman, and come help me. I know you're awake, watching my every move like a cow mooning after a bull. Being married to you is like having my neck in a noose. Bring some raw meat."

Her moccasins rubbed against the dirt floor.

He handed her his ancient prayer plumes of the hawk, passed down from his ancestors. She returned the sacred plumes to the mud walls of the hogan. Whoosh! The feathers infested into the mud, appearing like ancient artifacts of mischief. The mud kept the feathers moist, preserving their magic.

Weeping-Woman followed Jefe outside, the moonlight unkind to her narrow face. She may have been pretty had her bones not protruded from her cheeks. She was gaunt from a near-starvation diet, a self-imposed fast. Her long hair hung in strings to her buttocks, streaks of grey dominating her head. Even though her face was unlined, there was weariness about her, making her appear a decade older than her twenty-nine years.

He devoured the raw meat, specks of blood dotting his face and chest. He handed his bloody knife to her. "Clean it!"

"What have you done now, demon?"

He flung his arm out, slapping her.

Her head spun, and she looked at the tipi-moon teetering on the mountain top.

"Yes, woman, the great witch has returned to the people, but he will not gain more power than me," he spat.

"The babies," she moaned.

"And I will go out next week, and the next week, and the next until I have visited all the pueblos. I cannot allow this child to live, this...this reincarnation of the great witch who threatens all I have worked for." He yanked her hair and growled, "Because of your father, I am stuck between a rock and a cactus. Storm-Chaser will never tell me where the Reincarnation has been born nor when."

"Then go to a shaman from one of the other pueblos."

"If I do that, stupid, I will be caught and all the pueblos will unite against me. Flaco has been watching you, so don't go crying to your father."

Her eyes glazed over and she appeared to dissolve into the ground like a cockroach. *Her young son spied on his mother?* This thought made her resemble a crazy woman with disheveled hair, a goose-egg-size bump on the back of her head, and empty eyes, but this is how Weeping-Woman coped—escaping within her own mind kept her sane.

She giggled. It was not her own suicide she imagined but Jefe's death as she wiped his knife with her skirt. She then burned her bloodied nightgown.

Weeping-Woman rocked, naked, on her knees with her arms wrapped around her waist. "And a crying will be heard among the pueblos, the like of which has not been heard since the massacre by the white man. The Rio Grande will run crimson with the blood of innocence. So it is written. So it shall be."

"Shut up," he said and yanked her hair. Jefe lifted the blanket to the opening of their hogan and flung her inside.

The blanket flapped behind them, a cloud of dust from the dirt floor blowing from beneath.

The mountain lion jumped from the tree and spun until the lion vanished. In its place twirled a white falcon.

The falcon spread its wings and lifted into the night sky.

The tipi cloud folded its flap around the moon, pitching New Mexico into darkness.

4

Marcelina snapped open her purse and fished out the key to her shop. She flipped the *closed* sign to *open.*

The day went like any other work day at her shop, *Eternal Beauty.* Clipping hair. Plucking eyebrows. Dispensing homemade beauty products, a few dripping with rose hip seed oil milked from rose hips grown in her back yard.

The bell above the shop rang. It was almost closing time and the last customer of the day.

Pacheco Sandoval shoved the door open.

Quick, Marcelina put out her cigarette and rubbed the rouge from her cheeks, along with her flaming red lipstick. She splashed water on her neck, scrubbing off the odor of lustful perfume, her own creation.

Her heart fluttered at Pacheco, who was the head of the Brotherhood of the Penitentes, a fanatical arm of Catholicism ruling the Catholics in Madrid. One of Pacheco's goals was to root out witches and bring back the burning times.

"Good afternoon, Marcelina Rodríguez," he said in a voice booming like a fire-and-hell brimstone preacher. Even the brushes and combs rattled, causing hair lodged between the bristles of the brushes and teeth of the combs, to fly about the shop.

My married name is Martinez! Yet you persist in calling me Rodriguez, you son of a whore, as if I am still that little girl cowering before you, she screamed to herself. Instead, she was now a woman in her twenties, cowering before Pacheco. She frantically looked around her shop for an escape route.

He strutted about the shop, bow-legged on short legs with his fists on his wide hips, surveying *Eternal Beauty* with a sneer of revulsion on his swarthy face. He nodded in approval at a sign with an arrow pointing to statues of Saint Cosmos and Saint Damian, the Patron Saints of Barbers, guaranteeing a beautician's work.

Pacheco, however, was bad for business because he was a fashion terrorist. If not for Pacheco, she could experiment with elaborate hairstyles. In Madrid Catholic women were not allowed to have short bobbed hair, or permed wavy hair. Marcelina feared the Penitentes would forbid her from cutting hair in any fashionable style, even for Non-Catholic and non-minority women—if they ever discovered that heathen women were customers. If not for Pacheco, her profits could be greater. She would sell more makeup and fake eyelashes.

She might even design her own style of clothing, but if Pacheco had his way, women would be covered from head to toe with a veil to hide any beauty they possessed. Marcelina frowned at her shoes like her grandmother used to wear. Even though the company store sold silk stockings, ugly cotton stockings stuck out from her long skirt, making her look more turn-of-the-century than a modern 1930's woman. She hid her dangling earrings in the back of a drawer and wore them in secret with a mail-order hat cocked sexily over one eye. Marcelina dared not smoke or drink in public, even though Prohibition had been repealed.

Pacheco and Marcelina stared each other down, the fashion terrorist and the queen of the house of *Eternal Beauty*.

Marcelina, short and fat, with the eyes of a bullfrog.

Pacheco, short and stocky, with the eyes of a dead fish and complexion of a pirate.

"This den of beautification is where seeds are planted for women to work at what they do best—lead men into everlasting temptation so they might burn in the fires of hell," he roared.

And if any man knew about a living hell, it was Pacheco. She breathed a sigh of relief because he did not carry a torch to burn down her beauty shop. Instead, Pacheco dragged his dead wife behind him.

Agnes' bony face peeked around his pants leg, her eye sockets empty. Agnes looked at Marcelina with eye sockets begging for help. Her skeletal fingers were clutched in prayer, and her teeth clenched in her skull.

As always, pity moved Marcelina for this poor dead woman who was in all likelihood murdered by her husband. The punishment for adultery by the Penitentes is burial alive. Pacheco caught his wife in bed with his brother, when Marcelina was a little girl. It was rumored Pacheco's brother was buried alive. A couple months later, Agnes vanished, and the skeleton emerged at his side.

"Agnes needs a haircut," he said, matter-of-factly, like it was every day a skeleton got her hair fixed at a beauty shop. "I hear you work miracles in your house of beauty," he added, his lips cracking. Pacheco labored thirty years for a vengeful God and did not know how to smile. Pacheco's aim was to bring back the Spanish Inquisition to New Mexico. Who would have thought a saint like Pacheco could age? But after burning down Salia's house, a thick white stripe appeared across the center of his scalp, like a skunk.

Just like when she was a child, Marcelina could not save Agnes from her husband. All she could do was beautify her to cheer her up. She directed Pacheco to seat the skeleton in the beauty chair. "What is it you wish me to do for your wife?" Marcelina pushed Agnes against her rib cage, righting her so that the skeleton was no longer folded at the waist with her skeletal fingers touching her toe bones. *Have some pride, Agnes,* she said, but did not voice the words aloud.

"What do you think?" he said.

Her stomach ached and the brush shook in her hand. Pacheco was testing her. Maybe his visit to her shop was just a ruse.

"Perhaps an old-fashioned bun?" she suggested and grabbed Agnes by the hair to keep her from sliding off the chair. She shuddered to think what Pacheco would do to her if Agnes broke a bone in her shop.

He yanked his wife's beige skirt over her bony ankles, agreeing to a schoolmarm bun. "She always wanted to be a teacher," he said in a choked voice.

Agnes sat with her hands folded demurely in her lap, smiling at the mirror with big white teeth, looking happy for the first time in decades.

"Shall I shampoo her first?"

"But not with that perfumed soap. Use lye."

She gritted her teeth at burning her hands with lye. "I'm sorry, Agnes," she whispered to the skeleton as she laid her head back in the sink. "The lye must sting your skull, but at least lye is good for a headache. Surely a wife like you must get migraines," she whispered.

"Not too shiny," Pacheco said, shoving his head in the sink. "I would not like my wife to blind other men with her beautiful hair."

A bone of Agnes' neck was stuck to the edge of the sink, stabilizing the skeleton.

Marcelina marched over to a table and grabbed the *True Story* magazine before Pacheco should see it. He attended cock fighting and would have enjoyed the article *"I Never Lived Till Now, By Jack Dempsey"*, the former World

Heavyweight boxing champion who recently made a movie acting as a boxer. However, on the magazine cover was the actress Carole Lombard revealing her naked back and arms, and nails painted red, with matching lipstick and rouge. Had Pacheco noticed the magazine, he would have dragged Marcelina to the morada, the secret scary chapel of the Penitentes. He would accuse her before the Brotherhood of corrupting women's morals.

Marcelina ran to her bedroom and shoved the magazine in a dresser drawer. She yanked out a copy of *The Santa Fe New Mexican*. There was a picture on the front page of an opera singer named Catalina. Pacheco claimed he hated opera, calling it the devil's singing, because Salia had sung opera.

Marcelina marched back to the kitchen and slapped the newspaper on his chest, smiling mischievously. "I'll bring you a cup of coffee while you read this," she said, directing him to the living room. Pacheco liked old things and *The Santa Fe New Mexican* was the oldest daily newspaper south of the Mississippi River.

A fly landed on his nose. He swatted at the fly and then noticed the opera cover story. Pacheco yelped like the newspaper burned him.

The fly landed on her ear, chuckling so only she heard Lord Tez. She doubled over in silent laughter at Pacheco ripping the opera article from the paper.

Her laughter turned to sobs from the lye burning her hands as she scrubbed the skeleton's hair. Marcelina eyed Pacheco and then bent her head, whispering to Agnes, "The Devil knows more because he is old than because he is the Devil."

Speak of the devil, the fly said; *confess to her or I will.*

"I can't—hush, Lord Tez, or Pacheco will hear," she whispered.

You said you wished to clear your soul.

"I was joking," she said, rinsing the skull. Water ran through the eye sockets and out cracks in the vertebrae.

Have it my way then, shaken and stirred. The fly pointed its antennae to the living room, causing music to blare from her used Victrola. The skeleton started shaking to the song, *With Every Breath I Take*. Electricity shot through Marcelina's arms as Agnes' thoughts projected telepathically to her.

The fly told me what you did to me, Agnes said in a screechy voice, sounding like bone rubbing against bone.

Marcelina screeched—she spoke to Agnes before but this was the first time the skeleton ever talked back!

I know what you did to me, Agnes repeated.

Marcelina leaned over the sink, locking eyes with the skeleton's sockets which seemed to droop. "I'm sorry. So sorry," she mouthed at Agnes.

Marcelina closed her eyes, seeing Agnes with her skirts raised in the bushes fornicating with Pacheco's brother, the handsome Alfonso. "I was but nine years old and a good Catholic then," she whispered.

And so pious, Agnes added.

"Like every Catholic in the village, I was brought up to believe it my duty to report sinners to Pacheco. I didn't know the Penitentes would bury Alfonso alive. Every day, I am sick to my stomach about betraying you. What happened to you, Agnes, after you vanished," she said, placing trembling fingers on her lips.

A vision came to her of Pacheco drilling a hole in the morada, the holy shack of the Penitentes where they worshipped God in secret, the walls lined with skulls. Pacheco locked Agnes in the holy shack where she sat chained to a chair, thus ensuring she could watch him digging a grave. The Penitentes held torches, while Pacheco threw his brother into the six-foot hole, covering him with dirt.

Agnes stared through the hole at Alfonso's grave, imagining his muffled screams, his ragged nails scratching at the earth.

She refused food or water unless Pacheco unburied his brother.

The scratching from the grave stopped and Agnes screamed.

She sat there, day after day, her lips cracked, her stomach hollow.

In the first week, she miscarried Alfonso's baby, a lone tear slid down her protruding cheekbones.

After two weeks of not drinking any liquids, Agnes died.

Pacheco carried her corpse to his wagon and drove off.

Marcelina now stood with her shoulders hunched, shaking with silent sobs. "I'm so sorry. You have no idea my regret. Forgive me?"

The eye sockets watered and the skeleton nodded its head.

She leaned over and kissed the cheek bone. "I swear I'll make it up to you. I will one day take you to the ocean," Marcelina said, pouring a comforting hair conditioner on Agnes' skull to negate the acid sting of the lye. "You will like the ocean mist on your dry bones."

She dried the skull with a towel, pinning Agnes' waist-length hair to her scalp in a huge old-fashioned bun. A few strands of hair fell in curls to her cheeks.

Pacheco flicked his middle finger at the base of Agnes' skull.

Marcelina flinched at the sound of bone clunking.

"Cut those wayward hairs—a wife must not tempt another man. Let every wife see to only the needs of her husband," he said.

Marcelina did as ordered. "You look nice, Agnes, like an old maid," she said.

Agnes cocked her head at the mirror. Marcelina could tell by her stiff expression that the skeleton was not pleased.

"I have an old hat here that will go well with her dress," she said and dropped on the skull a round hat that hung past the ear sockets. Marcelina clipped some dime store earrings on Agnes and a necklace around her neck bones. The cheap pearls slung down the front of Agnes' white blouse, rattling against her chest bones.

"How nice! Agnes looks like she's all dressed up for church," she said to Pacheco.

He nodded his thanks.

Marcelina swept up the bang cuttings, dumping them into the dust pan.

Pacheco grabbed her wrist and squeezed until she dropped the dust pan.

He cleared his throat and held out a hand.

With a sulky look, she dumped the hair cuttings into his fist.

"Be warned, Marcelina Rodriguez, for beauty is vain. But a woman that feareth the Lord, she shall be praised," he annoyingly quoted the Bible, like always.

Pacheco walked out the door of *Eternal Beauty*, with his wife in his arms as if she was a bride being carried across the threshold.

Marcelina glared at his back, angry that he thought she might be a witch, else why not trust her with his hair cuttings? "Bring Agnes back any time," she yelled at him.

Pacheco did not acknowledge her.

Marcelina pressed her face at the window, flattening her nose against the glass.

Pacheco propped up Agnes against the front seat of his car.

That man is absolutely crazy. Marcelina snorted at the apple-red Ford, 3-Window Coupe Pacheco claimed as his own. The car wasn't even his but Salia's car. She had been the only woman in Madrid to speed down the Turquoise Trail in her own automobile, her reddish-brown hair flying in the wind, an act making her suspect with the Penitentes. Pacheco somehow ended up with her car. Salia was a most powerful witch. Marcelina was surprised the car wasn't bewitched to run over Pacheco, smashing him with its tires. The car should have become possessed and driven Pacheco off a cliff.

He better come back and pay me, Marcelina thought.

She sighed with relief when he slammed the car door and swaggered back to the shop.

Agnes waited in the car for her lord and master, her husband to return. The beige hat, way out of fashion, swelled from her large bun making the skeleton look rather silly. Her bony wrist was handcuffed to the door handle, and her skull was twisted around to *Eternal Beauty.*

Help me, Agnes pleaded

A tear rolled down Marcelina's cheek. She slid down the wall, bouncing on her rear. Marcelina somehow developed the ability to communicate with the dead. Perhaps the uplifting of the veil between the two worlds had always been there. She recalled at her stepfather's funeral that he reached out his hand from his casket and grabbed her wrist. And then there was her grandmother's funeral when Mama Sole lifted her hand from the coffin and slapped her. Marcelina had reeled back from the blow, screaming that the corpse came to life. The priest pinched her neck, marching her to the door, and flinging her from the church. "You are the devil's child for upsetting your parents, aunts and uncles," he had yelled.

The bell rang above the shop door and Pacheco, rubbed his face between his hands. "I would like a shave," he said, yanking his shirt tail from his pants, pulling at the buttons and ripping it off. He strutted to the coat rack, flexing his back muscles, showing off the deep, self-inflicted scars crisscrossing his back. He was regional head of the Penitentes, a group using self-flagellation to grow closer to God.

Marcelina pointed to the beauty chair. "I must sharpen the razor to give you a close shave."

She carried the razor to the back, swatting the blade across the sharpening strap.

He hurt Salia, the fly hissed in her ear.

Marcelina stared, mesmerized, at the sharpened razor in her hand, the silver blade so shiny she could see her pores.

And what about Salia's baby son?

She marched back to the shop and slapped shaving cream on his face until only his eyes were showing.

"If you touch my moustache, I will kill you," he said.

Like you did Salia, she wanted to shout. But Marcelina simply wiped his lip with a rag until his moustache hung wet from his face.

She efficiently shaved his face, sliding the razor down his neck, her hand trembling at the large vein on his neck bulging purple with life. *So full of blood. And I always believed ice water flowed through his veins. The Mayor of the Penitentes would bleed to death like an ordinary man. One whack across his neck and his head severed from his body.*

Marcelina imagined his head bouncing around her shop. She could mount his skull in her shop, like a trophy, the way Pacheco mounted skulls in the morada.

The skulls in the morada are of sinners. Pacheco is a sinner. He hurt my friend, Salia, she thought.

She held the razor against his jugular vein, her hand shaking and sweat dampening her lip.

He grabbed her wrist, twisting her hand, and the razor fell to the floor with a clang. "A warning for your brother, the priest. Diego thinks he is so important since Padre Gonzalez died. Tell the simple village priest that he is never to interfere with my work. Understand?"

Even though she wasn't on speaking terms with her brother because of his role in what happened to Salia, she nodded her head, rubbing her sore wrist. Marcelina would have a bruise come morning. She should have sliced the vein in his neck when she had the chance.

Pacheco grabbed a towel, wiping the shaving cream from his neck. He rolled his eyes around her kitchen beauty shop, sneering at the shampoos, conditioners, combs, and other beauty products. "But the very hairs of your head are all numbered," he said, quoting the Bible and pointing to the tattoo on his chest of a vengeful Jesus. The face consumed his entire chest. His nipples were the eyes and Pacheco shaved his chest, leaving only enough curly hairs to make a beard for Jesus.

"I know my head has numbers. Matthew from the Bible says so." Marcelina thrust out her chin because she, too, could read, though Pacheco thought all women stupid.

"The proverb means that your shop will not succeed." He walked to the door to leave and spun, smiling triumphantly. "I, on the other hand, am promoted Governor of the Penitentes."

"You are moving to Santa Fe?"

He nodded with a smug smile. "I am given a four-room, furnished house with the $50 a month rent paid for. There are over 11,000 souls in the city and 20,000 scattered about the countryside. I mean to make a great harvest and shut down the wild parties of the decadent capital that overflows with rich people."

"But I hear Santa Fe is no different from Madrid. Because of the Great Depression, children go to school without jackets, carrying lard and popcorn for lunch."

"The poor ones, maybe, but the capital is not suffering so much the effects of the Depression since it has little industry but a wave of wealthy people from other parts. They buy vacation homes or winter homes. Sometimes they move permanently because they come under the spell of our Land of Enchantment. Soon, I will be able to buy my own house once I have $1700, or I may wait until I have $7,000 and buy a fancy house. Your home kitchen beauty shop, on the other hand, is owned by Cerrillos Coal Mining and soon you will be evicted, thrown out on the street when Juan loses his job, like so many others have."

She reached for the table to keep from falling. Why would he say such a thing? "The company may own the house, but not my business. I do not owe my life to the company store," she said.

"Ah, but you do. A family such as yours does not need luxury goods."

She slumped her shoulders. The car. Refrigerator. Washing machine and radio—all bought at inflated rates on a payment plan from the mine.

Pacheco slammed the door to *Eternal Beauty* and marched to his car without paying. Mooching from the villagers was just one of his many perks. No one dared ask him to pay because to be brought up on charges by the Mayor of the Penitentes could mean a sentence of death.

It was unfair that Pacheco could move from Madrid so easily. He wasn't financially desperate to leave. Soon, he would be Governor of the Penitentes, a secret job but very important in the mostly Catholic state. He got the job by impressing the ruling state board of Penitentes by vowing to wipe out witchcraft.

She swiped her hands across the clean beauty chair. Nothing. Clean as a baby's rump. Pacheco wiped the chair down with the apron, and then took it with him. There was not one whisker from his face left anywhere.

"One day, Pacheco, you will not be so careful. Then you will know what it is to suffer. Stupid, so much for your harvesting of souls. Lots of farmers have been moving from Santa Fe to Albuquerque to look for work."

In times like this, she needed Salia. Marcelina lifted the pillow on her bed, tugging on a small photograph of her and Salia. They were both nineteen; sitting cheek-to-cheek with their arms around each other—best friends forever, blood sisters, partners in crime, and fellow sufferers of family.

Marcelina held the picture to her heart and wiped her tears. She concentrated all her new medium powers on the photo, begging Salia to cross over from the grave and talk to her like Agnes did.

Nothing.

Only silence.

Marcelina may now have the power to communicate with the dead, but Salia wasn't talking.

———

5

Pacheco placed the car in gear and the seat jerked.
His wife's skull hit the dashboard.

He shoved her back, holding her ribcage as he steered with one hand towards *Silver Coal*, admiring the neighborhood he now lived in, where the grounds were landscaped. The street was well-lit and smooth instead of dirt. The sidewalks were wooden. Each house had indoor plumbing, where one could crap without fear of freezing one's butt in winter. He ignored how run down the rest of the village had become since Samuel Stuwart's murder and the complete takeover by Oscar Hughes. Pacheco cared even less that he never organized a union for the miners like he promised. Besides, it was for their own good. To keep out the union, Hughes hired a former prison guard from the Deep South who had never brought back an escaped convict alive.

The Depression was not to blame entirely for Madrid's decline. It was Hughes himself. Employees had to buy their own equipment at inflated prices at the company store. Samuel Stuwart had provided this equipment free, but Hughes was stealing and keeping the money for himself. Plus, employees now had to pay rent for their run-down houses. Hughes even let the hospital decline so it was more like a pharmacy with the ability to help just minor injuries. No respectable doctor in his right mind would work at the hospital now. But there was a doctor in Madrid—a drunkard. Instead of buying new equipment for the hospital like he was ordered to, Hughes bought himself a shiny sky-blue, four-door Imperial Cadillac for $4,000.

Pacheco slowed his car and turned his head to the corporate offices of the Albuquerque and Cerrillos Coal Mining Company. He whistled. There it was. The blue special. Car of cars. An Imperial Cadillac. *The boss is working late,* he thought.

A woman walked down the brick walkway, seeming to float, she was that graceful.

Pacheco turned the steering wheel to the right, slamming his foot on the brakes. He hung his head out the window, like a dog, panting at her.

She swayed her shapely hips, her gold dress slinking to her calves, revealing the most gorgeous legs ever seen in Madrid. The woman was dressed in the latest style and wore a hat cocked fashionably to one side of her reddish-brown hair bouncing in unruly curls across her shoulder blades. She was exquisite with a beautiful face needing no makeup. Her lips were full and naturally pink. She had lush, long black eyelashes and eyebrows arched to perfection. Her cheeks were the color of a ripened peach, and Pacheco knew that if he sniffed her, she would smell like peaches.

Pacheco had only seen that much beauty packaged into one woman. *How can Salia be here? I saw her myself fleeing in flames from the house,* he thought, trembling with fear.

She walked with long strides, in the direction of Witch Hill, swinging a suitcase.

"Salia," he yelled in a hoarse voice.

She turned, smiling a dazzling show of snowy white teeth.

She swung her head back around and kept walking.

Pacheco cussed as he pushed at the car door. Damn thing was stuck. He lifted his boot, kicking at the window and shattering the glass. Pacheco climbed out the window, kicking Agnes on her cheekbone.

Panting heavily and choking on his saliva, he chased Salia.

He stopped and spun, his head darting everywhere.

She vanished!

Pacheco fell to his knees, yelling, "Salia! Salia!"

Silence—only his heart beating loudly.

He stood on rocky feet, dusting himself off, and dragged his boots back to his car, muttering. "How can she be here? Salia! She's dead!"

He drove recklessly, thinking about Salia's face at the window of the burning house, staring out like she didn't give a damn what the Penitentes did to her. And she was a mother! "Why did you make me do it, Salia? Why?" Salia's baby son burned in the fire. That was part of the deal Jefe cut with him for witnessing against his half-sister. Pacheco's aim was to bring back the Spanish Inquisition to New Mexico. Jefe could give a rat's ass about the Spanish Inquisition that centuries ago tried to wipe out Native American witchcraft and by its zeal, made the Indians turn even more to Tezcatlipoca, Patron of Sorcery, Witchcraft and Magic. What was important to Jefe was revenge against Salia's mother, his stepmother Felicita whose line ended with Salia's son.

"Why did you make me do it, Salia? Why? If only you had…"

There was a bumping sound and something flew in the air.

He slammed on the brakes.

Ah, his car ran down a woman. "Salia!"

Damn car door was stuck. He climbed out the door, holding his aching shoulder as he ran to the front of the car. *I've killed her twice.*

A woman lay face down on the road, her leg twisted so that her foot touched the middle of her back. She was moaning.

Oh, she's black. I ran over a Negro. Can't really tell who she is.

He hopped in his car and drove away, fish tailing the car, swinging his head from side to side, but there was no sign of Salia.

Pacheco made the sign of the cross at the thought of driving near Witch Hill to search for her. He always avoided the ruins but now drove slowly by the once grand Victorian house, looking forlorn like all abandoned houses yet, there was an air about the blackened walls, as if Felicita, La India, and Salia still spied from between the curtains. Hissing at all who looked back. Cursing those fool enough to stop, stare and shudder. The house seemed like it had a heartbeat of its own thumping against the still-standing three walls.

He cringed at the shattered window where Salia was last seen alive.

Pacheco drove home, turning the car into his driveway. He sniffed the car seat for any scent of peaches—this car had been hers. *It's now mine. Will always be mine.*

He sat in the car, staring into space and thinking that if only Salia had walked in this direction, she would see how he now lived and how important he was. His job at the mine was to pat the head of the miners as they bent their backs, entering the blackness of the tunnels. Pacheco was there at the end of the work day to show his support, his face blackened from rubbing his hands with coal dust.

Pacheco dragged Agnes into the house, throwing her on the couch, not bothering to cross her legs and seat her like a lady, the way he normally did. Pacheco didn't want a lady just now. He was consumed with Salia, brimming with passion for a girl raised by witches to be a witch. And what was a witch? A woman of loose soul!

While Pacheco brooded beside her, Agnes sat on the couch with her toes turned in and skull thrown back, her hat crooked on her bony forehead. Her arms were spread wide, her eye sockets staring at a carbide lantern hat, testifying to the fact that her husband finally had a paying job, though Pacheco did little work since he was a supervisor.

His lantern hat hung from one of the boots worn by the former mine owner, Samuel Stuwart. The pair of boots was mounted on the living room wall like an elk's head. The boots were like new when they came into his possession. Even though the boots were two sizes too big for his feet, he wore them until the soles had holes. Well, Samuel Stuwart had a hole in his soul, which comes of coupling with a witch. The rich man never had to polish his boots himself.

"Big Sam ordered servants around, and me. Bastard wouldn't let me build a union. His death was a matter of honor," Pacheco said in a surly voice.

Pacheco was now in debt up to his last rosary bead. He was more than happy to move to Santa Fe where he would take the prestigious lifetime job as Governor of the Penitentes, performing Sunday lay services at a bigger, more fanciful morada in rich Santa Fe.

"Governor Pacheco Sandoval," he said, feeling in a much better mood.

He flicked on the radio to hear the latest farm reports and grabbed a cold beer from the fridge, plopping down on the sofa. In May, the farms in the Great Plains were affected by a two-day dust storm traveling all the way to Chicago, depositing 12 million pounds of dust, or so the radio claimed. The storm then blew more dust as far as New York City. Luckily, the winds blew east and south so the Dust Bowl didn't affect New Mexico much, although the drought lasting the past three years did.

Pacheco cocked his ear to the radio, remembering how his father would have scribbled notes, mining the latest farm report.

All Pacheco mined was souls.

Earlier today, like a big shot, he sat with Hughes. Him. Pacheco—Manny Sandoval's son.

Another job he had was playing with the scales used to weigh the day's coal. Tilt the scales, in management's favor, a deed he was more than happy to do. He would be rotting in prison now if not for Hughes because when Pacheco first went to work at the mine, his job was to oversee the dynamiting to open a new coal vein.

Pacheco closed his eyes and chugged another bottle of beer, his seventh of the night so far.

How was he supposed to have known the mine was still occupied by men when he ordered the fuse lit? Pacheco had been told the mine was vacant, but couldn't remember who gave him that vital piece of information.

Hughes was a good man. He didn't press charges. "Anyone can make a mistake, Pacheco," he told him.

"Thank you, Sir." And he groveled like any coal miner.

"We'll keep this a secret between us. If the authorities ever find out, you might get the death penalty."

So Pacheco struck a deal with Hughes. Talks of a union were held that were merely a front to appease the men and get rid of the trouble makers from the National Miners Union who were sent from the coal fields of McKinley County to stir up trouble. Thus, did Pacheco's dream of unionizing the mine blow up like dynamite.

Pacheco now lay beside Agnes on the sofa, spooning her—a quality moment between husband and wife. The house was dark. He rested his chin on her collar bone, drifting off to sleep, snoring pleasantly beside the skeleton. His pants were stained with beer trickling from a full bottle he held to his chest.

He stirred, opening one eye. "Whasat noise?"

He tried to rise but the damn couch was like Jell-O to his drunken ass.

"Salia?" he said, slurring the name.

A woman, dressed in white, drifted slowly towards him. She had the soft, peachy skin of an angel. Hair like silk. Reddish brown curls whirling around her face.

"Love of my life," he said in a husky voice. "You look like a virgin, whore. What an anomaly—a virgin whore. That's how I like my whores. Come 'ere little whore, and lemme show you what I do to tight little virgins."

The ghost was shaking her hips, seeming to float more than walk. Other than the huge burning cross she held to her chest, he could see right through her.

"Light of my light", he said, laughing.

Flames shot out from the bottom of her bare feet. She was walking on fire.

The hair rose on the back of his neck and his moustache quivered.

Her blue-grey eyes stared back at him like a storm about to be unleashed.

He raised his hands to his face and screamed.

Salia turned her face to the right, revealing a hole burned on her cheek. On her other cheek, her skin melted across her golden neck.

"No," he yelled, placing his hands in front of him so she wouldn't come any closer.

Salia was like a burning oven—the heat of her body causing sweat to pour down his face.

"Leave me alone, witch! Go back to hell where you belong!

She threw back her head and laughed.

Pouf!

Salia ignited, vanishing.

Pacheco grabbed a blanket used to hide holes he burned in the sofa with cigarettes. He threw the blanket on the floor, extinguishing the cinders.

He dropped to his knees, scooping the ashes in his hands. The ashes felt like silk, just like her skin.

He cupped his hands to his nose, inhaling the scent of peaches. Salia always smelled of peaches.

"Salia!" He crumpled to the floor, scattering her ashes on his chest. He rubbed her ashes over his body, across his crotch, burying himself with Salia's remains.

"Come back to me," he whispered.

6

Reverse beauty is very profitable, and Marcelina was a rare witch with the gift. "Sit and I'll remove your freckles," Marcelina ordered a new customer with flaming red hair.

Marcelina grabbed a sponge floating in murky water. Whenever it rained, she walked to Bones Creek Cemetery to clean rainwater off the tombstones, squeezing the raindrops into a jar. Power pulsates with anything involving the dead—she wiped the woman's face, lifting her freckles onto the sponge. She tossed the dotted sponge in a container labeled *freckles*, to be used when a customer wished to spot a rival's face. Though one man did pay Marcelina to freckle his woman before asking her to marry him. Well, one lover's rose is another's thorn.

Marcelina sighed at the mirror and her own brown freckles. Alas, like a doctor, she could not practice charms on herself.

She grabbed a statue of a Catholic saint with a devil chained at his feet, Cyriacus, Patron Saint of Diseases of the Eye, and an exorcist. She handed the statue to her customer and rubbed her client's eyelids. The hair on Marcelina's arms crackled and with a jolt of electricity, she transferred to her fingers the power to make a person cockeyed. The woman's eyes were now straight.

Marcelina plopped down at the desk, her rump draping the chair, the wheels groaning. She frowned at her new Remington blue typewriter which cost the kingly sum of $19.95. She put one dollar down and was paying ten cents a day on the contraption. The keys were too small for her fat fingers so she licked a pencil, totaling up charges for homemade perfume, freckle removing, advice, haircut, and eye straightening. She would throw a penny in the church basket for the saint's share of her profit. With a deep sigh Marcelina put away the ten percent required to operate a kitchen beauty shop in a house owned by the Albuquerque and Cerrillos Coal Mine.

The woman paid the high sum for her services, knowing that complaining would result in being barred from *Eternal Beauty*.

"Shoo! Get out of here." Marcelina waved her hands at the woman who scurried away with her alligator purse nibbling at her hip.

Marcelina straightened her two copies of *Screen Book* magazine, a rag containing lives of the movie stars pulsing between the pages, all for ten cents. She swept the hair cuttings from the floor, wiping clean the chair. The woman was a new customer so Marcelina deposited the hair into a small paper bag marked with her name.

A fly beat at the window.

Marcelina yanked open the window and drew back her head from his fly breath.

I can tell you where to find La Llorona, Lord Tez buzzed.

She had been searching for weeks now for La Llorona, the legendary witch who was centuries old and occasionally left her grave at night.

La Llorona was the head of the Sisterhood of the Black Rose covens. Marcelina slid open a drawer and frowned at a dried black rose. The witch would not be happy with Marcelina for rejecting the black rose, but Marcelina needed to speak with her.

She swallowed the lump in her throat and said, "Fat lot of good your information about La Llorona will do me. How in earth do I resurrect a ghost from the Rio Grande?"

Trust me. Haven't I promised you riches with the magic I can teach you?

Marcelina slammed the drawer shut, dropped her broom, locked up the house, and walked towards the Atchison, Topeka & Santa Fe Railroad depot, her overnight bag banging her knee.

Lord Tez buzzed around her head, whirling about like a pesky fly.

7

The worst part of the Great Depression was that the coal mine was operating just three days a week and the men who were still working, like
her husband Juan, had their pay cut.

With shoulders heavy with economic worry, Marcelina slapped a dollar on the train station counter. "One ticket to Albuquerque," she said and
boarded the train, marveling that one could even travel as far as Los Angeles
or Chicago.

The fly danced on her head.

"Don't you dare use the bathroom on my hair," she hissed.

The train rolled by Witch Hill. Look. There at the second floor window, a lovely face stares, a prisoner of her own birthright. Salia—who never
wanted to be a witch, but when family calls, one has no choice but to obey.
So it is written. So it shall be.

Marcelina shook her head and Salia vanished from the window. *Poor
Salia, my long, lost friend. I must have imagined you.*

A coyote howled at the top of the hill. *Yes, there is my old friend and blood
sister, the coyote, Salia*—who had often borrowed her grandmother's piedra
imán, to turn into a wild dog and run with her pack.

The coyote looked at Marcelina as though it knew her.

She did not feel foolish waving to the wild animal.

Marcelina was disappointed though when the coyote turned its head
and ran from Witch Hill in the opposite direction.

Even now Salia turns her back. She cannot forgive me.

At the foot of the Cerrillos Hills, turquoise was once mined by Indians
since before the dawn of European history. The mines were now abandoned,
haunted by ghosts of Indians who died mining the turquoise or were murdered out of jealousy. As the train approached Cerrillos, coal was shoveled
even faster to give the train speed and prevent any ghosts from boarding. The
passengers breathed collective sighs of relief when Cerrillos was far behind.

The train stopped with a grinding noise at the Santa Fe Train Station.

Marcelina stood on the platform, rubbing her lower back while waiting for her connecting train. Juan was in Albuquerque playing baseball at the New Mexico State Fair with the state champions, the *Madrid Miners*, but her trip was a secret.

The train arrived in Albuquerque and even with a fly clinging to her hair, she felt like a queen, having never seen such wonders as the Alvarado Hotel Complex, which encompassed a hotel, train depot and baggage handling facility built by the great Fred Harvey chain in the design of a California Spanish mission.

At the hotel gift shop, the latest copy of *True Story* magazine, normally costing 15 cents, plunged from the shelf into her purse. Marcelina scurried out of the Alvarado, hugging her purse to prevent any pages from showing.

"Where is the river?" she asked Lord Tez, but the fly just twirled in circles. Marcelina fumed at his silence. She kept her eyes down as she strolled along the brick walkway. Albuquerque was a bustling city of English, Germans, Italians, Jews, Blacks and Spanish. There were a lot of homeless people due to the Great Depression.

She reached out an arm to a woman, yanking on her sleeve. "How do I get to the Rio Grande?" Marcelina asked, feeling as desperate as she sounded.

The woman pointed to the bus stop at the corner.

Marcelina took her place at the back of the line. She snapped open her purse, grabbing some homemade cookies, thick like biscuits, called bizcochitos, which was the official state cookie of New Mexico. She munched on her snack, swallowing the dry cookies and nearly choking on Lord Tez who flew out of her mouth, carrying a crumb.

Marcelina boarded the bus, gripping the seat edge, having never ridden before.

She twisted her head around, not wanting to miss a thing as the bus rolled through New Town lined with Victorian homes. When the bus turned into the main business district, she clucked her tongue at all the buildings closed because of the Great Depression.

For shame, she thought at the saloons lining the street. Albuquerque had one saloon for every thirty men, women and children. Ninety percent of the city budget was derived from selling liquor licenses. The town was an oasis for thirsty travelers and locals. The liquor business was thriving, even during the leanest years of the Depression.

"Conservancy Beach," the driver announced.

She climbed off and dragged her feet over to the man-made beach of sand imported from the beach of Galveston, Texas. New Mexico was landlocked but at Conservancy Beach there were bath houses and hamburger stands, closed now since it was nighttime. A few couples strolled hand in hand alongside the Rio Grande, sighing at the murky moon dangling over the river.

Marcelina waited for the couples to leave.

It was just her, the full moon, and the white rose on her head with a fly sleeping in the center.

She threw pebbles at the river, watching by moonlight rocks skimming across the water, the pebbles that didn't sink into the mud anyway. The Rio Grande was not very deep this time of year. Not in Albuquerque.

With each pebble she called loudly, "It is I, Marcelina. Show yourself, La Llorona. You have been after me since I was a child. I am here now, waiting for you. Come to me."

The wind whistled across the Rio Grande in all directions.

Ripples waved across the river.

The wind blew stronger, trees lining the bank swaying, with branches reaching out to the river.

There was a tinkling noise like bells ringing.

The tinkling grew louder and deeper until it sounded more like a booming.

The booming noise echoed in her eardrums. Marcelina stood paralyzed, her hair blowing wildly.

Then suddenly—silence.

All was still...

Until a loud piercing cry ripped the night. Cut the sky in two, appearing like lightning in the sky. A sound so eerie, her nose bled as she watched...

From the middle of the Rio Grande a hand reaching out from beneath the river...

Followed by an arm dripping mud...

Then a head surfaced, shaking to clear the nostrils so that fresh air might enter the lungs.

Finally, a woman rose from the center of the river.

La Llorona stretched out her arms, skating across the water towards Marcelina. Mud flew off her skin, the wind cleansing La Llorona. It was this woman who was crying. She was a creature vomited by the Rio Grande, a disgrace-of-nature with tears of blood streaming down her cheeks. La Llorona was a freak-of-clay, fast drying into cracked, dry earth. Her skin more like adobe than flesh.

No human being could make such a wretched sound.

Marcelina blew out her breath, along with a little more blood from her nose. She had done it—conjured up La Llorona, the Weeping Ghost, the dead witch surfacing occasionally, either on her own or because a witch from the Sisterhood of the Black Rose requested her services.

La Llorona wept for her drowned children as she searched the waters in hopes of resurrecting her children to save her soul from guilt and sin. She was tortured by a wretched eternal life and a peace eluding her for nearly three centuries. And so La Llorona lifted her mouth to the night sky and screamed, thrashing her arms about her head to bring up the cry from her toes.

The moon vibrated.

The stars dimmed.

In the middle of the sky was a lightning bolt, the high-pitched thunder stricken by La Llorona, from the depths of her very soul.

Marcelina hated La Llorona's cry, haunting her since she was a child. The screeching made her teeth ache and the hair on her head crawl. Yet she had no choice but to seek the witch out at Conservancy Beach.

La Llorona stepped onto the beach, wobbling on rusty legs. She shook her body like a dog, splattering mud.

Marcelina wiped some mud from her cheek, wrinkling her nose at the stench of fish, tin cans and worms. She clenched her hands into fists and shrieked, "Is it you who has been harming the babies at the pueblos?"

"Ah, you don't even wait for the mud of the river to dry on my parched skin before accusing me." She wrung her hands, sobbing. "I am parched for love. Dried up from loneliness. Thirsting for kindness. Have pity on me. See the cracks running down my skin—it is my heart that is breaking."

Marcelina felt like screaming, *why did I come here? To listen to your lies?* "How can a witch like you even have a heart?"

La Llorona pouted, playing with the ends of her faded wedding veil anchored to her head by a fresh rose sparkling with a black sheen, untouched by mud. "All I ever wanted was to be a good mother but I have always been plagued by slander. Hurt by gossip. Persecuted by rumors. Condemned by hearsay. Injured by jealousy. You wound me, Marcelina Rodríguez."

"My name is Martinez now. You know very well I am no longer the eleven year-old child whose birthday party you ruined," she snapped.

"I am not a murderess, Marcelina Rodríguez. Do not accuse me of such foul deeds. I am the innocent one. I have looked for my children for a long time now. If I did not love children, why would I seek my babies? My precious? My young?"

La Llorona twisted her hands and cried, but still Marcelina felt no pity, no matter how hard the hag cried.

Marcelina could stand it no more— La Llorona's crying driving her crazy. The high pitch sound of her screaming pierced her eardrums. Marcelina grabbed her shoulders, grimacing at her ice-cold touch. She shook her and the ancient crone cried even harder. "Stop it! I can't stand your wailing or your self-pity. Your cries send chills up my spine. You're going to make me deaf."

Like a chameleon, La Llorona switched from a pathetic old wailing woman to a young, vibrant one. She slapped Marcelina hard across the face.

Marcelina cuffed her throbbing cheek, tears stinging her eyes. She will have a bruise to explain to Juan. "You promised me that my baby would live, unlike my others. Will my girls, also, die from mysterious illness like the babies at the pueblos?"

La Llorona hummed a lullaby, rocking her arms, smiling at an invisible babe in her arms. "Beware, Marcelina Rodríguez. One burning with ambition is responsible for these foul deeds."

"Tell me who."

La Llorona merely smiled, opening her arms for a hug.

Well why not? Perhaps La Llorona will be an ally. You can never have too many friends in life or the afterlife. Especially, powerful friends.

The witch smacked her on the lips, and Marcelina squeezed her eyes shut, shuddering—her lips were so dry, like kissing a lizard.

"You are a good girl, Marcelina Rodríguez. I have something for you," she said, cackling just like the witch she was. She pulled from her pocket a sultry black rose, just like the one on La Llorona's own head. "My Sisterhood of the Black Rose has 13 covens, each with 13 members. The *Black Enchanting Rose* coven has only 12 members so there is an opening."

Marcelina jerked her head back from the razor-sharp thorn of the short stemmed rose. "I don't want the black rose. All the rose ever brought Salia was trouble. Unlike Salia, I have a free will."

"Very well, stay a white rose then. You lack courage," she snarled, tossing the black rose in the river.

The water boiled, the rose whirling, creating a downward cone, sucking some trout with it, probably to the bottom of the river.

Marcelina left La Llorona to her own night mischief which would last until the sun rose. Perhaps La Llorona would spend the evening in New Mexico, the Land of Enchantment and location of her *Black Enchantment Rose* coven. Or she might pay a visit to California, Texas, Nevada, Colorado, or Chicago where her other covens were located. La Llorona was even well known throughout Central America, Mexico, and South America.

Whoosh—there was a blinding light in the sky. Some witches, like Salia and her family, can turn into fireballs. The ball of fire was headed east, towards Texas, and was probably La Llorona. She had been wearing cowboy boots and speaking with a slight, Texas drawl. The *Black San Antonio Rose* coven probably awaited her this night of a full moon.

"You're still here?" she said to the fly on her nose.

I love you more than her.

"Then why don't you tell me what I really want to hear. Please, Lord Tez, where is Salia's piedra imán?"

But like always, the Patron of Witches was mum about Salia's extremely rare, shape-shifting stone.

She said, "You are lonely and need a cup of tea. A woman to see that you're warm. Someone to wipe the dust from your forehead and polish your mirror. If you tell me where the piedra imán is, I promise to find a full-size statue of you, like the one that vanished from Salia's house. I'll treat you better than those witches ever did."

The fly raised its skinny rear at her and farted, vanishing in a cloud of smoke.

"Ha! And I was going to take you to the state fair with me and buy you a hot dog."

Instead, she hopped on a bus alone to Central Avenue and Rio Grande Boulevard where the fair was being held only a few minutes ride from Conservancy Beach. She had only experienced the wonders of New Mexico's biggest yearly celebration through others' eyes, lips and ears, which is how Marcelina always lived her life—first through her parents, then through her friend Salia, and then through her husband Juan, and now through her customers at *Eternal Beauty*.

So it was with child-like wonder that Marcelina paid her three pennies to enter through the wooden arches with red, white and blue stars and stripes of the American flag draped over one arch. Over the other arch draped the New Mexico state flag with the yellow and red colors of Spain. In the center of the flag shone the ancient sun symbol of a Native American people called the Zia who believe that the giver of all good distributes gifts in groups of four. East. North. South. West. Summer. Fall. Winter. Spring. Sunrise. Noon. Evening. Night. And lastly, life itself. Childhood. Youth. Middle age and old age. These are all bound by the circle of life drawn in the middle of the state flag, with these four sets of four lines shooting out from the circle, looking like rays of the sun.

Oh, so many wonders to see! Where to go first, she thought.

Marcelina closed her eyes, twirled, stopped and then pointed.

She wandered through artwork from exhibitors as far away as Arizona.

She oohed and ahhed at the electro mechanical wonders on display by professors from the University of New Mexico. Marcelina wished she could stay until tomorrow morning because there was to be a flying exhibition of aerobatics. Witches can fly with magic, but how can a person soar through the air in a machine and not fall down? Surely the machine would be so heavy it would fall from the sky.

Now that she gave the idea some thought, Marcelina wasn't sure she wanted to witness the crazy flyers being squashed like bugs.

Tomorrow, there were to be games at the speed ring. Foot races. High wire acts and horse races. Too bad she had to be back in Madrid by morning. *I am like Cinderella.*

She bought an ice cream cone from a salesgirl who admired her necklace and bracelet.

"It's a Marlene Dietrich duplicate from that new movie *The Devil is a Woman*," Marcelina said.

"Lucky you. My favorite actress."

"My husband bought it for me," she said, her face beaming with pride.

She watched a Ferris wheel at the carnival, chocolate ice cream dripping on her double chin.

Marcelina dropped her cone, ice cream splattering her shoes. Riding the Ferris wheel were her husband Juan and his friend Tom Jackson. Seated between them was a busty woman with red lips and great white teeth. All three were laughing.

The fly hissed in her ear, *Only a whore would wear such red lipstick. Look how her breasts spill from her blouse, the slut.*

Marcelina ran to a carnival game cart with balloons and darts. She hid behind the cart, peeking out.

Her short, stocky Juan and the micro-skinny Tom were both dressed in dirty baseball uniforms, looking like sports stars no woman could resist. They stepped from the Ferris wheel, the woman with the tight dress bouncing between them, tossing her black hair.

All three lined up to play the balloon game.

"You play. You're the pitcher," Tom told Juan.

"Win a teddy bear for me," the woman said, batting her eyelashes at Juan.

The ice cream on her chin was drying, but Marcelina didn't care if she looked low-class. She fell to her knees, rubbing her aching heart.

She's beautiful and Juan wants her, the fly rasped. *She'll take his bat in her mouth with those big red lips.*

She paled, watching her husband win a teddy bear for another woman.

Lord Tez hissed at her, *Juan calls you his "little elephant", and turns from your bed.*

"Because it hasn't been very long since I gave birth," she mumbled.

Seven weeks is long enough. Juan only married you because he couldn't have Salia. Doesn't that woman remind you of her?

The woman was sleek and slim with skin like honey. Marcelina nodded her head, her lower lip trembling. "Juan is a good, loving, faithful husband."

"There," Juan said, bowing to the woman.

Marcelina bowed over, like he slugged her in the stomach.

See. He's begging her. Next he'll be down on his hands and knees, crazy in lust with her. When was the last time Juan wanted you? Poor man must be sex starved. And the fly laughed, its antennae wiggling.

Marcelina cuffed her hands to her ears and moaned. Lord Tez would drive her insane one day. "Shut up," she muttered.

The fly chuckled, and she swiped her hand in the air to shoo him away.

Tom said, "See, Marilyn, my friend has the best aim in New Mexico. Tomorrow, we'll beat the Bernalillo Lumberjacks and win the tournament. With my hitting and Juan's pitching, no one can beat the Madrid Miners."

Marilyn held the teddy bear to her lips, kissing it.

She's imagining Juan's lips, the fly whispered.

Marilyn sucked on the teddy bear's nose, lifting her eyes to Juan.

She's pretending she's sucking his baseballs. She wants his bat sliding into her home plate.

"Come on, Marilyn, we must go before your father gets home," a grey-haired woman yelled from the crowd lingering about the rides and games.

Tom grabbed her hand. "See you tomorrow?"

Marcelina never heard her answer because Lord Tez was driving her crazy with his seductive voice. *Tom's a referee to cover up Marilyn's game with Juan. How many times has your husband traveled to Albuquerque? To play baseball? Ha! More like he has been playing Marilyn. One day he'll just run off the field and never come home. You've got to outsmart her. Strike before you're struck out. It's the only way to play baseball, sweetheart. The only way to stay in the game is to strike her out. Play ball!*

She stumbled after Marilyn and her mother. Her stomach ached and her legs trembled.

Marcelina hid in the shadows, watching the windows of the house. Ah, there is the bedroom of the marriage-breaker. The harlot leaves her window shade pulled up and her light on while she undresses. She stands at the window, massaging her breasts and moaning at the full moon.

She's imagining Juan pitching into her big butt. He's your husband. Your property.

"Don't say that!" she cried.

You've got to act before Juan arrives to crawl through her window, sliding into home base—again.

She clawed at the necklace Juan had given her, fake pearls scattering.

"Yipes!" Marcelina dropped to her knees, frantically searching for the pearls.

You've got to steal your own bases, sugar, if you want to win. Remember the article in True Story?

She yanked the magazine from her purse and the cover blasting the article "HIS LOVE AT ANY PRICE Revealing Two Women's Deathless Battle for a Boy".

She sat against the wall, hugging her knees. Her makeup was smeared and her hair resembled a bird's nest. Her heart was in pieces like the necklace.

After 30 minutes the lights in the house flicked off.

The night was chilly but her head warm from a scarf cascading down her back, giving Marcelina the look of the Catholic woman always prepared for church with her head covered.

She slid the window up, removed her shoes, and tiptoed around the bedroom, touching Marilyn's intimate clothing with distaste.

The woman appeared lovely as she slept, her face freshly washed. The mark of the whore of Babylon, blood red lipstick, was scrubbed from her face, making her appear younger.

The fly skidded across Marilyn's forehead. Marcelina trembled with fear at getting caught in her bedroom, but Marilyn merely frowned.

Don't forget that you are not just an ordinary healer, Marcelina, Lord Tez whispered. *I, your patron, have given you the magic to absorb into your hands, the diseases you eradicate, such as that cockeyedness you cured earlier.*

She ran a hand over Marilyn's face, hovering over her eyelids and muttering a spell. "I am the beautician. Women come to me for beauty. And so, I grant reverse beauty to Marilyn. Now, my Juan won't want your pink taco," she hissed in her ear.

Marcelina whispered to the fly, "With her new crooked eyes, Marilyn will see her world as skewed and not so whitewashed. I am doing her a favor."

Of course you are, my sweetie. Marilyn will scream in the morning when she discovers her marred beauty, but the world is not a fair place, my dear. Play ball!

Marcelina climbed out the window after hitting a home run.

The moonlight highlighted her reflection in the window pane and flashed, illuminating the rose on her head. The white rose bloomed to a bright red color. The moonlight flashed back to its bluish hue. She reeled with fright at the red rose on her head, yet her heart beat in triumph. Tonight, she crossed a line with her magic and was no longer just a healer. There was no going back. The white rose turned red from the oils in her hair, filled with the power of red magic.

"But I promise to never become a full-fledged Sister of the Black Rose. I am a good Catholic—I swear it," she mumbled.

"Of course you are," Lord Tez hissed.

The last train left Albuquerque for Santa Fe in an hour. Lord Tez had deserted her, having worked his mischief. *It's his fault. He talked me into it. He is truly the Lord of Chaos.*

There was one more thing Marcelina wanted to do in the big city, and she bounced on the bus, approaching Old Town.

Marcelina blinked at the Grand Opera House on Railroad Avenue and 3rd Street. "Stop the bus!" she yelled.

The driver slammed on the brakes.

She ran down the bus aisle. "Hurry! Hurry!" she screamed, pounding the door.

The driver cranked the door open and she stumbled down the stairs, hurrying towards the opera house and a woman with long red hair standing at the steps. Marcelina clawed at the woman's elbow, swinging her around. "Salia?"

The woman jerked her arm away and shoved her so that she fell. "You crazy or something, grabbing a girl like that and scaring the crap out of her? Oh, maybe you're one of them what likes the ladies? It'll cost you extra, sweetheart," she said and winked.

The woman's face was heavily made up, not like an opera singer but like a prostitute.

"My mistake. I thought you were someone else." Marcelina dragged her butt away from the woman, and then pushed herself to her feet. She limped back to the bus, teary-eyed.

Marcelina shuffled into the Alvarado Hotel lobby. Often, she talked in her head to Salia. *Ah, my friend, how we always wanted to come to Albuquerque, but your curse kept you from traveling.*

She was embarrassed to be dressed so poorly compared to the fashionable guests at the hotel. The red rose sticking up from her head made her even more self-conscious. She took baby steps towards the Alvarado Hotel desk. "I would like to make a phone call, long distance," she said and yanked out a piece of paper from her wallet, handing it to a clerk.

"This is miner's scrip," he snorted.

"The village of Cerrillos gives 80 cents for every dollar," she lied— Cerrillos only gave 75 cents.

"This is not Cerrillos or Madrid, Lady, and your miner's scrip is worthless here. You'll need some coins." He crumpled her scrip, tossing it on the floor.

Marcelina had stolen Marilyn's purse, and she fished for some quarters.

The man showed her how to drop the coins in the telephone slot and dial the number.

"Madrid," the telephone operator answered.

"Betty Sue, is that really you?"

"Yeah," she said, cracking her chewing gum.

"Uh, what's your last name?" Marcelina said, testing her.

"It ain't any of your beeswax. Who's this?"

"Marcelina."

"Where you callin' from, Hon? You finally get a phone put in that shop of your'n?"

"I'm calling from a friend's house," Marcelina said feeling let down that she couldn't brag to Betty Sue that she was calling from Albuquerque, but her trip to visit La Llorona was top secret.

"You still gonna cut my hair Saturday?" Betty Sue said.

"Yes. Good-bye."

Marcelina hung up the phone, her face glowing in a way that only someone from a small village would understand. She had made a long distance phone call to Madrid, all the way from Albuquerque, and had seen electrical lights. In tiny Madrid, which had shrunk to about 1500 souls since the Great Depression, coal was still used for lighting. With a population of around 31,000, the big city even had royal roots, having been named for the Spanish Duke of Albuquerque.

Marcelina left the hotel, feeling like a queen.

8

Joseph Quill stood before the mirror in his room at the boarding house in Madrid. He brushed his head until his golden hair shone like the sun. Quill was dressed in a tuxedo with long tails. He was attending an opening at the *Engine House Melodrama Theatre and Opera*, some silly musical to get people laughing instead of mooning about the Great Depression, which had the coal mine running only two days a week. The opera was called *Revenge with Music*.

Quill actually lived in Santa Fe and his mistress, Sofia, was probably mad at him for not going home for the weekend.

He whistled as he steered his truck towards the theatre. He climbed out of his Dodge truck and shined up a dirty spot on the door of his pickup with his jacket but, hey, his tuxedo was black, just like his Dodge.

Flicking his ticket with his index finger, he strolled into the theatre, stopping in mid-stride, arrested by Salia Stuwart's portrait. On Salia's hair was painted a black rose, appearing moist and fresh.

With a shaky finger, he touched the rose which was damp. *Probably the paint sweating*, he thought. Quill sniffed his finger and the odor of a musky rose.

He cocked his head, examining the beautiful face of the opera singer who literally brought this theatre to life with her performances. Salia was once the star and owner of the *Engine House Melodrama Theatre and Opera*, burned as a witch by the villagers. From her blue-grey eyes flowed a heartbreaking vulnerability that would move any man to tears—even a rock like him.

So once again Quill had to harden himself against Salia Stuwart and what he must do. What he had sworn to do. He closed his eyes to her fragile beauty and shimmering sadness. He turned his back on the portrait, and walked towards his seat, only his steps were not as jaunty as before. His shoulders were rounded instead of straight.

Belinda Vasquez Garcia

He plopped down on his seat and brooded. *Why the hell did I even come tonight? Because I've always been a sucker for make believe. Like with Salia.* He laughed at the irony of his joke.

Quill moved his long legs so that an attractive woman could sit down beside him. He didn't pay any attention to her. He just stared, transfixed, at the empty stage, imagining what it must have been like when Salia was alive.

I'm obsessed with a ghost, he thought with disgust.

Eight rows behind Quill, Marcelina stepped on toes to reach her seat. "Move your duck feet," she said to one person.

"The seats are too narrow," she grumbled to Juan.

Her husband moved her about as best he could to make Marcelina comfortable. Juan then sat there, twirling his skinny moustache and looking miserable. "I am sorry, my dear, that I've lost my job, but I was not the only man let go from the mine. Had I any warning, I would not have let you purchase tickets to the theatre tonight."

Juan had returned from Albuquerque and banged the front door open, wobbling drunkenly at the threshold, his eyes bloodshot. "I have bad news—I've been laid off from the mine. We have a month to clear out of the house," he said and toppled to the floor. There was no more money for the baseball team to travel and the mine president, Oscar Hughes, was not a fan.

Marcelina groaned at the thought of being homeless, her hands trembling at the image of moving to Albuquerque where there was much established competition in the beauty business. *We shall just have to move to Santa Fe instead, but how to get the money to open a beauty shop,* she thought.

Marcelina was so afraid of moving away, her stomach hurt. Her family roots bored deep—her father and both grandfathers had been coal miners. She lived all her life in Madrid and never wanted to leave. "What if you can't find a job? So many are out of work—so many," she whispered to Juan.

"Don't worry, we will get by. Let's enjoy the opera and forget about our troubles for just one night. God will provide."

"Hush. The play's started," a man in front of her said.

"Oh, you shut up," she said, and Marcelina smacked his head.

Everyone clapped at the sweet young thing singing in the opera—*Revenge with Music,* a story set in Spain in 1800.

Half-way through the performance, Marcelina yawned and made a face when the actress sang another bad note.

Suddenly, the lights went out, pitching the theatre into a black hole like the most inner coal mine dynamited deep within the bowels of Madrid.

Seats creaked in the darkness.

Skirts rustled.

Boots tapped.

Then...

The sound of a woman crying raised the hair at the nape of everyone's neck. The crying had an echo quality, sounding like the sobbing came from within the walls and ceiling.

"It's Salia's ghost," voices whispered.

The sadness was palpable, a heaviness crushing their chests. The audience could hardly breathe the bittersweet oxygen of the theatre now smelling of peaches and vinegar. The odor filling the theatre was sour and sweet, just like Salia had been. She had always smelled like peaches fermenting in a tub of vinegar. The audience was punch drunk on despair.

The sound of a moving train caused their hearts to collectively quit beating.

Closer. Closer.

It sounded like the train was gaining speed and the engine headed towards the audience.

Everyone held their breath, staring at the light of an oncoming train.

The actors on stage hung their mouths' open as they felt the wind from the moving train rustle their hair.

The audience was stiff with fear as they gripped the arms of their seats, yet there was a thrill about the impending danger causing their adrenaline to soar, foreheads to dampen, and throats to dry out.

The east side of the theatre lit up so that the shadow of a train could be seen barreling along.

There. In front of the train. A ghost holding her arms up.

The ghost fell in front of the shadowy train and let forth a blood-curdling scream.

Pierre, the theatre manager, hissed from behind the curtain, "Salia, stop haunting! Quit messing around. Shoo. Go away. Turn on the rest of the lights!" He waved his hands, his fingers trembling. "Let me get on with the show," he pleaded.

A few in the audience jumped from their seats and quickly left the theatre. Wicked laughter echoed behind their backs. They ran even faster to their cars. A light glowed from the remains of the house at the bottom of Witch Hill. They muttered a prayer as they stepped on the gas, driving recklessly towards their homes. There had been two new performances since Salia's death. On opening nights at least one theatergoer was killed in a traffic accident. The Albuquerque and Cerrillos Coal Mining Company hushed the newspapers reporting the incidents, like the company did all unsavory happenings in Madrid. However, one Santa Fe newspaper reporter published a story that the ghost of the great opera singer, Salia Stuwart, haunted the theatre. The reporter was fired.

Above the stage was silhouetted the ghostly shadow of a woman on a swing, kicking her long legs. The ghost sang like a canary, sounding a lot like Salia.

The theatre grew cold and a gust of wind was felt as the shadow swung.

"Salia?" Marcelina whispered, staring up at the curvy apparition.

Whoosh!

The lights flickered until once again the stage was well lit.

Pierre walked briskly onto the stage. He coughed. "I hope you all have enjoyed our little, uh, diversion. Here at the *Engine House Melodrama Theatre and Opera* we like to...to...play with the latest technology. Throwing shadows upon the wall and such nonsense is part of the performance. The ghost... silhouettes. The theatre is old and the acoustics bad. We often hear strange sounds such as laughter and crying," he said and bowed.

Without any more fanfare, the orchestra played and *Revenge with Music* continued.

Marcelina left her chair and snuck around to the back of the theatre. "Salia? Are you here, my old friend?" she whispered.

There was a disappointing silence. Gone was the coldness rushing through the theatre, along with the sound of a phantom train. Salia's ghost acted her performance and left the theatre as quickly as she had come. Like she always did on opening night, Salia didn't want the audience to forget that this was still her theatre and she was the star here, and no actress could ever compare. In her haunting, Salia was every bit as possessive as Marcelina was with Juan. This was the reason her portrait still hung at the *Engine House Theatre* where the star's portrait of the current show should have hung.

Nobody would have dared remove Salia's picture from the theatre, just as no actress was allowed the use of her dressing room. The last actress insisting she have use of the large, luxurious dressing room, fled the theatre, catching the first train out of Madrid.

Marcelina tiptoed to the dressing room door that was sealed shut. She held her ear to the door, listening to a frantic pacing. "Salia?" she said through the keyhole.

The footsteps from the dressing room stopped and Marcelina dragged her feet back to her seat.

She noticed Marshal Quill holding his head in his hands and sobbing. And she had thought him a cold man.

———— ⧫ ————

9

Marcelina's twins screamed from the back room. "See to the babies," she yelled at Juan.

She dragged him from bed so he could take care of their three-month-old girls.

Marcelina marched out of the house and walked towards Witch Hill. Her chest felt tight with worry and her stomach tense. Juan had looked for work in Cerrillos but found none. He tried mining for gold in the hills south of town to pay for their move. Occasionally, he found a nugget to sell at the company store for $5. They had one week left before eviction. *What are we to do? Apply for Aid to Dependent Children? But where will we live,* she thought.

Marcelina wished she could ask Salia.

She walked to Salia's house and twirled atop Witch Hill, her black hair flowing behind her like lava. Marcelina pretended, as she always did, that she was Salia, imagining what it must be like to have long, shapely legs whirling beneath a twirling skirt. If only she could find Salia's shape-shifting rock, then she could transform into whatever she wanted, whoever she longed to be—she could stay young forever!

Marcelina spit at the big houses in the district the villagers call *Silver Coal* since the houses in that part of town were not as blackened by coal dust nor in need of repairs. At *Silver Coal*, there was meat on the table for supper every night, and children played in big yards with lush lawns. The miners were charged for a ton of coal a month, whether or not it was needed. Their kids were black from playing on mountains of coal piled up in their yards.

If Salia were here, she would loan Marcelina whatever money she needed. Salia had always been generous, especially with her only friend. Oh, how she missed her! They had been much alike. Both unloved and abused. Salia had always been there for Marcelina, rescuing her. They had saved each other.

With a heavy heart, Marcelina trudged towards the road and the mansion that once belonged to Samuel Stuwart. The mine manager, Oscar Hughes, now lived there. His wife, Mildred, acted like they owned the mansion, but the Stuwart nephew back East did. The nephew never actually came to Madrid, thus allowing Oscar and his wife to act like tyrants.

A car drove beside Marcelina, slowing down. Pacheco's small head barely topped the steering wheel. He hung his face out and chuckled. "I hear Juan is now a kept man. Is he sleeping late then?"

He laughed and sped past her.

She threw him a dirty finger, not caring if he saw. The roof of his car was piled high with strapped-on luggage. It must be moving day for Pacheco.

The worst part of being a beautician, who could work magic with hair, was that Mildred Hughes demanded that as part of the interest Marcelina owed the company store, she be at her beck and call to beautify her whenever Mildred requested. Mildred ordered she make beauty house calls.

Mildred doesn't even reimburse me for the calluses on my feet and demands I walk over on a Sunday. It's getting dark for heaven's sake.

She climbed the steps to the house.

The door flung open.

Marcelina screeched because the queen of Madrid opened the door herself. "Where are your servants?" Marcelina said.

"One came down with the flu so I kicked them all out, but you, Marcelina, are irreplaceable," Mildred said.

"If I'm so valuable to you, perhaps you can talk to your husband about giving Juan his job back," she said.

"Oh, I can't talk business with Oscar. He knows best about what man should work and what man is lazy. Come in," she said, pushing her into the house.

Marcelina rolled her eyes around the room. In school, she was not good at mathematics, but excelled at money. Such rich paintings, soft carpet, and the dining room set imported from Albuquerque. The pictures were worth at least five dollars each, or perhaps the exorbitant sum of twenty dollars. "Ah, and you bought a 12-tube Crosley radio. I have seen it advertised as both a ham radio and a regular one."

"Wood smears easily from greasy fingertips, so don't touch anything," Mildred said, slapping her fingers.

Marcelina was privy to gossip—a side benefit of her trade.

Mildred pinched her arm so she would hurry and, "Tell me some juicy gossip so I can broadcast it on my ham radio."

Marcelina narrowed her eyes at the large painting of Eustace, Mildred's daughter. How much hush money would she pay to keep quiet about Eustace's affair with another woman in Albuquerque? "I have some gossip for you, Mildred," she said.

Crash!

"Yi!" Marcelina screamed. "I...I have to go." A mirror falling by itself and breaking was a bad omen.

"Clean up the mess you made," Mildred snarled, shoving a broom at her.

"The mirror broke by itself," she cried, but everyone did what Mildred Hughes ordered. By the time Marcelina finished with the broom, the entire bottom floor of the mansion was spotless. She sat, wheezing, finding it difficult to breathe.

"Come now, Marcelina, no rest for the wicked. Follow me upstairs to work your magic on my hair. I am going to the opera tonight."

She felt faint, having skipped supper to come here. Marcelina stole a banana from a fruit basket, following Mildred up the stairs to her bedroom. She dropped the banana peel on the hall floor, figuring she'd pick it up on her way out, with Mildred none the wiser.

Mildred was so rich that she even had a radio in her bedroom.

Mildred flicked on the radio and plopped down in a cushy white chair. The radio announced President Roosevelt's fireside chat *On Drought Conditions* would be playing that evening.

Soon, Marcelina was caught up in the music on the radio, her big flashy earrings jiggling, black frizzy hair bouncing on her neck, swinging her wide hips behind the chair. A red rose dangled from her thick lips, saliva dripping on the petals. She lifted her hands and snapped her fingers while sweat stained the underarms of her candy-caned flapper dress. It was last decade's fashion, bought at a used thrift store. Her knees wobbled in flesh-colored nylon stockings with a rip down the left leg and holes in the right leg, but Marcelina refused to part with her precious stockings. She wiggled to the music and scanned a *Vogue* magazine that was on the nightstand.

Marcelina began Mildred's beauty treatment with a gentle wash, using the fragrant Armand Eau de Cologne Cleansing Cream. "When are your new servants arriving?"

"You're to fetch them at the coal mining office when you leave," Mildred said.

"I see," she said and yanked her hair.

"Ouch! Be gentle."

"Sorry, but I wanted to point out that you are balding so you must buy a bottle of Glover's Mange Medicine, Medicated Soap, and System of Massage." Marcelina curled her hair tighter, so that the roots strained. *I hope you lose all your hair, bitch!*

"You don't know what it's like to grow old—you're the same age as my Eustace," Mildred said.

"Speaking of Eustace...she is having sex with..."

"Unlike you, I'm fortunate to have money to indulge myself. Oscar keeps a safe stuffed with cash."

"There is a safe? Here?"

Mildred nodded.

Marcelina narrowed her eyes at the concoction of makeup in her bag—tools of her trade. "And you said your new servants aren't coming until I go get them?"

"That's right."

Marcelina quickly revised her plan of blackmailing Mildred with information that Eustace is a lesbian. Instead, she had been experimenting with lipsticks and eyeshadows, which Marcelina hadn't tried on any customer yet, but she brought the makeup with her, along with ordinary varieties. Hopefully, Marcelina wouldn't kill Mildred, her guinea pig. If the magic in the makeup was too mild, she could go back to plan one—blackmail.

"Is that Max Factor?" Mildred said.

"I have made this eyeshadow especially for you, my dear. The shade will open your eyes so big and pretty, I will be able to look into the pupils and...never mind. You don't want to know the technical details. Here, this red lipstick will loosen your lips so they are lovely and full."

Humming, Marcelina plucked a few eyebrows. She then filled in the arch with a black pencil and dusted above each eye with her special-formula grey shadow.

Mildred grasped the chair handles as the eyeshadow penetrated her skin. She sat stiff as a statue.

58

Marcelina waved her hand in front of Mildred and nothing—she was hypnotized. She placed a mirror under Mildred's nostrils, sighing with relief at her hot breath on the glass.

Marcelina painted blood-red coloring on Mildred's lips. "Now talk to me, Mildred. Where is your safe and what is the combination?"

Mildred spoke robotically, her eyes focused straight ahead and unblinking.

"Stay," Marcelina ordered, like Mildred was a dog.

She sashayed towards the exit. The closet door was slightly ajar. *Ooh, what nice dresses.* Marcelina knocked her butt against the closet door, bouncing it open.

The white mink coat looked familiar. She examined the inside and read the name stitched in gold.

She marched from the closet, screaming at Mildred. "You've got Salia's coat! How dare you!"

She reached back her hand and slapped Mildred, and her head snapped back, waking her up.

Marcelina screeched, running with the mink coat.

Mildred jumped from the chair and ran out the door, chasing her.

Marcelina jumped over the banana peel.

Mildred slipped on the banana peel, toppling down the stairs, screaming, with her arms and legs flying.

Mildred lay at the bottom of the stairs, her body twisted and broken.

Marcelina ran back up the stairs, opened the safe, grabbed the money, and scurried down the stairs. She nearly tripped on Mildred. She bent, placing her ear to her lips. Mildred's breathing was rattled.

She dialed the phone, but Madrid was having another power outage, which were more frequent of late.

"You'll be okay, Mildred. I'll get you to the hospital," she said, patting her hand awkwardly.

Mildred wheezed and whimpered like a wounded animal.

Marcelina covered her ears with trembling hands. She was not so good in a crisis. She picked up the phone but there was still no dial tone.

She did not know how to drive, nor did Marcelina know where the keys were.

The house was isolated and there were no neighbors to ask for help.

Mildred was no longer breathing.

Marcelina hated the woman but never wished for her death. However, superstitions always come true—*if a mirror in the house falls and breaks by itself, someone in the house will soon die.*

Marcelina opened all the windows so Mildred's soul could escape her body.

Then she waited and waited for Mildred to leave, but her soul was stubborn. "Very well. Have it your way, Mildred. If I had your pretty things, I wouldn't want to go either. Give my worst to your husband," she said, spitting.

Marcelina pried the Glover's beauty products away from her stiff fingers.

She grabbed a copy of *Photoplay* magazine with fashion designer Elsa Schiaparelli on the cover advertising her article on how a woman can still look stylish, no matter how small her income.

She, also, heaved a radio in her arms. There were dramas, comedies, and mysteries to catch up on.

They were moving to Santa Fe! She now had more than enough money to pay off their debt, put a down payment on a house and set up a beauty shop.

Marcelina clutched $4,022 in hot cash, humming as she stealthily walked home, dragging the radio behind her. "Happy days are here again..."

"Goodbye, Madrid! You can go to coal-mining hell!"

———

Part Two

Lust for Power

For what does a person live but to gain power in the world?

10

The shaman Storm-Chaser woke with a splitting hangover. Both his wives were yelling, making his head pound. He yanked a whiskey-stained pair of khaki pants over his legs. With shaky fingers he snapped the bottom two buttons, but it was enough to hang his pants low on his bony hips.

He wobbled over to the egg basket. His wives hissed and screamed, causing him to drop an egg on the floor. Women—his wives would be the death of him. What man can understand the heart of a woman? His wife, Spider-Woman, hinted that he should marry her great niece, Little-Dove, claiming she yearned for companionship after their daughter eloped with the witch, Jefe. Now, Spider-Woman didn't want the younger woman around.

Storm-Chaser lifted another egg from the basket, rubbing it across his stomach. He then broke the shell, pouring the egg onto a plate, and balancing the plate on his head. His hangover was sucked from his brain, through his skull and into the egg yolk.

The front door flung wide open. The sun ricocheted from a silver star, startling Storm-Chaser with blindness. He jerked his head, the raw egg sloshing the plate and splashing his face.

A man stepped through the doorway, blocking the light.

He blinked his good eye at a tall golden haired, amber-eyed man with a light tan. A U.S. Marshal. Storm-Chaser felt embarrassed to be caught with egg on his face, sitting barefoot with his pot belly hanging over his half-buttoned khakis, stinking of whiskey and tobacco. Like most Native American men, his chest had no hair. Instead, his 73 years were etched in wrinkles rippling across a chest sagging in folds to his belly. His iron-grey, mussed-up hair cascaded to his waist.

"Joseph Quill," the man said, kicking the door shut behind him. His spurs jingled when he stomped his boot, transferring the dust of the Pueblo to the wooden floor.

Storm-Chaser wiped his face, not bothering to cover the scarred hole of his right eye-socket with his leather patch. It was his experience that a white man couldn't stomach ugliness. He didn't expect the marshal to stay long.

Quill rolled his eyes around the dimly lit home of a prosperous shaman who traded his healing powers for food grown by his patients. Colorful corn hung from the ceiling still attached to the husks. Red dried chilies hung from the corners of a room smelling of garlic and onions. On one wall hung meat hooks with freshly butchered venison, chickens, sheep, rabbits, and sides of beef. Watermelons and cantaloupes bulged out from baskets. The iron griddle had some dough stuck to it from the morning tortillas.

Quill reached over to a plate and grabbed a warm tortilla.

"Do you wish to purchase my services?" Storm-Chaser said in an arrogant manner that assumed the marshal already knew who he was. Else why come to him in the first place?

"Why, old man? Do I look sick and need an egg on top of my head," Quill said, his eyes sparkling with amusement.

"There is much power in the egg. Birth. Woman. Lust. Rebirth."

"Yeah, yeah old man. They say you're a medicine man who can foretell the future. Cast love spells. Find lost animals. Bring about good weather. Cure blood diseases. Broken bones. Wounds. What have you."

Storm-Chaser rose from his chair, offended by the laughter in the marshal's voice. He buttoned a clean white shirt over his nakedness. "Why are you here then? To insult my hospitality?" he barked, a little more vicious than he intended. Quill still wore his dusty black hat. Storm-Chaser knew enough of white manners, and that hat should have been removed and placed across his chest as soon as he entered his home.

Quill waved the tortilla in Storm-Chaser's face. "Got anything I can wash this down with?"

Spider-Woman poured the marshal a glass of water, keeping her grey head bowed. "You must forgive my husband his manners. We are not often honored by a visit from a white man. Our ways are not your ways. Let me offer you some pemmican to eat with your tortilla," she said in a beggarly voice.

"Pemmican?" he raised an eyebrow.

Storm-Chaser watched, with an angry look on his face, his wife pound wild cherries, pits and all, into a mush. Spider-Woman mixed in strips of jerky and fat. They still had pemmican stored away in rawhide cases from

64

the winter that she could have served him. Why did she prolong his visit? He wanted the marshal gone!

Quill narrowed his eyes at Storm-Chaser. "What do you know of Salia Stuwart?"

Spider-Woman hit the bowl with such force of the pestle that she just might make a hole in the stone.

Storm-Chaser did not care to discuss anything having to do with Witch Hill in front of his number-one wife. Witch Hill brought back memories of dark years in his marriage when he was insane with lust for the witch, Felicita, Salia's mother. He motioned for Quill to step outside.

The question had jogged his memory—this marshal was the man with the light brown eyes who walked into the Mine Shaft Saloon after the house burning on Witch Hill. He had not found it odd then that a U.S. Marshal was asking questions about Salia a mere thirteen hours after the burning. Storm-Chaser had guessed the marshal was investigating Samuel Stuwart's murder which occurred two days before the Penitentes, those fanatical Catholics, stormed Witch Hill.

To the side of his apartment were his beehives, square brick boxes built above a foundation of boards. The hives were still covered with black wool blankets that had been tied down with rope for the night. A brick rested atop each hive. The pain of rheumatoid arthritis can be alleviated with bee venom. There were five hives in all.

The Pueblo was as busy as any village. The people all stopped what they were doing and acknowledged their shaman with reverence.

Storm-Chaser lifted his chin, striking a most shaman-like pose, as if he was all knowing. All seeing. All wondering what the heck their shaman was doing with a U.S. Marshal.

The people didn't wonder for very long. Soon, it was business as usual at the Pueblo.

Chickens ran around the yard with half-naked children chasing them, squealing in delight.

The smell of fresh bread baking in outdoor ovens permeated the air.

A group of women made pottery, running their hands over the clay, molding bowls and vases to be baked in a fire fueled by dung chips.

Women weaved baskets from a variety of grasses, willow wands and fibers, strips of bark and bulrushes.

At another end of the Pueblo women worked at an outdoor loom supported by two tree trunks. They wove homegrown cotton into clothing and made winter blankets from shorn sheep. The women made their own dyes from roots and plants.

Quill popped some chewing tobacco into his mouth and munched.

Storm-Chaser stared off into the distance towards Madrid. In the burning house, Salia whispered into his ear a secret he would never reveal, even if it meant his own life. "Salia was accused many times of being a witch," he told the marshal.

Quill shrugged his shoulders and spit. It was apparent by the look in his eyes that the marshal did not believe in hocus-pocus.

"You should beware of witchcraft, Marshal, especially a man of your influence. If a witch offers you food or drink, lay it aside for three days. Within that time, if the food turns to worms, its accursed nature is revealed."

"I'll remember that the next time I'm in Madrid and eat at the restaurant. The food tastes like it was cooked by a witch," Quill said in a dry voice.

"Any news of the Great Depression and this Roosevelt?"

"His New Deal is good for your people. Collier, the new head of the Bureau of Indian Affairs, is fighting for Native American rights, to preserve your culture and Pueblo lands. But you don't give a rat's ass about the Depression, the president, or Madrid's dwindling coal supply since the mines are only running a couple days a week. Your Pueblo burns wood along with dung, not coal. But okay, I'll play your game of let's *talk about something else because I don't feel comfortable talking about witch burnings*. Hell, you're not far from being a witch yourself."

"It is apparent you know little about my people or medicine men."

"What's this supposed to be?" Quill patted a wooden statue as tall as a man but resembling a bird with a blocked head and body and wings folded down. It looked like steps were on the inside of the wings.

"A thunderbird can produce thunder by flapping its wings, and lightning by opening and closing its eyes. A thunderbird can rip open a tree to find insects which it considers a delicacy." Storm-Chaser didn't tell Quill that the mark of the Thunder Spirit was his gift. The thunderbird was his patron, bestowing the power of lightning, thunder and all the fierceness of the skies. A man like Quill would never believe.

"So what do you know about the babies at San Felipe and some of the other pueblos?" Quill said.

He stared up at the sky as if in a trance and quoted, "And a crying will be heard among the pueblos, the like of which has not been heard since the massacre by the white man. The Rio Grande will run crimson with the blood of innocence. So it is written. So it shall be."

Just then a baby cried, startling them both.

Spider-Woman offered Quill a fresh tortilla spread with pemmican. Little-Dove stood behind her, patting a baby boy on his back to comfort him. She was a shy small woman with eyes like a doe.

"May I borrow a coin, Marshal?" Storm-Chaser said.

Quill absentmindedly removed a silver dollar from his pants pocket, staring intently at the baby, never once taking his eyes from the child. He didn't even notice Storm-Chaser lick the coin and press it to Little-Dove's forehead, instantly stopping her nosebleed.

Storm-Chaser dropped the coin in his pocket, rubbing his hands and smacking his lips. There was enough to buy a couple of whiskey bottles in Madrid. He would ride into town this afternoon.

Quill took the baby from Spider-Woman. The boy had a mass of black hair and grey-green hazel eyes, the color of a stormy ocean. His skin was fair.

Quill shook the baby, making him laugh. He kissed the child on his cheek, reluctantly surrendering him.

The baby smiled at Quill, and the marshal smiled back, lopsided and goofy-like.

"My grandson, Dark-Shadow, was born in Santa Fe," Storm-Chaser proudly lied. "You may have heard of his father, my son Wolfe, the great healer of Santa Fe, also known as El Curandero?"

Without taking his eyes from Dark-Shadow, Quill shook his head, no, that he never heard of his son. He seemed inordinately interested in the babe. He hadn't even tasted the pemmican Spider-Woman had given him but continued to stare at the baby, as if memorizing his face.

Storm-Chaser grew nervous at Quill's interest in his grandson and rubbed one bare foot atop the other. The night he brought Salia's son to the Pueblo, the tipi moon appeared to the Indian people after many centuries, proving that the boy was the reincarnation of the great witch Montezuma, but only he knew this secret and would protect the child with his life. Plus, the baby claimed his heart and was his grandson, regardless of whose blood flowed through his veins. Dark-Shadow was a fourth-generation witch, and his grandmother and great-grandmother had practiced black magic. Storm-Chaser vowed to raise the boy as a shaman to help his people, even if he was just one-quarter Indian. Dark-Shadow couldn't help it that he was, also, one-quarter Spanish and half-white, his father being the rich Samuel Stuwart who had owned all of Madrid, including the mine, besides various businesses in Albuquerque. Truth be told, Dark-Shadow was the late Stuwart's heir, and Storm-Chaser feared for the baby's life, if word got out that he survived the fire. The villagers, after all, had been trying to burn the baby as a witch.

"You named the baby Dark-Shadow?" Quill said in a curious voice.

"Yes. My grandson was born with a shadow at his back."

"We all were, old man, which reminds me about our previous subject. We were speaking about the babies," he said. Quill winked at the baby, cooing at him.

Storm-Chaser patted Quill on the arm, motioning with his head for the marshal to follow him to the back of his apartment.

Quill dragged his eyes from Dark-Shadow and walked beside Storm-Chaser, turning his head to have one last look at the baby.

Dark-Shadow stuck his fingers in his mouth and gurgled at him.

The man likes children, Storm-Chaser thought and smiled at the marshal whose eyes had a strange yearning when he looked at Dark-Shadow.

"I don't want my wives to know about the babies," Storm-Chaser said, leading him to the back of his apartment where there was a tipi. Storm-Chaser was half-Mescalero Apache and when his Apache blood boiled, it was then that he would sit in his tent, a relic from his youth when he wandered the plains with his father.

"What in tarnation is that contraption?" Quill asked and bent at the waist to look inside a short, round building made of bent branches hammered into the ground. It was covered with deer hides. Steam arose from the opening. Some four feet in front of this opening was the top half of a bull skull with horns. Inside was a pile of sizzling rocks, giving off steam.

"Ah, my wives have heated the stones of my sacred sweat lodge." Storm-Chaser rubbed his hands together in anticipation of sweating off the bad juices he encountered yesterday in Madrid where people stared at him with revulsion simply because he was Indian. Oh, they didn't mind taking his money—they just didn't want to touch his hand while doing so.

"What's a sweat lodge?" Quill said.

"It is good to sweat the bad juices from the pores of your body, and is one of the reasons I have lived on this earth for so many years. I wouldn't stand there, if I was you. My pit of rattlesnakes," he said with an amused look in his eyes. He never saw a man move more quickly than Marshal Quill. Not only did he jump away from the pit but at the same time, he drew his gun.

Quill smiled limply at him and placed his gun back in its holster. "Sorry. Habit," he said of his lightning reflexes. "Those snakes your pets?"

"My friends are still hibernating this time of year but when the weather warms, their deadly tails will be rattling. Snake medicine is very powerful, and the venom produces forty enzymes, proteins, and toxins used for healing. Tumors can be shrunk with the poison."

Quill coughed. "The odor of garlic is overwhelming."

Garlic grew in abundance around the apartment. "Garlic is a cure for dizziness and helps the blood provide oxygen to the brain. How many infants have died?" Storm-Chaser asked.

"All the male babies at the infected pueblos under the age of one, seemingly of the same disease. Babies who appear healthy and in the morning aren't breathing," Quill said with a sad look in his eyes.

"Did the babies have any visible symptoms after death?"

"Each had a sore around his mouth with three little marks. There was, also, a mark on each side of their noses."

"This is the work of witchcraft."

"I think, old man, that this is the work of a sick fuck."

"A man like you won't last long in these parts unless he learns to respect the followers of Tezcatlipoca."

"Tez who?"

"Never mind. You will learn. Mark my words," Storm-Chaser said and then muttered, "If you survive."

"So you vouch for all of the people at your Pueblo that they know nothing else about the babies?"

"I do vouch. It is a waste of your time to question any of the others. It will only upset them, this talk of disease and dying babies."

Quill whistled for his horse, a black stallion that came prancing from the front of the apartment. "Is this everyone at the Pueblo, living together in this complex?"

"My son-in-law lives apart from us in that direction," he said, pointing. "Jefe has an infant of his own. Perhaps you should warn him," he slyly added.

Quill mounted his horse and tipped his hat to him. "Next time I get a nosebleed, I'll know where to come, old man," he said, his eyes sparkling with humor.

"Or when you get sunstroke. You're not from around these parts are you, Marshal?"

"Denver."

"What's a Colorado Marshal doing sniffing around New Mexico?"

"That's for me and the federal government to know, and for you to find out with your mystical powers, old man."

Storm-Chaser said to his departing back, "A glass of water placed on the head of a patient soon begins to boil, resulting in a cure of sunstroke."

He laughed at his advice.

"Why aren't you driving a car like the rest of the white men?"

"On these potholed pueblo roads?" Quill said. The marshal winked at him. A gold scorpion necklace hung from a chain around his neck. Perhaps Storm-Chaser was wrong about the man. Just as his mark was the Thunder Spirit, maybe Quill's was the scorpion's sting. Storm-Chaser had a strange feeling about him—a surge of power was coming from Joseph Quill.

"When you run into the dark power of Tezcatlipoca then you will have need of my services, Marshal. My son in Santa Fe refuses to help anyone bewitched because he is afraid to admit his knowledge of sorcery. He fears jeopardizing his practice which is made up of a lot of white people. I have no such trepidation," he hollered at his back.

Quill waved a backhanded acknowledgment of the shaman's courage.

Storm-Chaser sighed. It was the same with all white men. No respect. No understanding of another's ways.

Always to their detriment.

11

Jefe's three disciples sat on the ground in a triangle. Between them was a dice tray woven of yucca leaves and grass. In one corner sat Big-Belly with thin, scraggly, greasy hair he regularly hacked off to the middle of his shoulder. He wore long leather moccasins that came to the middle of his thighs. Across from Big-Belly was the Bat, a midget four feet two-inches in height. The Bat was almost black in complexion with beady, darting eyes. Dead-Man-Walking sat beneath a shade tree because the sunlight was his curse. Dead-Man-Walking was as white as the Bat was black. He was one of the children of the moon, the rare albino Indian who many times is mistaken for a ghost. He had snowy white braids, white eyebrows and eyelashes.

Every man has a weakness and gluttony was Big-Belly's. He smacked his lips, sucking on the bone of an ass.

"Well, you are what you eat," the Bat said.

Big-Belly laughed, sounding like a pig mucking his nose in mud. He scratched at his testicles, yanked at his nose, cleaned out his snot, and rotated a finger in his ear, digging for gold, while he waited for the Bat to place his bet.

"I bet you my knowledge of lameness for your knowledge of sand imagery," said the Bat to the dead man.

Big-Belly grinned at the dead man, wondering if he would take the bet.

Dead-Man-Walking picked up the dice tray and flung it at the Bat, striking him in the corner of his eye. His power to draw a figure in the sand to represent a man, and then cause that man's death by using his sandy image was much greater than the Bat's power of making a man lame. The Bat was lucky to be let off so easy by his insult. Dead-Man-Walking was known to slice a man's throat simply because he called him a white man.

Big-Belly set the dice tray back on the ground, and the three men commenced their gambling. They concentrated on the game so none noticed a U.S. Marshal walk up to the tree. "Afternoon gents," Quill said, tipping his hat.

They jumped from the ground, surrounding the marshal with their arms crossed and their chests puffed out.

"I was wondering if I might ask you all some questions," Quill said, circling his eyes around the trio as if measuring who would strike first.

Jefe hurried out of his hogan, sticking his nose into the circle. "What do you want, Marshal? You're trespassing!"

Quill whistled, wrinkling his nose at the four sorry-looking hogans. "What in tarnation did ya all do to be kicked out of the Pueblo to this sorry place?"

Jefe stared back at Quill, and if looks could kill, Quill would drop dead.

"Folks say you're a witch," Quill said, chuckling at the ugly one. Well, the ugliest one of the bunch anyway. "I'm not afraid of you, Jefe. I've got some calabazilla to ward off the devil right here in my shirt pocket," Quill said, patting the herb in his shirt pocket.

"Liar!"

"Is it true with that cast in your left eye, you could give a baby the evil eye just by looking at him, and that baby would die? Or if you stare at a cake, it falls flat?" Quill smiled—it was not a nice smile.

"You are a fool and a dead man," Jefe snarled.

"Yeah, I'm a smart ass, with a nature to goad a man. Don't even think of paying me a visit in the middle of the night," Quill said, narrowing his eyes.

Jefe grabbed at a cactus, unmindful of the pain in his fingers from the needles poking through his skin.

Quill folded his arms, grinning. "You gonna fill your mouth with those cactus needles, Jefe, and shoot them into my heart? Well, don't waste your time, because I'm heartless."

"What the hell do you want?" he snarled.

"I plan to ask you all some questions. In fact, I was making progress with these men when you interrupted us."

Jefe turned to his men and growled low in his throat.

They shook their heads fearfully—they swore they said nothing!

Quill carefully watched the interaction between Jefe and the three men.

"I, alone, will answer any questions you have," Jefe said.

"Why? Did you cut off their tongues with that sharp knife sheathed against your leg?"

Jefe reached for his knife, clutching the handle. "I am their leader," he said.

"This is America first and an Indian Pueblo second. In America, these men have a right to speak and as a lawman, I have a right to question them."

"Very well. You may question my men."

"Alone. You mosey on back to your hogan and jack off, or whatever it was you were doing. Don't come back until I'm ready for you," Quill said.

Jefe spun and stiffly walked towards his hogan.

"Oh, and Jefe, stand by the door where I can see you. Don't even think of using a sow's ear to eavesdrop with magic."

Quill grabbed the Bat by his neck and walked him over to a secluded area, out of earshot of the others. He questioned him about the deaths at the other pueblos.

The Bat whined, claiming he knew nothing about dying babies. He darted his eyes and pulled at his dick, a sure sign a man is lying.

Quill then questioned Big-Belly who laughed and said he didn't even know where any of the other Pueblos were.

"Shit! Your breath stinks like a donkey, fat man," Quill said, taking a step back.

"And I think you screw donkeys, Marshal."

Quill punched him in the gut, and then walked back to the shade tree and Dead-Man-Walking.

The dead man sat silently, staring straight ahead.

"You a retard?" Quill asked. From the corner of his eye, he could see Jefe grinning at the growing frustration in his voice.

Jefe leaned against the wall of his hogan with his arms crossed and flatly told Quill, "We have no male babies here. What do we care if baby boys of the other pueblos are dying? If this is why you have made this mission of mercy to warn us, then your trip is in vain. Get on your horse and ride, Marshal, and keep riding."

Quill opened his eyes in shock at a woman limping from the hogan carrying a golden-haired, dark-skinned baby with lime-green eyes. He frowned, trying to remember if he heard of any recent kidnappings.

"Anjelica is a girl—my daughter," Jefe snapped at him.

"Ah. Beauty and the beast," he responded.

Jefe flinched.

"What happened to your half-sister, Salia?" Quill said.

"Good riddance—Salia got what she deserved."

"How so?" Quill said, glaring.

"When you kill a man as powerful as Samuel Stuwart, you can expect the coal miners and the Penitentes to rise up against you," Jefe said.

"It was never proven that Salia killed her husband. The villagers took justice into their own hands," Quill spat.

"I have my own question to ask, Marshal."

"Go on."

"I am Salia's closest living relative, since her baby son, also, burned in the fire."

Quill could barely contain his anger at Jefe's grin, when he mentioned his dead nephew.

"This makes me heir to all that belonged to Salia. There is something missing from her house that was mine. I would like you to investigate this theft."

"What exactly was stolen?"

"A rock."

"Gold?"

Jefe shook his head *no*.

"Silver?"

No.

"Turquoise?

"A plain-looking lodestone but magnetic," Jefe said.

"You're wasting my time," Quill snapped, mounting his horse.

"I demand equal justice like the white man. My property has been stolen and I want it back. I need that rock," Jefe screeched. He was shaking like a lunatic.

Quill tipped his hat and turned his horse so that his back was to Jefe.

"A man like you won't last long in these parts," Jefe screamed.

Quill turned around, leaning on the pommel of his saddle, the leather creaking with his weight. "Yeah. I been told that already. I'll be back," he said, narrowing his eyes at all four men. "You can bet your red assholes on that."

"Don't return without my magic rock! Do you hear me, Marshal?" Jefe screamed at his back.

Quill's answer was to kick his horse into a trot.

The eyes of Big-Belly, the Bat and Dead-Man-Walking darted between the marshal and Jefe. What was going through their minds was the bet they intended to place on how soon Jefe would kill Marshal Quill.

———

12

Storm-Chaser sat cross-legged in his tipi, a hand-me-down from his Apache blood. As a boy, he lived on the plains following the buffalo. Now, sheep grazed behind his apartment.

He lit the ceremonial pipe given the people by the Thunder Spirit. His mentor passed the pipe onto him many moons ago before crossing over to the spirit world.

It had been pouring all day at the Pueblo. He puffed, concentrating as he smoked, his mind engaged with images of the sun.

Smoke engulfed the tipi.

Wings flapped above, and with each flap, thunder boomed in the sky.

Storm-Chaser stepped outside into a surreal world that had a dream-like quality. A thunderbird, the size of a man, circled his head. The bird had a blocked head and a square body with blinding silver feathers. By beating its huge wings, the bird caused the wind to blow and the sky to thunder.

Storm-Chaser placed his hand over his forehead, shielding his eyes from sparks of light shining from the bird's feathers. "It is good to see you, old friend," he said.

The thunderbird squawked, and lightning flashed from the sky with each blink of its eyes.

Storm-Chaser smiled and said, "In two hours is my grandson's christening celebration. The rain you have brought is welcome; however, it would please me if..."

The thunderbird floated to the opening of the tipi where smoke billowed from the pipe of the Thunder Spirit.

The thunderbird swirled around the tipi, dissipating with the smoke, transforming into a billowing gray cloud.

The cloud was lifted up to the sky and floated away, leaving the Pueblo in sunshine.

The thunderbird stopped the rains to allow Storm-Chaser's guests to travel in comfort to the christening party.

Native Americans, dressed in their colorful finest, walked over from their apartments.

All bowed as they entered the shaman's home.

Several of the men handed Storm-Chaser a bottle of whiskey as payment for his previous services, in honor of his grandson's party.

"Bring out the boy," Storm-Chaser ordered Spider-Woman.

His number two wife, Little-Dove, sat at Storm-Chaser's feet, resting her head sadly on his knee while Spider-Woman shuffled on soft moccasins to a back room of the apartment where a baby, nearly nine months old and wrapped in a fine-spun shawl, bounced on a blanket.

Spider-Woman ran her fingernail down Dark-Shadow's cheek and drew blood.

He stiffened, punching a tiny fist out.

She cooed to him, and he relaxed.

Spider-Woman exposed her sharp incisors and bit his ear.

He spit at her but didn't cry.

She spit back, knowing who this boy was—Salia's son. Spider-Woman had been midwife at his birth and watched Salia hang the eagle-shaped bag around the baby's neck.

Spider-Woman stroked the bag and smiled meanly at him. "You are grandson of my enemy Felicita. Your grandmother was my husband's lover," she hissed.

She carried Dark-Shadow like a sack of potatoes into the front room, his arms and legs kicking, his face reddened.

Storm-Chaser took the baby from her and held him up in the air triumphantly.

Everyone cheered, except for Spider-Woman, who stared sullenly at the floor.

———◆———

13

The moon outlined a hunchbacked man driving a wagon with a skinny boy riding shotgun. Two women rode in the back, one smoking a pipe like a man and the other huddled in the corner with her head buried in a blanket.

Weeping-Woman bounced in the back of the rickety wagon, the wooden boards banging against her shoulder blades. She clenched the side so tightly, her fingers drained of blood. *The babies*, she thought, her shoulders shaking with sobs. Her pupils stung as if bumble bees feasted upon her swollen eyeballs. Since the night of the tipi moon she wept enough tears to flood the Rio Grande.

Two-Face kicked her leg. "Quit crying, you stupid woman. Your sobs woke me."

Liar! Two-Face had not been sleeping. Her stepdaughter spent most of her time spying. Two-Face puffed on a cigar, blowing smoke in her face. The masculine side of her face was hard and spiteful.

Weeping-Woman acted like she was comatose, hiding her deep hatred of her stepdaughter and husband.

A dozen years ago on a thirsty summer day, Jefe stumbled upon Weeping-Woman at the creek. The bottom of her skirt was tucked into her waistband, and her sleeves rolled up. She was barefoot with water up to her knees. She was bent over, her rump sticking up, swishing a basket of wheat. Sweat ran between her breasts, giving her brown skin a shiny sheen.

Weeping-Woman heard a noise and spun. She dropped her basket and backed away from a hideous man, knowing who this animal was. Her father warned her to stay away from Jefe, but...surely; there could be no harm in taking a sip of the bottle he offered. Wait until she told her girlfriends she tasted a cola! She never drank anything so refreshing or tasty before, though a tad bitter.

While she drank the cola, he poured a few drops of red oil onto his palm from a little container hanging from his neck. He reached behind her ear and rubbed her skin.

"That tickles," she said, giggling, feeling the oil creeping into her ear and penetrating the big vein in her neck leading to her heart.

He squeezed her knee, running his tongue around her ear lobe. "You are so good looking," he grunted.

Me? Her reflection in the water showed a girl with eyes too wide apart, a face practically lipless, and a flat nose.

Beside her, Jefe's handsome face rippled in the water. How could she have thought him ugly a moment ago? He was the most gorgeous man she ever laid eyes on!

It was summer and she wore no underwear. His hand crept beneath her skirt, poking her. She squeezed her thighs together, sighing. No one ever touched her there before.

Weeping-Woman threw him on his back, ripping the clothes from his body and writhing against him, moaning.

Jefe laughed at her.

When her father found out she was in love with Jefe, Storm-Chaser tore at his braids, moaning. "I will need a urine sample from Jefe for you to drink so I can reverse his love spell, daughter. Get one for me," he barked.

"I can't just ask my boyfriend to pee for me," she said.

"No? But you have access to that part of Jefe's body don't you?" And for the first time ever, her father struck her. He then locked her in the bedroom, which was a very small room but afforded privacy. Jefe visited her that night. Though he couldn't' enter the room, there was a hole in the wall. It was all Jefe and the bewitched girl needed. The next morning, Storm-Chaser smelled Jefe around the hole so he sealed it shut.

She then burned down the apartment to go to her lover.

Her father was furious and even more angry when he found out she was pregnant—he kicked her out!

Jefe dragged her over the threshold of his one-room hogan, announcing to his daughter that he married Weeping-Woman because she was pregnant. "This is your new mother," he told the then thirteen year-old Two-Face.

His daughter hissed at her new stepmother, who was only a couple years older than she. Two-Face was filled with an unhealthy jealousy when it came to her father and did all she could to make Weeping-Woman miserable. So did Jefe. A Pueblo man normally joins his wife's family. Jefe and Weeping-Woman should have moved in with Storm-Chaser, which is why

Jefe married her. He had planned to gain more power through the shaman. Her father rejecting them would be the first of many disappointments Jefe would find in his wife.

As for Weeping-Woman, she was not born with the name she now had. It was only after her wedding night that she was renamed. Everyone at the Pueblo now called her by her name of sadness.

Sanity fleetingly entered her mind at night, when she slept alone. Weeping-Woman remembered her father once said he could reverse her bewitchment, if he had a urine sample from Jefe. One morning, she arose early, tiptoeing from the hogan. By now, a very pregnant Weeping-Woman knew her husband's habits. She hid behind the bush Jefe watered every morning. She held a cup, catching drops dripping from the leaves.

With her father's help, she quenched her thirst of her husband. His stench no longer made her feel she would die without him, but Weeping-Woman pretended to still be obsessed by love.

But because she drank Jefe's urine while pregnant, Flaco was born a watered-down version of his father—thank goodness! And he was the last child she would ever give Jefe. It was a well-kept secret that her mother dabbled in witchcraft—even Storm-Chaser didn't know Spider-Woman was a member of the Sisterhood of the Black Rose witches. Weeping-Woman begged her mother for a potion to make her barren. But last winter, a little half-white girl named Anjelica was born to Jefe by a rich whore in Santa Fe who died in childbirth.

Too bad the baby was left behind this day with a relative of sorts. Anjelica would have laughed at the wagon jostling along the road. She was a happy baby, so unlike her father. Weeping-Woman lost her heart to the precocious child.

The wagon rounded the final bend to their destination, and the Santo Domingo Pueblo rose from the earth like a desert sand castle. The ancient Pueblo was a miraculous complex of apartments, molded from sun-baked adobe bricks. Ladders leaned against the walls to allow the dwellers to climb from apartment to apartment, and floor to floor.

The Puebloans had always been farmers and for centuries lived in rectangular apartments, which is why Jefe felt the people were never powerful like the fierce Comanche or Apache who once roamed the plains as if the entire country belonged to them. Jefe flicked at the horse to make it go faster.

He scoffed, "Apartment dwellers. Bah! Living in an apartment, one loses a sense of nature and the power evident in every weed. Each flower. In the stars. The sun. The moon. The Puebloans are addicted to their things, furniture, and jewelry. And a little piece of real estate with a ladder leading down to earth."

It was because of Jefe and his disciples that the Pueblo ladders were yanked through the windows at sunset and the windows shuttered. The first story rooms were used as storehouses. Only the shaman, Storm-Chaser, was not afraid to live in a first story apartment.

Weeping-Woman frowned at the 8 x 10 room that was added since she last visited her mother. The room hung off the side near the chicken coop and must have been built for the newest member of the family. Jefe heard about the christening of her new nephew and demanded to go, even though they were not invited.

Alongside the Pueblo were the remains of the apartment Weeping-Woman set on fire so she could escape to Jefe's waiting arms and marry him. Nevertheless, her heart twisted, and a sense of pride and longing swept over her. She gripped the sides of the wagon, her eyes sparkling with both joy and dread—Weeping-Woman had coming home.

———————

14

At the christening party, Dark-Shadow was being passed around by all the female guests. The baby smiled with a dimple digging into his right cheek. The child was truly beautiful, with big grey-green eyes, long lashes, and a thick mop of black hair. His skin was fairer than most of the Indian babies. He was a big muscular boy with large hands and feet.

Bam! The front door was kicked open. Jefe stood at the threshold, breathing heavily, and sounding like a wild bull. His head was lowered, his eyebrows raised.

Weeping-Woman stood beside him, her head down, believing she was hiding her black eye and swollen lip.

Jefe shoved her aside, barging into the apartment, his act meant as a deliberate offense. If the door had been left open, this meant all who passed by were invited to enter, but the door had been closed. In any case, Jefe should have announced his presence and waited for Storm-Chaser to welcome him into his home.

Two-Face swaggered behind Jefe, mimicking her father. However, she didn't seem comfortable in her voluptuous, lumbering body.

Storm-Chaser raised an eyebrow at Jefe's filthy bare feet—another insult. He snorted at Jefe's wooden bowl and spoon. It was an Indian custom for all invited guests to a party to bring their own eating utensils. Even worse, they had not been invited, which made Weeping-Woman feel even more awkward, especially since she was a daughter of the household.

Storm-Chaser motioned with his head for Little-Dove to take Dark-Shadow. The baby's lip was trembling.

Jefe violated another etiquette rule—he should have walked to the right of the room and waited for her father to ask him to sit to his left and behind him. Instead, Jefe marched to the center, standing in front of his father-in-law with his hands on his hips, glaring down at Storm-Chaser.

The shaman stood and Jefe strained his neck at him. Storm-Chaser always seemed a foot taller than he was. He had the power to fill an entire room with his presence. He may have been old but his body was still muscular and lean. All the power of the Thunder Spirit electrified his veins. Storm-Chaser scooped a piece of bread into the bean pot, ignoring Jefe's hostile stance. "You may as well come in, daughter," he said without looking at Weeping-Woman.

She wiped her eyes with the backs of her hands, bending her head to enter. Her limp was more pronounced than usual. She had only seen Storm-Chaser from a distance these past five years, hiding behind a tree or big rock, peeking out with starving eyes at her imposing father who once showed her all the love for an only daughter.

Weeping-Woman walked to the left, sitting on the floor with the other women, her legs modestly folded to one side. She looked around the room with hungry eyes.

The room was sparsely furnished with a rough small table and bench. Home-made colorful rugs covered the floor. A basket served as a trunk with a pair of scissors on top. A kiva fireplace dominated a corner of the room, the fireplace serving to heat the apartment and used for cooking. All baking was done outside. Honey was spread on fried bread as dessert. There was dried rattlesnake meat. Corn on the cob. Deer seared outside over an open pit. Her parents offered quite a feast. Weeping-Woman was filled with sadness that they never welcomed her son, Flaco, so warmly. Storm-Chaser once remarked that Flaco would grow up to be like Jefe. He had looked at his grandson with distaste when making his prediction. Weeping-Woman had marched home, vowing to never visit again when her father was at home.

Flaco ran up to the table and stuffed his face. For one so skinny, the eleven-year old had an appetite that was small compared to his father's hunger for power—Jefe did not yet notice the ceremonial pipe of the Thunder Spirit dwarfing the decorated cradle.

Two-Face arrogantly marched to the right of the room and sat on the floor, cross-legged, with the men. The feminine side of her face could be seen by the women. Her masculine side faced the men, who looked painfully at Jefe, but none dared reproach him for his daughter.

The women, however, whispered among themselves.

Two-Face jerked her masculine face in their direction. Except for Spider-Woman, the others lowered their eyes like she stripped them naked. They all blushed.

Two-Face did not acknowledge Spider-Woman or vice-versa. Two-Face snorted at the women, turning her attention back to the men. Each man scooted back a notch, isolating Storm-Chaser and Jefe at the front of the room.

Two-Face reached her hand into her knee-length moccasin, and Weeping-Woman looked at her father in alarm. Storm-Chaser smiled. Ah, or course he knew she gripped a knife.

How tiresome the feud between her father and husband, and she made things worse by marrying Jefe. Weeping-Woman blinked her eyes at a kerosene lamp hanging from a corner of the room. With a similar lamp she burned down their other apartment. Spider-Woman squeezed her hand, and Weeping-Woman fought the urge to bury her head in her mother's lap.

The men in the room sat as if on pine cones, watching Jefe grow more impatient with each scoop of Storm-Chaser's spoon.

Her father finished his beans, set his empty bowl down, and with amusement, turned to Jefe. 'You have read too many fairy tales from the white school you attended as a boy. You act like the wicked, fairy godfather, angry at not being invited to the christening of the shaman's grandson. Do you intend to curse Dark-Shadow for my insolence?"

Jefe had no sense of humor and very bad manners. Though he had not been offered food, he helped himself from a pot of beans, scooping some into his bowl. He grabbed a tortilla from atop an iron griddle and dumped some green-chile stew on top of his beans. He pulled out a wicked-looking knife and the guests scooted back a few inches.

Weeping-Woman stared aghast at the knife. Was her husband so stupid that he would attack with so many witnesses?

Jefe snorted, slicing at freshly butchered venison hanging from a meat hook. He then flung his knife at one of the many woven rugs covering the room and the handle vibrated. "Bah! Why this christening party, old man? You have always been caught between two worlds," he spat.

"It is true, Jefe." Storm-Chaser said his name, which means *boss*, in a disrespectful, mocking tone. "I have great admiration and much respect for *The Christ*, the greatest shaman who ever lived. Even I cannot raise the dead. The powers of *The Christ* were greater than Montezuma, the most powerful sorcerer who ever lived."

At the mention of Montezuma, Jefe dumped the remainder of his beans on the floor.

Storm-Chaser narrowed his eyes at the waste. Jefe delivered a great insult to him by not eating all the food he impolitely served himself, and by dirtying the floor. "Perhaps murder turns your stomach. Every boy child who has been born within six months of the tipi moon has been killed," Storm-Chaser said.

Jefe sneered. "There must be a disease going around. Don't tell me that you also believe in the legend of Montezuma and the return of the tipi moon. Do your job, old man—find a cure for the babies!"

"I shall find out who is responsible," he said.

Jefe passed between the fireplace and the seated guests, more ill-manners on his part. The guests leaned back as he made his way to the cradle, each man nodding respectfully and coughing like a pinto bean stuck in their throats.

Jefe stopped at the cradle, glaring at the baby and the pipe of the Thunder Spirit which he always coveted. "Where did you find this boy?" he barked.

"Dark-Shadow is the son of my son."

"Wolfe is more woman than man. Perhaps his male lover gave birth," he said, laughing.

"The boy was born in Santa Fe and is my grandson. That is all you need to know," Storm-Chaser said, holding his head stiffly.

Jefe snorted. "You have yet to take Flaco under your wing and teach him the way of the shaman," he said, shoving his son at Storm-Chaser.

Flaco ducked his head and jumped in front of the fireplace.

His father and grandfather stared each other down.

Flaco leaned over the cradle, his tangled hair brushing Dark-Shadow's face, causing the baby to blink his eyes and turn his face away.

Flaco was wild looking, like a Mustang. A mass of hair fell to the middle of his nose. His voice was high-pitched and sounded like a horse whinnying as he hummed a song to the baby, rocking the cradle.

Flaco tickled Dark-Shadow on his chin.

The baby laughed.

Weeping-Woman's eyes shone at her son as he reached into the cradle and picked up the boy christened Dark-Shadow.

Flaco was stronger than he looked and lifted the baby high in the air. He hurled him higher above his head, let go of the baby's armpits, and stepped back to watch him fall.

Weeping-Woman jumped and caught the child. She spun to Flaco. "I am Dark-Shadow's aunt. You must take care of your little cousin," she said in a shaky voice and placed the baby in his cradle.

"If you ever harm him, Flaco, you will answer to me," Storm-Chaser barked, but stared at Jefe when he said this.

Flaco stared mindlessly into the fire, as if hypnotized by the flames.

A resounding slap echoed in the room. Flaco held his hand to his ear and opened his mouth with a soundless scream. "Leave your little cousin alone," Jefe ordered, shoving him across the room. He frowned at his son sitting cross-legged, still staring at the flames. Flaco rocked, lost in his own world, whinnying like a horse.

Jefe placed a hand around Dark-Shadow's neck.

Storm-Chaser rose to his feet.

Two-Face grabbed the knife handle sticking out of her boot.

Jefe merely lifted the buckskin bag, shaped like an eagle that hung from the baby's neck.

"His mother made the bag. Poor woman died in childbirth," Storm-Chaser lied. "I hear your half-sister had a child. Too bad for you her house burned. As Salia's closest relation, the house would have been yours."

Jefe grunted. "Since our grandmother's death, we were not on speaking terms. I searched the ruins, and both Salia and her boy perished."

"You found nothing at Witch Hill then?" Storm-Chaser said, examining him through half-closed eyes.

"Merely a few trinkets," he said suspiciously.

Gifts for the baby were piled on the floor beside the cradle. All the guests had brought gifts, including Jefe, who reached into his pocket and pulled out an egg.

Quick as lighting, Storm-Chaser snatched the egg and threw it on the floor.

Whoosh! The egg burst into flames, catching the rug on fire.

Jefe stared intently down at Dark-Shadow.

The baby looked back as though hypnotized.

Storm-Chaser jumped between them. He reached behind, pinching the baby to bring him out of his trance before Jefe could do any more damage.

Dark-Shadow screamed. The cradle rocked with the kicking of his legs and the swinging of his arms.

"You're scaring my grandson with your ugly face, Jefe."

"Hypocrite! You, old man, shamed my father by sleeping with his wife, Felicita," Jefe snarled.

"Leave your stepmother out of this. Felicita is dead," Storm-Chaser said in a weary voice.

"I still remember the two of you riding across the Pueblo in that fancy buggy of hers, Felicita using her whip on any who got in her way. Many times I have wondered if she took the whip to your back, old man."

"The way your grandmother, La India, took a knife to your face, Jefe? The dead are best forgotten, but it must be hard for you whenever you look in a mirror and see your grandmother's handiwork. Do you think then that my backside looks like your face?"

Jefe raised his fist as if to strike him. "It was you, old man, who stole my grandmother's piedra imán!"

"Why would I wish to harm La India by stealing her piedra imán and thereby guaranteeing her death? She was a harmless prankster. Fool! Look at me. If I had a shapeshifting stone, do you think I would be so old? I could turn myself into a young brave, just as your grandmother stayed young though 135 years of age. I could have immortality."

"Bah! You're the fool, giving a christening from the white man's church," Jefe said and spit.

"Take your man-woman daughter and return to one of your whores! I hear one recently died giving birth to your bastard. You shame my daughter and dare to show your face in my home! And take your wife with you—my daughter is not wanted here so long as she is with you."

Weeping-Woman stumbled to the exit, crying.

Flaco still rocked by the fire, humming a tune and smiling at the flames.

Two-Face made a filthy gesture with her hips, and then swaggered behind Jefe who walked stiffly.

Flaco rocked, staring into space.

Spider-Woman clucked her tongue, helping her grandson to rise. She gave him a hug, but Flaco stood unmoving, his arms hanging limp at his sides. Flaco never formed a connection with anyone, not his father, nor half-sisters, nor grandparents. He was an emotionless, detached boy, with a deep abiding fear of his father. "Your place is with your mother," his grandmother said, leading Flaco from the apartment and shoving him at her daughter.

Weeping-Woman pulled her son to her chest, ruffling his hair. He cringed at her touch. With a heavy heart, she watched him clench the wagon seat like a statue.

Her mother stared forlornly back at her, waving.

Weeping-Woman rocked, whinnying like her son.

Storm-Chaser sat with his legs crossed, facing his guests. He cleaned his pipe with jerky movements.

The cleaning of their host's pipe was a sign that the party was over. One by one, they stood to leave and drifted from the apartment.

So much negative emotion came from the direction of Jefe's departing wagon that the air cackled with it. The guests crossed their chests, muttering silent prayers for protection from Jefe.

No one noticed a mountain lion leaning against the outdoor oven watching Jefe.

It appeared as if the lion was laughing.

15

Dark-Shadow screamed as if the baby was in pain. He seemed to hurt wherever he was touched and had the runs.

Little-Dove cleaned up the baby, rocking him in her arms.

Spider-Woman burned *cachana* as an incense to purify the house from illness. She then wrestled with Little Dove for the baby, which made Dark-Shadow cry even louder.

"Enough! Leave the boy to me! Get to bed—both of you," Storm-Chaser barked, his voice cracking with worry.

Little-Dove surrendered the baby to Storm-Chaser. She scurried from the room with Spider-Woman pinching her.

He cradled Dark-Shadow in his arms, rubbing his cheek against his little face. The baby whimpered. "I'm sorry, little One, that Jefe brought you a bewitched egg. He is beyond stupidity. To think I would allow him to break the egg over your head. If any of the egg white would have touched the soft spot on your head, you would be dead."

Dark-Shadow screamed, his face reddening even more.

He stared down with worry at the baby, suspecting he suffered from the evil eye which is a forceful, deliberate stare witches use to drain the recipient of health. He patted the baby's back. "I know. I know. Do not fret. I shall heal you," he said in a soothing voice, offering him a toy made from two rattlesnake tails. The rattle normally made the boy laugh but he lay in Storm-Chaser's arms with his arms hanging limp. He mewed, sounding like a kitten stuck in a well. The baby was burning up with fever and gulped in shallow breaths of air, his little chest barely rising, his face screwed up with tiny wrinkles.

The quickest cure would be for Jefe to reverse the bewitchment by patting the baby's head or rubbing his temples.

Rage filled him—the evil eye was Jefe's gift for his grandson! Storm-Chaser never in his life felt more like killing a man. Dark-Shadow's breathing was now so shallow, he appeared dead and soiled himself again.

Storm-Chaser cracked an egg, emptying the yoke and egg white into a bowl, setting the bowl on the floor beside Dark-Shadow.

Jefe's eyes appeared in the bowl, one eye black in color, the other grayish-yellow with a scar running down the middle. Dark-Shadow kicked his legs, flinging his arms like he was reborn. He let out a healthy cry.

Storm-Chaser rubbed ashes from the fireplace on the baby to protect him from Jefe and his band of witches. He placed a yellow ear of corn alongside him to shield the baby from supernatural attacks. Lastly, he sang a few words, blessing a small necklace containing a coral bead. He placed the necklace on Dark-Shadow to protect him from future assaults of the evil eye.

The baby's tears were drying and he had the hiccups.

Storm-Chaser lit a red-tipped match, extinguishing it in a cup of water. He dipped his finger into the water, and Dark-Shadow sucked the drops from his skin, the phosphorus from the match curing his hiccups.

Storm-Chaser lay down beside him, stroking his cheek, singing softly until the baby fell asleep.

He wasn't through with Jefe yet. The shaman normally just provided cures, but he was in a vengeful mood. Storm-Chaser watched his enemies closely and was aware that Jefe could see to his left with his damaged eye. Well he would no longer!

Storm-Chaser took a poker from the fireplace and with a thunderous yell, poked the left side of Jefe's damaged eye floating in the bowl.

At the same moment he stabbed the eye, he heard Jefe scream, and a hand appeared in the bowl, covering the left eye.

The vision faded from the bowl.

Storm-Chaser reeled in shock because Dark-Shadow could have died. He trembled, moaning, "I should have thrown Jefe out immediately. I should have known my worthless son-in-law would do the boy harm, that he would be jealous because of Flaco. Thank goodness Jefe doesn't know who this child really is and thinks the boy's father is my son. Jefe would never believe a child born of such an effeminate man could be the Reincarnation of the great witch, Montezuma."

He covered his face with his hands and rocked, crying for the grandson he almost lost and for the son he never had.

He stumbled to bed, ordering Little-Dove to take care of the baby. The boy was hungry so Little-Dove woke the wet nurse, a young second cousin, to feed him.

When the apartment was in complete darkness, Storm-Chaser cocked his ear at a noise. He could have sworn there were sounds coming from the direction of the baby's crib—a woman's voice, softly humming. He had heard the tune before, and the notes crawled beneath his weathered skin. The humming was a requiem tune of the spirit of the witch, Salia, the same lullaby her ghost sang in the burning house.

Storm-Chaser knocked the side of his head with his hand. Sometimes he heard a ringing in his ears. Perhaps it was because his ears were so old that he thought he heard Salia singing—Dark-Shadow's mother.

If his hearing had been more acute, he would have heard these words hissed into the baby's ear in a hoarse voice.

"Hush, my darling, if you never say a word.

Grandma's going to kill you a mocking bird.

Hush, my Boy, if you never cry.

I promise you, you will never die."

The baby cooed at Felicita leaning over the cradle, her face a ghostly white, her hair sweeping her filthy feet. She stretched her neck, swallowing with difficulty.

She floated to a mirror, her head held up regally. She twisted her head, twirled, jumped, but a ghost has no reflection.

Felicita vanished in a puff of smoke.

Of its own accord, the cradle continued to rock like an invisible hand moved it.

Hush, my darling, if you never say a word.
Grandma's going to kill you a mocking bird...

———

16

Jefe screamed, cupping his left eye with his hand. He could no longer see to his left nor fake blindness for trickery. His enemies could sneak up on him to the left. He tore at his hair, foaming at the mouth. "Bastard! I'll get you, old man!"

He grabbed the sacred plumes from his hogan. He climbed a large rock and stood naked with his arms spread wide as though he was about to take flight. Jefe threw back his head and laughed. Of course—why murder the old man whose days are numbered? Kill the grandson he is so proud of, solving two problems at once. He would weaken Storm-Chaser with grief, thereby assuring the shaman did not mingle in his mischief. Storm-Chaser would have no alternative but to pass his secrets and the pipe of the Thunder Spirit onto Flaco. The shaman was too proud to let anyone but his grandsons have the pipe. Jefe would even seem generous and suggest that Flaco live with him. He should have thought of this before the old man took Dark-Shadow under his wing and protection.

"Bah! Some protection! Finally, the old man has become weak." His blood pounded with the exhilaration of revenge. Though Jefe would be weak from the transformation, he would visit Storm-Chaser in the morning, just to see how the old man was coping.

He stabbed hawk feathers into his hair, and then dug a knife into his wrist until blood dripped. He closed his eyes, muttering an incantation. Jefe dipped his head, breathing deeply, conjuring an image of a hawk, until his eyes shone reddish brown. His black eye turned the color of wine. Veins ran down his blind eye, dripping blood across his cheek. The blood did not blind him. On the contrary, the blood sharpened his vision until he could see as far as a hawk with his good eye. Two miles away was a cactus upon which hung a rosary, maybe Storm-Chaser's beads. He zeroed in on the cross hanging there and spit. His saliva dripped down the rosary beads, and he laughed, power pulsing through his body.

He flung his arms wide and raised his head to the heavens. He called out arrogantly for all to hear, "I go without God and without the holy virgin."

Feathers grew across his head and his body, blanketing his nakedness. His broken nose became a twisted beak. His toes curled into claws. Jefe's arms became wings.

When the transformation was complete, he had turned into a large, graying hawk.

He lifted his wings straight up and shot into the sky like a rocket.

How great to be airborne again, and catch a tailwind, gliding through the night sky. What a rush!

The hawk flew towards Santo Domingo, his eyes glittering.

Jefe flip-flopped in the sky several times, showing off.

The Santo Domingo Pueblo came into view.

The hawk dived nose down, and then straightened into a smooth landing.

When Jefe was grounded, he shook his head, ruffling his feathers.

Jefe rocked, walking in the funny manner of birds, more graceful in the air than on land.

He turned his beak in the direction of his father-in-law's apartment.

Jefe let out a cackle of delight.

17

Jefe heard a growl. A cougar leapt in the air above him.

Squawk! Squawk! He fluttered his wings, trying to take flight.

The cougar landed smack dab on top of him and took a swipe at him with its razor-sharp claws.

The hawk cried out and was in such excruciating pain that it metamorphosed into a half-naked Jefe who lay there with a broken arm, two crushed feet and a chest scraped of flesh. Blood oozed from his wounds. A few feathers clung to his cheeks, arms, and chest. He had grown back to his normal size, but the bottom half of his body was still a hawk, so he looked like a giant bird man.

Jefe cussed at himself for his stupidity. All these weeks he sensed he was being watched, both in the air and on land. This mountain lion was at the ball park, and he discounted the creature as harmless. "Show yourself, for I know you are no mountain lion." he snarled.

The mountain lion spun until it vanished—in its place stood U. S. Marshal Quill, his spurs jingling, a mocking look in his golden eyes.

"You! I should have killed you from the start," Jefe said.

"You and whose army, Jefe? That rag tag group you call your disciples?"

"You came sniffing about the babies. If you care so much, why didn't you stop me before tonight?"

"Because now you threaten what's mine—Dark-Shadow."

"Why do you care about the shaman's grandson?"

Quill merely looked at him.

The marshal just shapeshifted from a cougar into a man, and the truth finally dawned on Jefe. Every foul word imaginable vomited from his mouth. "It was you who stole my grandmother's piedra imán, you son of a whore!"

Quill yanked off his necklace, flinging it on the ground. The gold scorpion medallion came alive, growing a foot, with long tail and pinchers, dragging the chain across the ground. On eight legs the scorpion walked towards Jefe, waving its pinchers at him.

With his unhurt arm, Jefe dragged himself, crying out from his broken bones scraping against the ground.

The scorpion caught up to Jefe, crawling up his naked leg, and broken arm. The scorpion grabbed Jefe's flesh with its pinchers, stinging him several times before Jefe was able to grab the scorpion, and toss the creature.

"Well done. My scorpion landed on its back," Quill said, laughing.

Jefe lay there spitting and cussing, calling for the shaman who could cure a scorpion bite with garlic.

"I doubt Storm-Chaser will come to your aid," Quill said, seeming able to read his mind. "The old man is deaf in one ear and only hears what he wants to out of his other ear. Besides, why would he help an asshole like you? Bringing an egg to kill a baby in front of a shaman? His own grandson? You always were a moron, dumb shit."

Jefe breathed heavily, sweat dripping down his face. He grasped his leg where the scorpion bit him several times. "You are no ordinary law man who just happened to find a shapeshifting stone. Reveal yourself, coward, so that I may know which sorcerer I am about to kill."

"You haven't the power to kill me. You always were the bullshitter, Jefe."

"Take off you mask!" he snarled.

"Very well, I'll humor you. The last wish of a dying man." Quill ran a hand over his face, and in his place stood a tall, muscular Spanish man. His tan was a shade darker than before. His golden hair had changed to black and hung to his shoulders. His eyes were lime-green. Arrogance shone from his face. Standing before Jefe was his greatest enemy, the head of the Las Cruces witches.

"Lucas Monterrey! You have been masquerading as a US Marshal," Jefe whispered. He flushed red and started screaming every insult he could think of.

"Given the history of your family, I wouldn't insult mine."

"That's why you nosed around disguised as Marshal Quill, asking about Salia. You wanted my piedra imán so I wouldn't defeat you."

"Keep your sister out of this!"

"But why do you care about Dark-Shadow?" And then Jefe realized, "That old bastard lied—his son, Wolfe, didn't father Dark-Shadow. The infant fell from the sky, and just like Montezuma, has no father. Dark-Shadow is the Reincarnation of the great witch Montezuma."

Quill simply blinked his eyes at him.

"The Reincarnation is mine! His power belongs to me," Jefe said for if a witch kills another, the magic of the dead witch can be absorbed by the witch who killed him or her. "You plan to kill the Reincarnation, and gain his power? I have already killed him. You are too late," Jefe spat.

"You have not killed the Reincarnation, else I would not be able to best you," Lucas said.

"Perhaps," Jefe said in a weary voice. The scorpion's poison seeped through his veins, his ambition disintegrating, and his hypocrisy at an end. He was so damned tired.

Jefe closed his eyes and saw a vision of a woman coming for him. The image filled him with warmth. He wanted nothing more than to give into death. He sighed and said half-heartedly, "I hope Dead-Man-Walking beats you to Dark-Shadow and kills the boy."

Lucas laughed. "That bloodless phantom? Unless you order him to hunt down the Reincarnation, I doubt the dead man would do so on his own. He is, how shall I say it? A jackass perplexed by his role in life. Invisible during the day. Yet visible at night. He shines with his own illusions. The dead man thinks he is the Reincarnation and is convinced, because of his rare lack of color, that he is above all other men including you, Jefe."

"I hope the Reincarnation lives. With any power I have left, I curse you, Lucas Monterrey, with all my being and all my might that the Reincarnation will grow up, hunt you down, and kill you. Even you will never be more powerful than the Reincarnation, unless you put an end to him while he's young."

A muscle moved in Lucas' jaw.

"I've gotten to you, haven't I, Las Cruces whore? You better kill the baby now, while he is weak, before he knows what he is." Jefe looked hopefully up at him. He could still have his revenge against Storm-Chaser through Monterrey.

"Unlike you, I do not fight babies," he said, kicking dirt in Jefe's face.

"Promise me you will kill the Reincarnation as he sleeps in his cradle. I have cursed you," Jefe screamed, grasping his boot. "If you don't kill the Reincarnation now, he will surely kill you."

Lucas stomped on his good hand and Jefe yelped. "Let's put an end to this charade, shall we? You are the one who is cursed, Jefe."

Jefe's only chance was to try to fly away. He changed back into a hawk, fluttering his broken wing.

Lucas spun, turning back into a mountain lion.

Jefe felt the lion's jaws around his breast, remembering the hurt he felt when he suckled at La India's breast as an infant. If only his grandmother had not watered down her milk, giving him only enough power to sustain him, his life would have turned out differently.

It was hard to die with regrets and unfulfilled ambition, a lust for power that was all consuming. Even at the point of death, Jefe still wanted more powerful magic.

Again, Jefe saw the woman he had once called mother coming for him. La India was the woman who placed his lips on her ninety-five year old breasts and suckled him the best a selfish grandmother could. She had raised him since birth.

It wasn't Grandma's fault. I never really knew her. La India wouldn't tell me her real name. Perhaps now...

La India walked towards Jefe with outstretched arms. She was flesh and blood with her long black hair spun into braids dancing on her bouncing breasts, filled with the aphrodisiac of power. He could suckle at her breasts and grow strong again, filled with the power of her witchcraft.

For Jefe there was gold at the end of the rainbow—his grandmother, La India, wore a skirt with wide horizontal stripes, the colors of the rainbow, her smooth face lit like the rays of the sun.

"Mother, you've come," he said in a raspy voice, sounding like a bird wheezing. He lifted his good wing to her, and his beak twisted to the side as he tried to smile.

She bent to her knees, lifting his head onto her lap.

He puckered his mouth to her bosom. *I'll live now. Her power will be my power, and I will yet defeat Monterrey.*

La India unbuttoned her blouse and a nipple winked at him.

Jefe struggled to rise so he could suckle.

Ah. At last. He pushed his beak against her breast to start the milk of power flowing.

She reached her hand back and gave him a resounding slap, cutting his beak with her turquoise wing. La India pushed her thumbs into his eyes and shoved his head away.

He cried out, sobbing for his mother.

She floated away, vanishing into a rattlesnake hole a short distance away.

The last thing Jefe felt before he died was a sting upon his cheek from the only woman he ever really loved.

A kiss before dying—Jefe's power passed into the lion Lucas had transformed into.

All that remained of Jefe were a few hawk bones and feathers.

The mountain lion licked its paws. It arched its back, flexing its muscles which had grown thicker since consuming Jefe. The mountain lion spun until it vanished, and in its place stood Joseph Quill, U.S. Marshal, rocking dizzily on his boots.

He snapped his fingers and the scorpion turned back into a necklace, the scorpion an inch in length. He clasped the necklace around his neck, mounted his horse and rode away.

Quill appeared broader in the shoulders and taller in the saddle. There was a determined clench to his jaw and a glitter to his eyes shining golden in the moonlight.

He narrowed his eyes and looked to the right. He could see in the dark as well as any mountain lion.

He burped, rubbing his stomach.

Eating an enemy is always bad for the digestion—power gave one heartburn. He needed a whiskey to rid himself of Jefe's bad taste. "Piece of shit never took a bath," he muttered. He spit, wiping his mouth with the back of his hand.

Quill turned his horse in the direction of Madrid and the Mine Shaft Saloon.

He rocked on his saddle, his chin resting on his chest. He yawned, his sleepiness the aftermath of eating a full meal. Quill closed his eyes, nodding off to sleep. The Mine Shaft Saloon stayed open all night. He had plenty of time to get there.

Quill was snoring when his horse passed the Bones Creek Cemetery on the outskirts of Madrid. Not even a coyote howling from the grave of

Samuel Stuwart, who had been unfortunate enough to be married to Salia, woke him.

The coyote sat on the grave, once more lifting its head to the moon and howling.

There was loneliness to that howl.

There was sadness.

The coyote lay down on Samuel's grave, resting its head on its paws and whining itself to sleep.

Quill's horse at least knew where it was going, and piano music coming from the saloon woke him.

He tied his horse up front, placed a cigar to his lips, and lit a match.

He sighed deeply, wanting more than a glass of whiskey. He needed a whole damned bottle. Then maybe this tightness in his stomach would go away.

Jefe was right—his dying curse settled like a rock in his gut.

With any power I have left, I curse you, Lucas Monterrey, with all my being and all my might that the Reincarnation will grow up hunt you down, and kill you.

Quill pushed open the swinging doors of the saloon. "Hey Shifty," he yelled to the bartender. "Got anything I can wash down a curse with?"

He treated Jefe's curse the way he did any threat. In humorous fashion.

That was just his way.

Part Three

The Dead Live Again

For who can divine the mystery of death?

18

July 1, 1940
Santa Fe, New Mexico
Montezuma Avenue

The sign in the shop window read:
ETERNAL CAPITAL BEAUTY & AFTERLIFE
& Out of This World Health
SÉANCES by appointment only

Marcelina and her family had been living in Santa Fe for nearly six years. In that amount of time she established a successful business in the Plaza. She had two beauty chairs and a helper beautician. In a darkened back room, Marcelina conducted séances. The séance room was furnished with a table, chairs, Ouija board, Spirit slates to write messages from the dead, and Spirit trumpets used to turn up the volume of whispered voices of ghosts. Her greatest pride, however, were her six-year-old twin girls.

Her daughter, Carlotta, had been cleaning the same spot for the last half hour with her eyes closed, swaying her hips to an invisible song. In that amount of time, her twin Isabella had cleaned a glass window, dusted the beauty shop, and wiped down the two beauty chairs with a damp rag.

Both girls had straight, jet-black hair pulled back from their faces with a hair pin, coffee-brown eyes more slanted than round, thin eyebrows, full lips, high cheekbones and small noses, slightly bent in the center. They had sturdy frames. Marcelina fed the girls sparingly to prevent her daughters from having the weight problem that plagued her since birth.

With a sullen look, Carlotta cleaned the hairs, one at a time, from the sink. Her excuse for being lazy was that she was always hungry.

"Carlotta, you better get to work and finish cleaning the shop before Mama comes in here," Isabella said.

"Shut up! You're not my boss."

They heard Mama stirring in the back where the house was. Quickly, Isabella finished the mirrors. Carlotta swiftly swept the broom across the floor.

"Bring me my coffee, Carlotta," Mama yelled from a back room—her office.

She rolled her eyes. Why didn't Mama ever ask Isabella to fetch her coffee? Why was she her personal slave?

Because they love Isabella more, a masculine voice hissed in her ear. *They don't want your sister to break her pretty back.*

Carlotta bit her lip and blinked back her tears. Everything *the voice* told her was true. Isabella was always the favorite, even though the sisters looked alike. Despite that they were formed from one egg, split apart, forever separated by family ties. Why did Mama and Papa love Isabella so much? It wasn't fair. Carlotta should have been the favorite of at least one parent. They should have split their love in half instead of giving all their heart to Isabella and leaving none for her. Isabella was the daughter of the house. Carlotta was the slave.

She ignored Mama summoning her and violently swept the floor, leaving a few straws on the tile. How she hated her sister, the perfect Isabella who never got in trouble.

Good day, sweetheart. Runt of the litter. Heart of my heart. The voice caressed his words in her ear, tickling her ear lobe. *Doesn't your sister look pretty this evening? No wonder they love her more*, the voice hissed.

His breath fogged the mirror, making her face fade as if she was an illusion, a little girl who never was.

Carlotta screamed and dropped the broom—the fog ate her head so she was headless in the mirror.

"Carlotta!" Mama screamed louder from her office. "Do not make me come in there and cut your head off."

See. What did I tell you?

Her headless figure in the mirror ballooned to the size of Mama.

What a pretty picture! Without a head, your mother can't order you around, can she?

With her skinny arms, Carlotta could barely lift the coffee pot but she poured a cup, splashing the floor. She mimicked Mama's voice, "Bring me my coffee, Carlotta. Bring me my coffee, Carlotta." She held the cup to her mouth and spit.

Isabella was watching so for good measure, Carlotta took a broom straw from the floor, the dirtiest one, and stirred the coffee. She threw the straw at her sister and stuck out her tongue. Carlotta marched to the back room where Mama's office was.

Carlotta came to an abrupt halt, nearly spilling the coffee. She gulped at a razor Mama was sharpening.

Mama grabbed the cup, slurping the black liquid. "Coffee's cold!"

"I'm sorry, Mama."

Carlotta looked defiant and not the least apologetic. Mama's double chins trembled as she tried to hold her tongue and be patient with her. No matter how kind she was to Carlotta, the girl was so rebellious. "Quit whining. Look at me and what the damage bearing twins did to my body. I have one chin for each of you girls. It's your fault I'm fat and have lost the glow of youth. A mother transfers her beauty to her daughter and with each girl, she fades. You and Isabella have given me a pair of crow's feet around my eyes, and a line on my forehead. Look here. You gave me this wrinkle, Carlotta," she said, stretching her neck.

Carlotta sulked at the floor.

"I must hurry," Mama muttered, buttoning her coat so the buttons were askew—the hem was six inches higher on the right.

"Can I come to the séance tonight?" Carlotta said.

"No."

"But I've never met your dead friend. What's her name—Selena?"

"Salia. And you can't behave in front of the living, much less the dead." Mama waddled to the shop exit. She gave Isabella a hug and said, "Keep an eye on your sister. Your papa will soon be home from his prison shift. Tell him if Carlotta gets into any trouble."

Carlotta threw a dirty finger at her back.

When Mama was safely gone, Carlotta touched the purple bruise on her swelling cheek and winced. She grabbed her sister's arm, shoving her to the back and a door leading to their four-room house.

Carlotta dragged out a box of tiny dolls from beneath the bed. Mama made a doll for every customer, each with a bit of human hair plastered to the head. She played with the dolls, torturing them.

Isabella ignored the sobbing of the magical dolls that collectively sounded like a mewing kitten. She played solitaire, a card game she was an expert at.

Carlotta zipped open the folds in the dolls' stomachs, sprinkling chile seeds, dirt, and rags, making mama's clients in real life, cough, groan and vomit all over Santa Fe. Carlotta giggled at the thought that some felt fingers scratching inside their stomachs. Others felt a fist moving about inside their stomach linings. They not only felt these phenomena but could see one side of their stomach move to the side, stretching beneath their ribs just like when a woman is pregnant with a kicking fetus. Only they weren't pregnant. Most likely, each woman ran for Mama's popular elixir, guzzling the foul-tasting liquid in hopes of finding relief.

Carlotta turned the dolls around, examining the dual faces. There was a face to make the victim sick. If she turned a doll over, there was a face to deliver the victim to her grave. What would Mama do if she wiped out her business by killing her clients through these dolls?

Carlotta stared at the graveyard faces of the dolls, imagining the morning after with a good portion of the women in Santa Fe lying dead in their beds. Their faces grey like ashes and bodies putrid from the stink of death. Their hands ice cold and eyes vacant.

The first to become deathly ill would be the richest.

Kill them, the voice hissed in her ear.

Carlotta picked up the doll representing Mariah Hanson. In her other hand she held a knife.

Isabella stood over her sister. "You do that and I will tell," she swore.

Carlotta dropped the knife, her face pale. "I'm bad sometimes because I hear voices," she said.

"You're such a liar. You always blame others."

"Anyway, why does Mama have a death face for her dolls, if she never intends to kill her clients?"

"Mama would never do that. It's just that the spell requires it."

"You're such a know-it-all," Carlotta said, narrowing her eyes. She should try making her own doll of Isabella. Carlotta paled at this thought. Isabella was her identical twin. If she made a doll of her sister and choked it, would she, too, die? It seemed at times that she and her sister were both one doll. Her sister with luminous complexion—the face of the living. She with dull complexion—the face of the dead. Carlotta screamed, throwing the basket of dolls in the air.

The dolls came crashing to the ground—Carlotta laughed. There would be quite a few headaches and sore muscles in Santa Fe.

Isabella sighed down at the dolls, some of whom were twisted and crying. She picked up the dolls from the floor, emptied their stomachs of all foreign matter and gently placed the dolls in the basket, straightening the limbs and the necks.

In Santa Fe, the women all sighed because Mama's elixir finally worked and once again, all was right in their world.

Mama made more money off her addictive elixir, called *A Whiff of Heaven*, than anything else in her beauty shop.

19

Marcelina drove her 1933 Chevy Standard car on North Alameda Street. She was proud of her seven year-old, battered, gold-colored car. It was a coach, with only two-doors. True, the back seat was ripped by Carlotta while playing with a knife. Carlotta, also, stabbed Isabella on her leg and though Marcelina sewed her up, Isabella had a nasty thigh scar.

Santa Fe is one of the oldest settlements in America and it showed. The streets were narrow, and all the buildings made of mud. A city ordinance required all construction to be adobe. Hence, the capital appeared as it was in the 1600's (except larger) when the Catholic Church and Spain nailed up a sign proclaiming:

Holy Office of the Spanish Inquisition
Established 1626, New Mexico.

Marcelina jerked to a stop in front of twelve bumps on the paved road where twelve witches of the Sisterhood of the Black Rose were buried—La Llorona's original coven. Numerous times over a span of centuries, the graves were flattened, only to bump out again.

With modern paving, the problem seemed solved. Every decade or so, the city of Santa Fe tore up the pavement, flattened out the graves, repaved, and voila—the bumps returned in the morning, lifting up the pavement without cracking it!

Recently, an exorcism was attempted by the Archbishop of Santa Fe but to no avail.

A puffed-up Pacheco then had the idea of exhuming the witches' remains with the Penitentes screaming out prayers and lashing their backs with blood flying everywhere. Lo and behold, the next morning, the bumps reappeared. The witches must have returned to their graves.

Pacheco then accused Santa Fe of harboring witches and being a safe haven for magic.

The Archbishop, under pressure from the governor, threatened Pacheco with ex-communication, including all the Penitentes, if they didn't fall more in line with traditional Catholicism. "The pope declares you renegades..."

A car honked behind Marcelina, and she emptied her head of thoughts of Pacheco, crossing herself in the Catholic fashion as her car went bumpity bump over the witches' graves.

She drove up Palace Avenue, admiring the lovely homes of the rich. She slammed on the brakes in front of the La Posada Inn, which had originally been a Victorian mansion built in 1882. The present owner four years ago placed adobe on the external walls, creating a façade of Santa Fe architecture.

Betty Sue, the former telephone operator from Madrid had moved to Santa Fe and worked at the La Posada. Betty Sue reported calls coming through the phone line from Room 256, even though the phone was disconnected. Room 256 had been Julia Staab's bedroom. Julia died in 1896 and was the original owner of the property.

Marcelina walked from the parking lot, swinging a large bag containing the tools of a medium's trade.

She entered the hotel and the La Posada owners handed Marcelina a black and white picture of Julia and her husband Abraham. Julia had chubby hands and wrists, and a pretty face. Her husband looked like a tyrant. "Abraham kept Julia and their eight children under his iron thumb. Julia's hair turned white overnight after their youngest child died, and she retreated to her room. Even though they had the other children, she just stayed in that room, refusing to eat much and not sleeping. Some say Abraham was having an affair and murdered her. Others say she hung herself."

"You most likely stirred up Julia's ghost with the renovations to her house," Marcelina said.

"We don't think the construction caused Julia to appear. The furnace broke, and workmen couldn't unlock the furnace room door. That's when we first heard a woman's voice from room 256 claiming that this was her house and wondering why the furnace wasn't working. She said she'd fix it and the furnace suddenly started working."

"Julia's ghost was always here," Marcelina said. "She was just dormant, silently haunting the grounds, not making her presence known. That's how it works with the dead who have not found peace. And then something happens to disturb them and make them realize there are others here. Julia doesn't know she's dead, but now she's aware there is something odd because others have invaded her home."

"Julia likes to bathe. The bathtub water sometimes runs in the middle of the night, though no one's turned it on. We don't let guests stay in her room any more, else they get spooked," the owners whispered.

Marcelina looked up the stairs to a closed door and the number *256*.

Her shoe scraped against the staircase as she climbed, the maple floors squeaking, sending chills up her spine.

Marcelina unzipped her bag and took out a Spirit trumpet, an instrument allowing mediums to hear voices from the grave. She placed the Spirit trumpet to the door of room *256*. The horn-shaped speaking tube amplified a faint whispering, "I'm in here. Don't come in. I'm dressing." Footsteps patted across the floor.

Marcelina flung the door open.

The room was empty and silent, with chilling cold spots. A depressive atmosphere was overwhelming, and made Marcelina want to cry. The others felt it, too.

The trio dragged a table over to the coldest spot in the room. They sat shivering, though there was a roaring fire in the fireplace. For normal séances Marcelina required four others, seated in a star shape with her at the head. Betty Sue joined them, along with a waitress who had seen Julia's face appear in the bathroom mirror and then vanish.

Julia's photograph lay on the middle of the table, looking up at them with wide eyes.

The five held hands. Marcelina concentrated, staring at the photo of Julia, who had a hand on her husband's shoulder. Marcelina made a face at Julia's hairstyle that was pulled back with pins, looking like a sausage on each side of her head.

"We know you're here, Julia," Marcelina said. "Reveal yourself."

The table shook and they all grabbed onto it.

Whoosh! The fire went out.

A translucent lady, clothed in a fancy, silk black dress, materialized. Her hair was white, sticking up from her head like a crazy lady. But the woman was the same in the picture—Julia Staab.

Marcelina looked at her kindly. "Don't blame yourself because your son died. Let go of your sadness."

Julia vanished and the books flew off the bookcase.

The fireplace turned off and on.

The new owners were pushed from their chairs by invisible hands.

Betty Sue screamed, gripping her ear. "She bit me!"

"Get out!" a voice yelled. A lamp lifted off the table and crashed on the floor.

Marcelina said, "Julia was locked in this room by her husband because she was insane and a danger to her other children. She killed her son. Run for it!"

An invisible hand tugged at Marcelina's purse.

The room was now so cold, her teeth were chattering.

Whoosh! The electricity went out and the hotel darkened.

Marcelina felt her way out of the room, stumbling down the stairs. She ran screaming towards the parking lot. She held her hands out in front since she couldn't see. There was no moon out. She screeched, moving faster, guided only by the buzzing of a fly. "Ah, Lord Tez will see that I am safe. Where is the car? I should be there by now."

Yet, Marcelina ran until she landed in a pond.

She climbed from the water, her shoes muddy and her hem soaking.

"Where did Lord Tez lead me?" She stumbled out of a clearing and into a tree-infested compound of three purple buildings.

One of the buildings was windowless with a crude wooden cross on the door—the morada of the Penitentes, their secret chapel! This compound was the headquarters of the ruling state group, headed by Pacheco.

Cars and trucks were scattered about, but Salia's old car was missing so Marcelina figured she was safe from Pacheco.

Curious, she poked her head into an unoccupied building. The soft glow of a kerosene lamp illuminated the room. Outside was a cistern filled with perishable goods. The Penitentes was a medieval, flagellanti order going all the way back to the 1200's in Spain. They were condemned as heretics and went underground, resurfacing during the Black Death plague in Europe. This room was the Deposito where food was cooked over an open fire during Holy Week when the Penitentes conducted a week long vigil, ending in the crucifixion on Good Friday of one of their members.

Screams were coming from a third building and she tiptoed over, spying through a crack in the door. Blood splattered the walls. Dozens of men were stripped to the waist, their faces scrunched in pain as they flogged their backs with whips made from amole leaves. Some wobbled on their knees, frothing at the mouth in agony.

One man stood with his whip around the neck of another, choking him until the man passed out, banging his head on the floor.

A car came roaring into the compound.

Marcelina peeked around the building, squatting and hiding. *Salia's car!*

Pacheco sat arrogantly behind the wheel, the skeleton Agnes beside him, all dressed for chapel.

Marcelina tiptoed away, her heart beating faster at the crude head-stones in the Penitentes cemetery at the south end of the compound.

A fly appeared on her ear lobe, laughing into her ear.

"You think it's funny, Lord Tez, that you led me to the Penitentes? I'll take my chances with the crazy ghost."

This time, the fly led her back to her car, performing somersaults in the air.

She jumped behind the wheel, her hands shaking and her foot pressed hard to the gas pedal. She sped towards the Plaza to pay a professional business visit to Wolfe, the great healer of Santa Fe, whose skills made her feel lacking.

"I wish to buy rattlesnake broom," Marcelina said, looking at the floor when she spoke. She was acutely aware of Wolfe's narrow lover, Rudolph, hovering around him, touching him like a wife. "I, also, need something to calm me. See how my hands shiver so I can't count the money to pay you."

"Your hands always shake when it comes to parting with your money, Marcelina," Wolfe said with a wry smile. He handed her a small bottle of oil.

She sniffed the oil and the odor of stinky feet. "Ah, valerian root," she said, sprinkling a few drops on her tongue. Her shakes subsided.

"Do you ever see your son—Dark-Shadow?" she said.

He looked at her with steely eyes and slapped the rattlesnake broom in her hand.

She counted out four dollar bills in his palm. Too bad it wasn't September; else she could find the bright yellow, woody plant called rattlesnake broom and not have to pay for the leaves and stems. Wolfe was a plant mystic and could provide any type of plant all year round.

She mumbled her thanks and hurried to visit an old lady. Marcelina instructed the woman's daughter to steep a bit of rattlesnake broom for twenty minutes. "Have your mama drink a tea from the mixture and then add the remainder to her bath water to ease her arthritis. But save a bit of tea to give her at bedtime to help her sleep. Call me when the pain becomes bad again."

She kissed the old woman on the cheek, charging nothing for her healing services since they were poor.

Charity always put Marcelina in foul mood. On the way back home she got mad at herself for helping the poverty-stricken family— one of many poor people that she lessened their pains with her healing skills, all for free.

But deep down, Marcelina knew she could never refuse when someone asked for her help.

———

20

"Are you going to stand there all day looking stupid?" Marcelina barked at Carlotta.

"No, Mama."

"Then get out of here and finish your work before I change my mind about letting you go to the movies with Isabella."

"I'll work hard today. You'll see."

Marcelina sighed deeply. She opened her arms. "Come here," she said.

Carlotta climbed on her lap and Marcelina rocked her. "What am I to do with you?" she said.

Carlotta shrugged her shoulders.

Marcelina stared into her black coffee.

Isabella shuffled into the room. "Mama," she said in a tentative voice.

A cigarette, burning to ashes, hung from Marcelina's mouth. She was hypnotized by her cup of coffee and her reflection in the liquid. *Look at me, with a neck like a fat turd.*

"Mama's stuck in her dark places again," Isabella said.

"Is she in a trance talking to dead people?" Carlotta said and jumped from her lap. She kicked her mother's shin.

"Mama? Can you hear me? Come back, Mama," Isabella said, shaking her shoulder. "Please come back from the black hole."

Marcelina blinked at her daughters. "What?" She rubbed her aching leg.

Carlotta scurried from the room.

Isabella stroked her cheek. "We were calling you, but you were lost somewhere else. There is a new customer waiting who asks specifically for you. Shall I tell her to come back some other time?"

"No. Just help me up, darling."

Isabella pulled on her arms, helping her to rise. Marcelina walked from the back of the shop, leaning on Isabella. Her eyes were still glazed so Carlotta waved her broom as she passed, swatting her rump.

The stink of solution used to perm hair brought Marcelina back to her senses and business as usual.

A new customer complained of thinning hair. Marcelina trimmed and shampooed the woman, rinsing her hair with a homemade product. She wrapped the woman's fingers around a full bottle. "Rinse daily with the *Yerba de la Negrita* solution and your hair will thicken within four months. Five dollars," she said, holding out her palm.

While the woman debated whether or not to pay the exorbitant fee, Marcelina gave her daughters a look. Carlotta swept the customer's hairs into her dust pan. Isabella carried the dust pan into the office. Marcelina stretched her neck to make sure Isabella placed the hairs in an envelope. Marcelina saved her hair clippings to make what she called a *client doll*.

The customer opened her purse, counting her bills out, one at a time. "Five dollars is a lot of money," she said in a surly voice, "but you do have a reputation—the solution will be worth the money if it works."

"Like you said—I do have a reputation. Here—take a complimentary guest bottle of *A Whiff of Heaven*. Take a sip anytime you hurt anywhere. I'm sure you will be back to buy a bigger bottle," she said, smiling meanly, and handing her the addictive solution.

The woman walked towards the exit, holding her purchases to her chest. She almost knocked over Betty Sue.

"Marcelina! I need your help. I have a date," Betty Sue said. Her husband died the year before and Marcelina nursed her through her grief.

Marcelina patted her friend on the back, offering Betty Sue a cup of soothing chamomile tea for her nerves. "I'm happy for you." She then cut her hair, snapping the scissors, and styling her hair like a work of art.

"Do you want to have lunch on Sunday? You can tell me all about your boyfriend," Marcelina said.

"Yes! I have so much else to tell you. Did you hear about the Mine Shaft Tavern in Madrid burning down on Christmas?"

"Well, now I believe in Santa Claus again," she said, dryly.

"Yes, well it did have the longest bar in the state and lots of drinkers. But my biggest news is about Salia."

Marcelina's eyes popped open.

"There are rumors in Madrid that Salia not only haunts the theatre but that she haunts the ruins of the house at Witch Hill. There are reports by frightened villagers that a fireball flashes in the sky above Bones Creek Cemetery, and her ghost is seen those nights at Samuel Stuwart's grave. Her body is balled up at the headstone, her ghost sleeping on his grave. Before sunrise, she flashes into a fireball again and soars across the sky."

Betty Sue went on talking about other news from Madrid.

Marcelina was thinking—*but a fireball? Why would a ghost turn into a fireball? Why not simply vanish into the spirit world like other ghosts, who slip back through the crack between the two worlds until they return to haunt the living again?*

A fireball? The same phenomenon Marcelina witnessed at the house at the bottom of Witch Hill after Salia came running from the house in flames and then rolled around the ground like a ball of fire.

Marcelina could hardly wait until her last customer left. She threw some bologna sandwiches together for supper, ordering her girls to clean up.

She left Juan napping on the couch.

Marcelina drove to Bones Creek Cemetery and parked with her headlights off.

She waited all night for Salia to appear.

She went every night for a month, but Salia never came.

Finally…she sat behind the wheel, staring at Samuel Stuwart's elaborate resting place. "This is ridiculous. I have conjured Salia myself with a séance. Of course she's dead. I've seen her ghost myself and looked right through her because she is transparent. Salia is not alive. I'm wasting my time and gas here," she mumbled.

She drove back to Santa Fe, cursing Madrid—a place filled with both bad and good memories. Marcelina swore never to return.

Still nibbling at the back of her mind was the fact that Salia's ghost was seen in the graveyard flashing into a fireball, which made no sense.

———

21

Marcelina snapped the lock in place. Whenever she attempted to communicate with Salia, she wanted no one else in the room.

She drew the flowered drapes closed and lit a fire in the fireplace. "So Salia will not be so cold," she muttered.

Marcelina lit a candle on a small round table. She placed on the tabletop Salia's one-armed doll. The doll's hair was scorched, unlike in the painting above the fireplace where the doll was undamaged, except for the missing arm.

Marcelina laid out Salia's other treasures—a shiny silver button and a turquoise rock. Next to the rock was a piece of chocolate cake, Salia's favorite.

She grabbed the Bible that Salia stole from the church. On the inside Salia scribbled—*if people judge so harshly, then what is the use of God?*

And lastly, Marcelina placed on the table a dried black rose, a flower loathed by Salia. The black rose was meant as a test, to make sure that if Marcelina was lucky enough to conjure Salia's ghost, that the spirit was truly her.

Marcelina placed her fingers on a heart-shaped piece of wood that was on a Ouija board. She closed her eyes, seeing the past and Salia placing her hand on the Bible. "I swear nothing will ever come between Salia and Marcy, best friends forever," they had both said.

"There. It is done. We have sworn our friendship on your holy Bible," Marcelina now recited.

The heart-shaped wood slid across the Ouija board, spelling out the words: *I especially remember Judas from the Bible.*

"I'm sorry, Salia. Please reveal yourself to me. Please, Salia," she cried out. "You have not been to visit me in such a long time."

She squeezed her eyes tightly, willing Salia to materialize, imagining her in the cemetery in Madrid, scratching at her grave, her coffin shaking.

There was a knocking on the coffin—Salia's secret knock.

Marcelina opened one eye—the knocking was coming from the end table.

The table lifted into the air, spun, and floated to the floor.

The smoked painting of Salia, La India, and Felicita, spun on the wall.

The pages of the Bible fluttered, stopping at the Song of Solomon 8:6, and lighting up the words—*for love is strong as death; jealousy is cruel as the grave.*

"I miss him, Marcy." Salia's voice shook with sobs. "Help me" she whispered.

"Oh, Salia, I have always helped you and been here for you. Please, please forgive me."

A fog rolled from the ceiling, covering the used, chaise lounge chair Marcelina saved for months to buy.

An overwhelming scent of peaches filled the room.

The fog cleared and Salia now lay in repose on the chaise lounge, her right arm thrown over her head. She was dressed in a flimsy, flowered robe, one nipple peeking out. She hummed with a voice like a canary, "Marcy, my sweet, you have always been able to see right through me. Throw that disgusting flower away. The black rose...brings back too many memories," she said, her voice cracking. Salia stroked her forehead like it pained her.

The transparent Salia seemed so fragile, like a whiff of air might blow her away. Marcelina could see right through her to the back of the chaise lounge and a tear in the fabric Carlotta made with a knife. The rip appeared to cut Salia's heart in two.

Marcelina snatched the black rose, shoving the flower in the Bible, and slamming it shut.

Salia glowed now that the flower was gone.

Marcelina shyly approached her. "Does it still hurt to be dead?"

Salia moved her face so she could see her burn scars. "I am now as ugly as you, Marcy."

"Don't be cruel."

Salia smiled sweetly. "What do you want, Marcy? What is it this time?" she drawled.

"Why do you still turn into a fireball?"

Salia floated above the lounger. "I must go. I'm searching for him, you know."

"Samuel?"

She nodded. "Take care, Marcy. Beware the Penitentes. Look what they did to me," and Salia turned her face to the left, revealing her burned flesh.

"Where is your piedra imán? I will take care of your magic rock. Poor stone must be starving and thirsty. Did you hide it?"

"What makes you think I ever had my grandmother's shape-shifting rock?"

"How else could you become such a great opera singer?"

"Ah, such little faith in my talents. You wound me, Marcy. I was a musical genius, an overnight success."

"Yes, but you couldn't do that without the magic rock. I know you, remember? You were always tone deaf. Don't go! I need your help, Salia. It's been so hard all these years," she cried out. "No one understands..."

Her ghost vanished in a puff of smoke.

"Salia, come back to me," Marcelina weakly called out. She toppled to the floor and fainted—like every séance with Salia.

When Marcelina woke, the room was in darkness. There was a bump the size of an egg on the back of her head.

She turned on the lamp and sat before a mirror, examining the crow's feet around her eyes, a couple of wrinkles on her forehead, and smoking lines around her mouth—tiny lines now but deeper every day, or so it seemed. Perhaps she should not examine her signs of aging so often.

Marcelina ignored her aching head and cracked open an *aloe vera* leaf, rubbing the juice on her face. The Egyptian queen, Cleopatra, claimed *aloe vera* was the secret of her great beauty and twice a day Marcelina indulged in the ritual. She was going on twenty-eight, and an obsession with staying young was why she became the beautician, and searched for Salia's piedra imán. She wanted to eat like a pig, yet be thin. She longed to walk into a room and turn heads, everyone gasping at her beauty.

Like La India, Marcelina would stay young forever, if she had the shape-shifting stone.

Except La India was never obsessed with beauty, just immortality.

Just.

To live forever. So little to ask.

If one never aged, then one would never die, unless a woman was murdered, like Salia.

———

22

By the light of a summer moon Storm-Chaser stood bow-legged, his grey hair tied like a horse's tail. A breeze blew his loose, made-for-sleeping-comfort underwear around his skinny, hairless thighs. Though he slept off most of the effects of the whiskey he earlier guzzled, Storm-Chaser was a bit rocky on his feet. A cigarette dangled from his mouth, and he aimed his eye at the end of his rifle. He pointed the barrel at a coyote darting between kiva ovens, resembling bee hives rising from the ground.

A real coyote always ran with its tail hanging straight down. This coyote scurried away with its tail sticking straight out and was fat. "Stupid Witch! May my aim be true and my bullet deadly," he roared and pulled the trigger.

The coyote yelped, fell to the ground, and picked itself up. It was obvious the animal was in pain, yet, the coyote ran.

"Coward! You needn't shiver so. I will grant you a peaceful death and not follow you back to your lair," he yelled.

Storm-Chaser was too old to be messing with witches. His bones creaked when he sat on the ground. He sprinkled sand in front of a fire into four piles—black, yellow, white and blue. Only the white and black sand was not dyed, the white having blown over from White Sands, conjured during a healing ceremony. White sand represents life. Storm-Chaser shuddered at the coarse black sand representing death, which usually comes uninvited. The particles blew over on their own from the Pacific Ocean and the volcanoes in Hawaii. Sometimes he found piles of black sand in his sweat lodge, which he gladly accepted as tools of a shaman's trade. Now, the black sand came in handy to discover if the witch he wounded would die or return to extract vengeance.

He blew a fistful of red powder into the flames and sparks jumped, sizzling in each pile of sand, causing the sand to snake across the ground.

The white sand formed into the coyote, red blood seeping from its side. Like any wounded animal, the coyote pointed its nose towards home. The animal was in obvious pain but moved southward in the direction of Madrid and away from the Santo Domingo Pueblo.

The blue sand became a dark sky and the black sand painted buzzards whirling in loop-de-loops, following the trail of blood.

The yellow sand swirled into the shape of a cave in the Ortiz Mountains.

The coyote staggered to the entrance of the cave—literally, a hole in the wall.

Buzzards perched on trees outside and waited.

The coyote's right side was drenched in blood. It stumbled into the cave, swinging its head and growling. Its tongue hung from its mouth, saliva leaving a trail on the ground.

One more paw forward.

And then the next.

And the next.

Until...

The coyote fell, black sand swirling around its still body.

The painting burst into life, no longer sand but images like a crystal ball. The images played like pictures at the motion picture theatre in Santa Fe. Storm-Chaser leaned forward, peering into the moving painting.

The coyote turned into Big-Belly. The fat man did not have a piedra imán, but there are many spells a witch can use for animal transformation.

Jefe's disciples have learned more powerful magic since he vanished, Storm-Chaser thought.

From the back of the cave walked a ghost glowing with white luster, his feet not seeming to touch the ground. The ghost appeared out of focus, wiggling about, but it was an illusion due to his chalky skin. He was Dead-Man-Walking, the albino, another of Jefe's disciples.

Dead-Man-Walking knelt beside Big-Belly and touched the blood rushing from his side.

"Dead-Man," Big-Belly rasped.

The albino blinked his white lashes.

"Storm-Chaser... shot...," he said, gasping.

Dead-Man-Walking cocked his head at the blood trickling from the corners of Big-Belly's mouth. He watched, with the eyes of a man fascinated by death.

126

Storm-Chaser thought, *Bah, what a cold man. He has grown no closer to Big-Belly even though they have lived together for combined protection for five years. The Bat, Big-Belly, Dead-Man-Walking and Two-Face are paranoid, all of them caught up in their own self-importance that whatever made Jefe disappear is after them, too. They sleep beside each other, share the same food, hunt and fish together. They steal and kill jointly. As far as Dead-Man-Walking is concerned, their relationship is strictly business. Now, he witnesses Big-Belly die—merely a business transaction that did not go as planned.*

Dead-Man-Walking offered no words of comfort. He spoke of no lasting regret, sentiment of loss, or hope for a dying man. He said nothing of intent to try to heal him, or stroked his hand. All he stated was, "The shaman must have used a magic bullet. What a big, stupid target you make. I should have sent the Bat instead."

"Comfort me. Don't let me die alone," Big-Belly whispered.

Dead-Man-Walking yanked back his head so that he was out of reach of the dying man. He wasn't about to let Big-Belly latch onto him at the moment of death and take his spirit with him.

Two-Face and the Bat scrambled into the cave. The Bat tripped over Big-Belly's corpse because he was pulling up his pants.

Dead-Man-Walking scoffed at the two of them.

Neither one had the grace to look embarrassed.

Storm-Chaser agreed with Dead-Man-Walking that sex was why Two-Face and the Bat weren't very powerful. Storm-Chaser had slept with many women but lusted after only one—the witch Felicita, and look what desire gave him, a missing eye.

The celibate Dead-Man-Walking labeled the intercourse act sexual folly. And for what? Two minutes of pleasure weakening a man and making him vulnerable.

Two-Face stared at the corpse. "Just as Storm-Chaser banished Jefe, he's now killed Big-Belly!"

"It was your turn to scout the old shaman but you're drunk, as usual," Dead-Man-Walking said, glaring at her.

She looked at Big-Belly with fearful eyes. "It will take much to kill Storm-Chaser. Much planning. Much magic."

He drew his knife, slicing open the body, looking for the magic bullet that killed Big-Belly.

She bent at the waist and vomited.

"Know your enemy," Dead-Man-Walking preached, which is why he fished inside Big-Belly's innards. The heart is a man's life. And within the heart beats the tale of his years on earth. Every day. Each hour. All the minutes and seconds. A man's life is mapped out in veins criss-crossing beneath the skin and beyond. All veins lead to the heart, eventually, through one path or another. Thus, he massaged Big-Belly's heart, searching for any softness Storm-Chaser may have planted or any heartache the shaman might have used to weaken him with emotion. He searched his heart for any hardness or hatred Storm-Chaser might have projected on Big-Belly, for too much negative emotion can be a man's undoing.

Nothing!

"I need a drink," Two-Face said, wiping her mouth with the back of a shaky hand.

"You've had enough! Quit sneaking behind the cave and breaking into our liquor. We risk imprisonment stealing that whiskey, and you drink up our profits every time you take a bottle."

She covered her head to protect against his blows, but Dead-Man-Walking held up in triumph a bullet looking like any ordinary bullet. "I will examine this bullet and see what magic the shaman has used to kill Big-Belly. Drag his body outside for the buzzards."

The Bat swallowed and looked over at Two-Face, but she was sitting with her head slouched and tangled hair brushing her ankles. Her moods were unpredictable when she was thinking of Jefe, lost in memories of her father.

The Bat picked up a fat ankle in each hand, dragging Big-Belly to the exit. The Bat was small but he had bulging muscles. He was filled with nervous energy. He talked fast, and walked fast, darting about like a rodent. Living in a cave suited him. He was born with extraordinary eyesight and could see like a bat.

Dead-Man-Walking kicked Two-Face in the leg. "Tell the Bat to take my rifle and kill a few of the buzzards after they've fattened up on Big-Belly. Make us some buzzard stew. I want to smell meat cooking in this cave when I wake up," he said.

She didn't move. However, her toes twitched, revealing she heard.

"Stupid slut wants everybody to feel sorry for you. Poor little orphan. Daddy's girl. It's been five years since the shaman made Jefe disappear, and still you mourn the bastard."

"I'll go help the Bat," she sniffled, dragging her filthy bare feet from the cave.

Dead-Man-Walking stretched his arms above his head and yawned. The sun was rising from the east. It was the albino's bedtime. Being a creature of the night was a curse upon his head because he was more visible at night when his skin shone with a crystal sheen, which made his life as a witch tricky. No matter how quietly he moved, his shine gave off one hell of a noise.

Dead-Man-Walking lay on the ground to sleep the day away.

Storm-Chaser blew on the painting, freezing the images which turned back into sand.

The sand swirled above the fire, extinguishing the flames.

Storm-Chaser was startled to see Dark-Shadow standing beside him, sleepy-eyed. The little boy had the uncanny ability to just suddenly appear. Dark-Shadow wasn't even aware that at times he seemed to move in shadows. At nearly seven, he stood a few inches taller than other boys his age. Spider-Woman berated Storm-Chaser for spoiling the precocious boy who was his joy in his old age.

Dark-Shadow stretched out a hand to his shoulder and gently squeezed.

He covered the boy's hand with his own gnarled hand. "It is nothing, Grandson. I merely killed a coyote lurking about. The only damage I have suffered is a sticker lodged in my toe."

Dark-Shadow led him back to the house, and seated him on a stool. He gently worked out the sticker from his toe like his grandfather was a wild, wounded animal in need of comfort. Indeed, Dark-Shadow softly spoke words of nonsense to calm him. It was uncanny how Dark-Shadow seemed to feel his pain as he pulled the sticker from his foot.

"You have a kind touch. You will make a fine shaman."

"Like you, Grandfather?"

"Better. May I sleep with you? I don't wish to disturb my wives."

Storm-Chaser climbed into bed with Dark-Shadow, brushing the sleepy boy's hair from his forehead. He would have gladly killed Jefe to protect Dark-Shadow, but he had no idea what happened to Jefe. He only hoped that Jefe was deceased because his death meant Dark-Shadow was safe.

Storm-Chaser held his grandson close, inhaling his scent of wood chips.

He closed his eyes and slept soundly with the small boy held safely in his arms.

23

Dead-Man-Walking tossed and turned. He felt like a trapped animal, with the other three hanging from his neck like an albatross. Well, there were only two now and he damned Big-Belly for dying. He needed the others to defeat Storm-Chaser so the shaman's power will pass onto him through death. Dead-Man-Walking may be white as snow but he was a dark angel, believing it was only a moment of time before he came into his own to be worshipped for who he was and the destiny he was born to. His future shone brighter when Jefe vanished, and he became leader.

Two weeks after Jefe did not return home, the four disciples confronted the shaman.

"Good riddance! I am happy for my daughter and Flaco," Storm-Chaser had said.

The Bat and Big-Belly held Two-Face back else she would have done something stupid, like get herself killed. Storm-Chaser was poised to strike back, and Jefe had been a selfish teacher, keeping his magical secrets mostly to himself, doling out tidbits when it suited him. The power of the four of them together could not defeat Storm-Chaser. They had no choice but to climb back on the wagon and drive away, promising the shaman they would return.

Storm-Chaser had laughed. "I will enjoy killing each of you."

They then moved into the cave, convincing each other it was for the best, to combine their magic and increase their powers to eventually avenge Jefe.

Dead-Man-Walking secretly rejoiced at Jefe's disappearance. Half the time, he wished Jefe's daughter vanished with him. Two-Face was still furious with her stepmother for taking Flaco and Anjelica, and moving in with the shaman after Jefe went missing. Two-Face whined for days afterwards that she had no family, until Dead-Man-Walking slapped her. "Shut up," he had said. He grabbed her by the neck, walked her to the nearby creek and threatened to drown Two-Face.

She considered all her family traitors and disowned her half-brother. It was a shame, because Flaco might have been a better ally and was now eighteen. Dead-Man-Walking did confront Flaco about joining them, but the boy was bitter.

Two-Face did what she could to irritate Dead-Man-Walking, egging him on to slap her, kick her in the butt, and punch her stomach, and begging him to bite her. She would close her eyes and call him Jefe, just as she did with the Bat when they curled up together in a corner of the cave. She was one twisted cunt.

The Bat now shuffled into the cave—alone.

"What's she up to now?" Dead-Man-Walking said.

The Bat shrugged his shoulders and yanked at the feathers of a buzzard.

He groaned. The Bat was a terrible cook. And Two-Face was useless half the time, crying and screaming for Jefe.

Dead-Man-Walking went outside and approached her huddled figure.

She softly said, "I know you think I'm crazy. But as long as I can pretend that you or the Bat is my father..."

"It's been six years, and we must accept that your father is dead."

"I just want him back."

"Does it matter if Jefe returns alive, as a ghost, or as a zombie?"

She jerked her head up. "What do you mean?"

"We must begin experimenting with ways to bring back a dead witch."

"Or a missing one," she said and for the first time since Jefe vanished, she smiled so that one half of her face softened like a woman.

24

Carlotta eyed Isabella opening a box of Jolly Time Popcorn and pouring the kernels into a pan. When the toast popped from the toaster, Isabella opened a box of Velveeta and slid out a pitcher of Kool-Aid from the fridge. She proceeded to make three toasted cheese sandwiches for dinner.

With her sister occupied in the kitchen, Carlotta slyly looked around the living room, eying Mama's purse. Mama was dressing in the bedroom. The little girl snapped open the purse and yanked out a cigarette. Carlotta lit a match and puffed. Mama smoked so much, she would never miss one drag—a penny, yes, but not a *Lucky*.

Coincidentally, an advertisement blared out from the radio, "Ladies, try a *Lucky* instead of a sweet. Get *Lucky*. Your hips won't swell."

Which proved to be false advertising—Mama was a chain smoker.

Carlotta took a few glorious puffs of the cigarette.

She's coming, the voice warned.

Mama's footsteps pounded the hallway from the bedroom, sounding like an elephant.

"Yipes!" Carlotta looked around for a place to hide the cigarette. She flung it to the floor, bringing her shoe down hard. She fanned her small hands at the smoke and twisted her foot to extinguish the cigarette.

"Mama, how pretty you look," she said, swallowing the cough in her throat. "Where are you going?"

"Is dinner ready?"

"What witchcraft are you using tonight?"

Wham!

Carlotta cried out, holding a hand to her reddened cheek that was already beginning to swell with Mama's handprint.

"How many times have I told you that I am not a witch? I am a healer, for the good of the people," Mama barked.

"Of course, Mama," she said, blinking back her tears.

Carlotta followed Mama into the kitchen, wondering what exactly she was up to, dressed in her very best with a white feather in her hair.

They ate in silence, Mama staring at the wall like in a trance. The cheese stuck in Carlotta's throat, and she looked around the room, wondering if there were any dead people in the kitchen.

"Dinner was good," Mama said to Isabella. "You," and she pointed to Carlotta. "Clean up. And don't get into trouble while waiting for your daddy to come home. Remember that I, also, have a mirror behind my head like Tezcatlipoca."

The hair raised on the back of Carlotta's neck. She scooted her chair from the table, eying the back of Mama's head. There was no mirror, but that red rose on her head seemed to grow from her scalp so maybe...

Mama marched back into her bedroom with her head held stiff like a regal queen. She was dressed in her finest evening clothes, a purple concoction of lace and chiffon ballooning around her hips and down to her ankles.

The bedroom door slammed and the lock snapped in place.

Carlotta tiptoed to the door, placing her eye on the keyhole.

Mama pulled out a worn blanket and unrolled it, revealing some strange items. Carlotta couldn't make out what the items were but if the things had anything to do with witchcraft, then the stuff had to be as odd as Mama.

Yuck! Mama was stripping down to her birthday suit.

She stood naked on the blanket, her dress, petticoats and underwear spread around her.

Carlotta held a hand to her mouth to stifle her laughter. If Mama knew that the sight of her naked body made her convulse with giggles, she would kill her.

What is that story in the Bible the nuns teach at school—the one where Noah curses his son, just because he catches his father naked. Well, no wonder. Noah must have looked as silly as Mama does.

Mama opened two boxes and held one in each hand. She sprinkled the contents of each box over her body. She threw the empty boxes on the floor and stood, with her arms held wide.

Mama was a sight to behold, covered in white powder, looking like a big fat mass of cookie dough. She took three steps towards the south, spun around and took three steps to the north.

Mama turned in the direction of the bathroom window and ran.

There was a splash followed by a noise sounding like "hoot, hoot". Then silence.

More silence.

More.

More.

More silence.

Carlotta pulled a hairpin from her head and picked at the lock.

She shoved the door open and tiptoed into the bathroom—no sign of Mama or her evening clothes. Only a half-filled bathtub containing magic white powder, steamy water and a breeze from the open bathroom window— the only means of escape, a bathroom window much too small for Mama's gargantuan buttocks to fit through.

Carlotta balanced on the edges of the tub, looking out the window at an owl flapping its wings. The owl had a white feather and a red rose.

Mama turned into an owl!

Carlotta screamed and fell into the bath water. She jumped from the tub, shaking the water from her body. She was drenched with wet powder.

She screeched, holding up her arms, looking in the mirror for any feathers growing. Yet, Carlotta was disappointed that she was still a girl and had not turned into an owl like Mama did.

———

25

Marcelina flapped her wings and headed south, towards Albuquerque. She was that rarest of birds—an owl with multi-colored feathers, the bright shades of her evening gown. The white feather stuck out of the top of her head, beside a red rose.

She flew across Route 66, part of a grand highway system linking Los Angeles to Chicago via Albuquerque. Route 66 was responsible for the success of hotels and restaurants sprouting along the highway.

Marcelina hadn't been to the opera since moving from Madrid. She flew to Albuquerque for a performance by an opera singer who went by the name of Catalina, which means *Cat*. The singer intrigued her because Salia had a lot of cat characteristics, due to an invisible, magical cat bone. And there were other similarities. Catalina refused to star in motion pictures. Salia, also, refused to perform in movies. Her family curse had prevented Salia from leaving Madrid, but a movie director once offered to come to Madrid to film her—Salia turned him down flat. "Because, it is dangerous to have your photo taken. A painting or drawing is no threat because it merely resembles a person. But a photograph is an exact image taken in time. With a photograph, a witch can perform image magic against you," she had told Marcelina. Native Americans are especially proficient at image magic, and Jefe would have used Salia's photo to hurt her.

Marcelina sailed through the open door of the Grand Opera House to a back room and softly landed her claws on the carpet. She folded her wings over her face and was transformed back into a woman clothed in her nicest evening gown.

She seated herself in the front row of the theatre, like any normal woman might. Yet, when the real purchaser of the theatre seat arrived to claim her chair, Marcelina showed her claws, and the woman scurried away.

Marcelina never felt so self-conscious in all of her life. A few white owl feathers stuck out of her hair beside a red rose. She sneezed and feathers fluttered about. She felt so out of date at the opera house wearing an old-fashioned, poufy gown. The theatre was filled with hundreds of women in narrow, draping, evening gowns. She squashed her orange dress down, feeling like Marie Antoinette awaiting the guillotine on Halloween. Her knee-length hair was swept up, exposing her neck. Being a first-rate beautician, she was painfully aware of the latest styles of hair brushing the shoulders, which unfortunately didn't look good with her chubby cheeks.

Marcelina was curious to know what this Catalina looked like, since the posters and newspapers only had drawings of her character. Earlier, she walked to the Santa Fe Public Library to look the singer up in the encyclopedia. Again—no photograph, or painting, or drawing, or anything displaying the singer's image. Rather odd for someone so famous. Catalina was a European actress from Spain, having sung and acted upon the European stages and on Broadway in New York City. It seemed Catalina burst upon the European opera stages right after Salia was burned. She recently appeared on Broadway in *Anna Karenina*, and the performances were said to be similar. In fact, Catalina was compared to Salia when she performed that opera and the opera *Madame Bovary*, which is what brought the singer to Marcelina's attention.

And so, butterflies flew around her stomach and her heart beat faster when Catalina made her entrance upon the stage.

Marcelina was disappointed that she did not resemble Salia. However, she did sing like a canary, sounding a lot like Salia's ghost.

She did not notice six seats to her right sat Marshal Joseph Quill. He leaned forward with an intense expression on his face, his eyes following every move Catalina made upon the stage.

———

26

Her piedra imán is what made Salia such a great actress and gave her the ability to sing. Catalina performed upon the stage as well as Salia, a performance so uncanny, everyone in the theatre held their breath, waiting for her next move or note.

With her piedra imán, Salia could transform into anyone she chose. Marcelina cocked her head at Catalina, trying to picture her friend. Of course Catalina didn't look like Salia but there were similarities. The way she moved with the grace of a cat. Her dazzling smile, sexiness and charismatic way. She was just as charming. Her laughter, sounding like ice tinkling in a glass, was the same. And her figure was just as breathtaking.

Catalina's face was harder than Salia's had been, but she was lovely. The opera star had flaming red hair, whereas Salia's hair was reddish brown in color. Catalina's eyes were an emerald-green, instead of blue-grey.

Her eyes may be a different color, but the eyes are the same. Cat-like. The eyes reflect the soul.

There was something about the way Catalina tossed her head and the manner in which she placed her hands on her hips when she sang.

She leaned forward and looked at Marshal Quill sitting in the audience staring intently at Catalina.

The Marshal looks smitten, she thought.

Salia always did have a way with men, the fly whispered into her ear. Lord Tez sat upon her shoulder tickling her ear with a feather.

"Catalina is not Salia. She can't be," Marcelina said.

"Sh," someone said.

"Shush," another said.

The fly bit her ear and she jumped. Blood dribbled from her ear, staining the white collar of her evening gown.

Lord Tez departed as quickly as he had come, leaving a fiery burning in her ear. He buzzed in front of Marshal Quill who frowned at the fly.

Catalina stopped her singing, snapping her fingers.

The lights came on.

"You were told not to take my picture. I heard the clicking of your camera," the singer screeched, pointing.

The offending photographer was escorted from the premises.

Catalina smiled at the audience, sweetly apologizing for the interruption. The show continued where it left off.

Marcelina wondered about the singer's acute hearing ability. *Cats have tremendous hearing,* she thought with excitement.

Marcelina stood with everyone else and clapped when Catalina bowed for her third encore.

The singer lifted her hands as if to say, *no more please.* She gave the audience one last, radiant smile before leaving the stage.

Marcelina stepped on a few toes to reach the aisle. She elbowed some ribs as she snaked her way to the back of the theatre.

She gave a hearty knock on Catalina's dressing room door.

A French maid peeked out.

"I would like to see Catalina," Marcelina said, stretching her neck and feasting her eyes on the singer sitting at her dressing table. "Tell her I am an old friend."

"Mademoiselle Catalina never receives visitors after a performance, even those claiming an old friendship," the maid said, lifting her nose in the air.

Catalina dropped the tissue she was using to remove her makeup. She cleared her throat. "Louisa, tell the woman to come in."

Louisa stared with astonishment at her mistress. She lifted her nose even higher, like Marcelina was a fly on a French pastry. "You may enter, but just for a moment. My mistress needs her privacy."

"I know who you are," Marcelina said to Catalina.

"I don't know what you mean," she said with wide-eyed innocence. Catalina continued to remove her makeup, ignoring Marcelina's reflection in the mirror.

"Salia, don't you recognize me? I am your best friend—Marcy," she said in a soft voice.

Her eyes grew cold. "I've never seen you before in my life!"

Her dressing room overflowed with bouquets of roses and other flowery concoctions. A long diamond necklace hung from Catalina's neck to her waist. She had changed from her stage costume to a shimmering gold chemise dress that moved with her body, sparkling like real gold. She was a woman of the world, yet there was weariness to her emerald eyes. Her face was tense. For all her smiling and success on stage, Catalina did not seem to be a happy woman.

"What perfume are you wearing? It smells exquisite," Marcelina said, sniffing like a dog.

"Chanel No. 5. Coco is a friend of mine, though lately she has been accused of collaborating with the Nazis. We differ on our politics." She frowned. "Here—try some of her perfume."

And the world-class singer did an astonishing thing—she rose to her feet and dabbed a few drops from the bottle behind Marcelina's quivering ears. Her fingertips lingered on her right ear, softly stroking her ear lobe. "There. You smell as good as me now," she gently said. She cleared her throat. "What did you say your name was?" A curtain fluttered across her face. She plopped down in her velvet chair, once more the ice cold actress.

"My name is Marcelina."

Catalina rapidly blinked her eyes, staring at an open jar of cold cream. "Please leave now. I have a date and must dress."

"You know who I am. Don't pretend. Not with me, Salia. How I have missed you, my old friend. My blood sister. Remember?"

"Please leave before I have you thrown out, and quit calling me Salia," she said in a choked voice.

"You are disturbing my mistress. I will call security," Louisa said.

Catalina grabbed her maid's wrist. "No. It's okay." She glared at Marcelina. "Go! Get out of here before I change my mind!"

"I see I am mistaken. I am sorry for you." Marcelina spun on her heel and marched from the dressing room, her arms held stiff by her side.

As soon as the door slammed, Marcelina burst into tears, crying hysterically.

She ran, bumping into theatre goers, shoving them out of her way.

Marcelina ran behind the theatre and turned back into an owl.

She flew over Route 66, this time headed towards Bones Creek Cemetery in Madrid.

27

Marcelina perched on the tree closest to Samuel Stuwart's grave. She was well hidden in the leaves, her wings tucked by her breast. She fluffed her feathers for warmth.

With her large owl eyes, she followed the movement of a bright light speeding across the sky from the southwest direction of Albuquerque.

The light grew bigger, proving this was no ordinary light. Witch lights the villagers term this kind of phenomenon. Often a kaleidoscope of witch lights dance in the sky before settling down to earth in a circle.

Tonight, there was but one lone witch light growing larger, until a ball of fire hovered above Bones Creek Cemetery.

The fireball landed near the graves of Marcelina's parents and stepfather. Marcelina growled low in her throat, thinking of her stepfather. She spit and a gob of saliva slithered down the tree trunk.

The fireball rolled towards Samuel Stuwart's grave, stopping before the headstone of the ill-fated owner of Madrid.

The fireball sizzled to a pile of ashes.

The ashes flew in the air, rising to a height of about five-feet eight inches.

The ashes fluttered, bonding to form the shape of a woman.

The ashes turned to clay, and the clay to flesh.

Marcelina recognized the flaming red hair that was so bright, the woman's head still looked like it was on fire. It was Catalina who stood before Samuel Stuwart's grave.

Catalina held out her clenched fist and moonlight shone on an ordinary-looking rock. She twirled. Faster. Faster...

Until in her place now spun a sleek coyote chasing its tail. The coyote was reddish tan in color, an odd color for a coyote.

The coyote lifted her head to the moon and howled. It was a plaintive howl and the loneliest Marcelina ever heard.

From all directions gathered a pack of coyotes, forming a circle around the lone coyote sitting on Samuel Stuwart's grave. Catalina, the coyote in the center, lifted one paw as if to say, "hello my old friends".

In answer, the coyotes licked her, washing her face with their tongues and playfully nicking at her ears with their teeth. One stuck its tongue up her nostril.

Catalina twirled in the center of the coyotes, slapping her tail in their faces.

She stood upright on two legs—her bottom legs transformed to the shapely legs of a woman, the top legs to slender arms, but the rest of her still coyote.

Catalina spun—transforming into a woman with a furry tail and coyote head.

The tail vanished and only the coyote head remained on a woman's body.

When the coyote stopped twirling, Marcelina caught her breath because the coyote vanished, and in its place was a different woman than Catalina.

The woman, who now stood in the center of the pack, had reddish brown, flaming copper curls. Her emerald-green eyes were now blue-grey. Salia was dressed all in white, which made her copper-colored hair stand out even more.

Salia collapsed, falling to a rumpled heap on top of the grave where she wept, causing the coyotes to let out a plaintive whine.

Each wild dog gave her a final lick upon her face, a kiss good-bye before turning their tails away from Bones Creek Cemetery.

Salia lay atop the mound of dirt, beneath which Samuel was buried. She was bent in the fetal position, her hair in riotous curls, blanketing her body from the cool summer night. Marcelina could not see through Salia like when she visited as a ghost. Salia appeared to be a flesh and blood woman.

Marcelina clutched her wing to her heart. *Salia. Oh, Salia, you have returned. Still beautiful and young. Untouched by the fire that consumed most of the house at Witch Hill.*

She flew down from the tree and grasped the dirt with her claws to anchor herself on the earth. Marcelina always had difficulty walking as an owl, rolling from side to side. Birds were meant to fly, not walk. She made a hooting sound.

Salia stirred. She sat up and twisted her eyes with her fists. She cocked her head and stared at the owl with the big eyes.

Marcelina's beak became a nose.

Her big orange eyes turned black in color and smaller.

Her bright feathers transformed into a ballgown.

Before Salia's shocked eyes, the owl turned into Marcelina, standing with her arms wide open. "Salia," she cried out.

Salia arched her back like a cat when it's startled. Marcelina half expected her to hop sideways, like a cat does when it's surprised.

"Salia! It's me. Marcy."

Salia jumped up and ran, her bare legs flashing towards the trees, her white dress flicking at her thighs.

She disappeared into the woods behind the cemetery, seeming to move through the trees, as if not made of flesh but of spirit. Perhaps, she was a ghost after all, and Marcelina scared her since she didn't conjure her up at a séance.

Marcelina chased after Salia. *Running after a ghost?*

A fireball was always Salia's favorite mode of air transportation—a skill she learned from her mother and grandmother. Six years ago at the burning house at Witch Hill, one spark lifted slowly upward from the ball of fire that was the burning Salia. The spark flashed across the sky like a shooting star, headed east towards Europe and the theatres awaiting any great opera singer, beckoning her with open arms.

Of course! For the first time it dawned on Marcelina—*how can anyone with the ability to flash into a ball of fire burn from the flame?* Salia would have needed a new identity to make her way in the world after her death was advertised in the nation's newspapers as an "accidental fire" set by the smoking opera singer. Salia had been a famous singer, and her face well known to opera lovers who traveled from all over the country to Madrid to see her perform. With her magic stone, her *piedra imán*, Salia could shapeshift into another woman. And Salia's *piedra imán* went missing when she did—because the shape-shifting stone never left Salia's possession!

Marcelina heard a noise behind her and spun.

Salia had circled back and was hiding behind Samuel's headstone. Her teeth were chattering.

"Salia, you're alive? You're not a ghost?"

Salia darted from the headstone, her feet flying.

"Oh, Salia, surely you're not afraid of me? Of Marcy? All I want to tell you, Salia, is that I'm sorry," she yelled.

Marcelina turned back into an owl, flying after her.

Salia finally realized it was hopeless to flee from a flying owl that could see in the dark. She stopped running and sadly stared up at the owl.

Their masquerade was at an end and it was Marcelina, the woman, who looked back at her. "Salia?" she said, unsure of her welcome. She held out a one-armed doll. A peace offering.

Salia reached out a hand, hugging her doll to her chest. "She smells like death, like the ashes from my house at Witch Hill," she said in a tiny voice. Salia rocked the doll in her arms, singing the twisted lullaby her mother, Felicita, used to sing.

"Hush, my darling, if you never say a word.

Mama's going to kill you a mocking bird.

Hush, my darling, if you never cry.

I promise you, you will never die."

"No," she said in a childish tone and threw the doll on the ground. "I had a baby, Marcy," and her shoulders shook with sobs.

"Salia?" she said again, panicking. She had rejected her doll, a reminder of her childhood; perhaps Salia rejected her, too.

Marcelina turned to leave, her head hanging down, her shoulders rounded.

"Marcy! Oh, Marcy, how good it is to see you."

They went into each other's arms, hugging and crying. They giggled and laughed.

Salia smiled softly with full sensuous lips. Her small nose turned up slightly. Her skin was the color of peaches shining luminous in the night. Her perfume smelled like a peachy Chanel Number 5.

"So your dream has come true to act and sing upon the world's opera stage. I'm glad," Marcelina said.

"I should have known you'd find me out, old friend. Who but you knew my secrets? Who but you shared my pain? Ah, Marcy. That all seems a lifetime ago."

"It was. You're Catalina now."

"Do you...do you think they liked me?"

"The audience loved you, Salia."

"But they love Catalina, not me," she said, with a stricken voice. "And I've grown weary of being the toast of Europe. I want to start over—to come home. Oh not to Madrid. But to America. To New Mexico. I've bought a home in Albuquerque, where I can be closer to Stu."

She speaks like her husband is still alive.

"After all these years, it still hurts. I miss him so much. He loved me above all others. No one else ever did. Grandma loved Mother, and you love your Juan. But Samuel chose me when he could have had any woman."

"I always thought you made him love you with magic."

"Our love was real, and it destroyed him—Marcy. They killed him because of me, because he dared to love me!"

"I know," she said patting her hand. "But how did you escape your family curse, Salia, which would strike you dead if you left the Madrid area? The curse states that once an Esperanza of the blood comes to this land, if he or she is the last Esperanza, then that Esperanza cannot leave because his or her very soul is constructed from the mud of this valley and so rooted to this land. If the last Esperanza is uprooted, he or she will die like an ancient oak ripped from the land that nurtures it."

"So it is written. So it shall be," Salia said in a flat voice and looked at Marcelina with hooded eyes. "The roots of the house burning freed me from the family curse. All those good Catholics freed me from the family curse. They burned me, remember, and left me for dead. The good people of Madrid didn't even give me a funeral. They treated me like a dog," she said bitterly.

Marcelina didn't remind Salia that there had been no body to bury. "But you're here now. In Madrid. You have visited many times over the last dozen years," she said.

"It amuses me to haunt Madrid. This damn village haunts me. I may look like a woman of the world but inside, I am still the same Salia. Madrid still has the power to hurt me."

"So you haunt Madrid as a coyote, ghost, shadow, other women, and as yourself. And what of me, Salia? Did it amuse you to haunt me? To be conjured up at my séances, so ghostly, that I could see right through you?"

Salia laughed. "It was a great joke, no? You should have seen your face the first time I came to you, transparent. Priceless," she said, lifting her eyebrows.

Ah, here was the old Salia—a mischievous gleam sparkling in her eyes, but..."Your prank was not funny! If I wasn't so happy to find you're alive... all these years. All these years, I thought you dead. I mourned for you. I cried daily for you. I died a little inside, Salia."

She pouted. "Come now, Marcy, we are united but minutes, and already you scold me. I am still your Salia and you are still my Marcy." Salia licked her cheek like a cat. "Come. Let us sit beneath this tree and talk," she said and reached for her hand, leading her to an enormous tree across from Samuel's grave.

"You are the same Salia, yet you are so very different than what you were." Marcelina suddenly felt shy and certainly old next to Salia, who still looked nineteen. *Due to her piedra imán,* she bitterly thought. She felt awkward next to Salia, like a clumsy ox, a bullfrog walking around on hoofs. Marcelina was so out of date. Salia was dressed like a Paris fashion model and looked like a movie star, a sophisticated French prostitute, a high-class falutin' broad. "All that stuff is true then? Your designer is your friend, Coco Chanel?" she said in a voice filled with awe.

Salia nodded her head. She was dressed like a rich woman, in a long, sleek, white evening gown that came to her ankles. A gold ribbon hung from each side of her long-waisted gown with silk pleats cascading down the dress. Long silver and gold necklaces fell from her neck to her waist, bouncing against the gold brocade of rich fabric, forming a V at her collar. Salia was ultra sophisticated. Oozing with international class not found in the likes of New Mexico. Catalina was much sought after in rich and powerful circles for her wit and icy manner with the gentlemen. Catalina was an untouchable goddess, very elegant.

Salia placed her arms around her, and Marcelina felt reassured. Salia shivered and Marcelina hugged her like she did when Salia was a child, drowning in the misery of a three-generation witch family. They both saved each other when they were young.

Marcelina rested her head on Salia's shoulder. "How I've missed you, my friend. I've needed so much to talk to you. When you materialized at my séances, you never stayed long enough for a good girlfriend talk. Pouf! You would vaporize as if just saying, 'Hi, Marcy. Got to go, Marcy.'"

"You witnessed me haunting the theatre in Madrid," Salia said, giggling. "It was so funny to see some of my former torturers running from the theatre, scared of their own shadows."

"There were a few accidents on the road because of you," Marcelina said.

"I know," she said soberly. "But I am not to blame for their bad driving."

"They deserved it, after burning your house down, thinking they were killing you. And what of your poor baby?"

"Please, let's change the subject, Marcy," Salia said and wiped her eyes.

"No one understands but you what I've been going through," Marcelina said.

"Becoming a witch isn't easy."

"I'm not a witch. I'm a healer."

Her eyes twinkled. "Mere healers do not have the power to turn into owls."

Marcelina blushed, her chest swelling with pride. "It's a slick trick, no?"

"What trick? You and I both know that animal transformation is red magic," she said, scoffing. "You are in denial, Marcy. You are as much a witch as I am, though I was born to inherit my...gifts," she said with irony.

"So, you still have a difficult time accepting your fate?"

"Fate is hard to swallow when it's forced down one's throat."

"You are doing well for one whose fate was shoved down her throat."

"As I said, with power comes responsibility. Let me show you what I have been up to since the war broke out in Europe." Salia jumped to her feet and spun, hugging her piedra imán to her chest.

She stopped spinning and rocked a bit dizzily. She now had blonde hair, wore glasses and was dressed in the uniform of...

"You joined the British army!" Marcelina squealed with delight.

Salia wore an army cap and jacket, beige shirt, skirt, and tie, stockings and serviceable shoes. Her features were slightly different; her blue-grey eyes now brown.

"But what did you do?"

"I am a member of the Women's Auxiliary Air Force. Of course, we didn't fight in active combat and I grew quickly bored and vanished. I suppose I'm AWOL," she said, frowning. "I found a more worthy cause." Salia spun and her outfit turned to a nurse's uniform and her hair to brown. "Oh, Marcy, you should have seen them, the poor wounded men. I wish I had your healing skills. I tried...but my mother and grandmother were never really healers. Those witches were better at breaking people than fixing them."

Salia and Marcelina walked leisurely back towards Samuel's grave, catching up on the years in between their separation.

"I paid a visit to Jefe, or I should say, my ghost did," Salia said.

"Oh, how priceless! I wish I would have been there!"

Salia described what happened and both women rolled on the ground, laughing hysterically.

Marcelina picked up Salia's one-armed doll and dusted her off. "I have two girls. Identical twins, Isabella and Carlotta," she proudly told her.

"I'm glad for you, Marcy. You always wanted children," she said in a broken voice.

Marcelina slapped her hand to her mouth. "Oh, my God, how careless of me. I forgot. I'm sorry about your baby dying in the fire, Salia."

"It's better this way," she said in a soft voice.

"Better your son died?"

"I would have made a bad mother with her as a role model."

"Felicita," Marcelina said and crossed herself.

"Really, Marcy, you are tiresome with your Catholic gesture of always making the sign of the cross."

"Old habits die hard. Besides, I don't like speaking of your mother in a cemetery."

"Felicita is not buried here." Salia said, her face tightening into a hard mask and eyes glittering like steel.

"Where is she buried then?"

"Her body simply vanished."

"What?!"

"Oh, don't worry. I think my grandmother buried her somewhere and refused to tell me."

"You think?"

"Please change the subject."

She nodded her head and smiled. It was heaven to be around Salia again, breathing the same air and walking beside her in the moonlight.

"And so you are the beautician."

"How did you know? You never stuck around a séance long enough for me to say."

"I have passed many times in front of your *Eternal Beauty*. Once, you nearly caught me staring in the window. So you finally fulfilled your dream of making beauty?"

"And you, Salia, are the great actress and singer admired the world over."

They stopped at the grave of Salia's husband and she rocked, hugging her stomach. "I loved him so much. He was so good to me, my Samuel. I am filled with so much guilt, that I feel sometimes I shall die, killed by my own heart and strangled by my own lack of forgiveness."

Marcelina placed an arm around her shoulders and squeezed. "Salia, it's not your fault your husband was murdered. You gave him a son. The boy made him very happy."

"You'll never understand. How could you? I betrayed Samuel!"

Salia reached behind the elaborate, life-size tombstone of her husband and yanked out a whiskey bottle. She popped the cork and took a drink. "This night I won't drink alone. Here," she said, handing the bottle to Marcelina.

Salia nervously lit a cigarette. She paced, puffing on a cigarette, occasionally grabbing the bottle and taking a swallow. It was as if she forgot Marcelina was there and was talking to herself, berating her relationship with Samuel.

Marcelina believed she was talking gibberish. "You loved Samuel and he loved you. Madrid was jealous and killed him. End of story," she said.

Salia sniffled. "Do you mine leaving us alone?"

Marcelina gave her one last hug, kissing her on both cheeks.

"We'll speak soon. I promise," Salia said.

"You better not vanish, Salia, as you did before."

She didn't respond. Her head was bent, her eyes glued to the name *Samuel Stuwart* engraved across the marble base of an elaborate white marble statue carved in an uncanny image of her husband. The statue looked so real, it seemed Salia could reach out a hand and touch Samuel.

Marcelina hid behind the tree she earlier perched on and spied. She was reluctant to leave, fearing to never see Salia again.

Suddenly—cracks appeared in Samuel's statue.

Moisture slid down the marble like drizzling rain.

He is crying, thought Marcelina.

Salia dropped to her knees, pulling at weeds around the grave. "Hello, darling. Sorry I couldn't come last night," she said.

A man's voice came out of nowhere. He sounded angry, his voice boiling with pain. "It's been six years!"

Marcelina looked with wide eyes at Samuel Stuwart materialize, dressed in a snowy white linen suit. He stood in the same arrogant stance he postured in life. Samuel leaned nonchalantly against a tree, yet it looked as if he held up the tree instead of the other way around. His arms were crossed in front of his chest. Moonlight lit up his face. He had the same autocratic expression of a man who owned the world, but his eyes lit up for only Salia.

Her tears have conjured him from the dead, Marcelina thought. She looked up at the statue of Samuel Stuwart, expecting the statue to be gone, thinking the statue must have come to life. But the statue still posed on the marble base.

The white-suited Samuel was still there, too, leaning against the tree, moonlight glittering on his blonde hair.

Marcelina threw her arms over her head and screamed, running away from Bones Creek Cemetery as fast as she could.

Samuel and Salia just stood there, staring at each other, both breathing heavily.

———

28

Samuel opened his arms wide. "Well here I am, Salia. Isn't this what you wanted?" he said, his voice dripping with a sarcasm belying the pain in his face. "You sleep on my grave some nights!" His eyes glittered with anger and lust, love and hatred. "You wanted me alive, so here I am. Your love has brought me back from the dead, my dear." He threw back his head and laughed. When he stopped laughing, tears shone from his sad blue eyes.

She walked slowly towards him.

He didn't meet her half-way. Samuel leaned against the tree, appearing for all intents and purposes to be relaxed, but his chest moved rapidly as if it hurt to breathe the life-giving oxygen of the cemetery that still had the smell of death from a funeral earlier in the day.

Salia stood inches from him, staring into his eyes, unable to fathom whether or not he was happy to see her. She wasn't sure how he crossed over from the grave, why he was here with her now. She only knew she dreamt of this moment, wished for this time, thousands of days over the last six years. "Oh, Samuel! How I've missed you. I come to the cemetery to be with you, hoping you'll come back to me. Now, here you are." She looked at his face with wonder, remembering every beloved line on his face and each hair on his eyebrows. "Is it alright to touch you?" And she reached out a trembling hand.

"I'm real—flesh and blood, darling."

And it was he who could stand their separation not a moment longer as he reached out to Salia, cupping her cheeks between his big hands.

Funny, she didn't remember his hands being rough and callused. A rich man like Samuel always had such smooth skin.

He smashed his lips against her lips.

She clung to his shoulders, feeling faint.

He groaned, smoothing her wayward hair back from her face. "I've waited for you all these years. Dreamed of you. Missed you. Hungered for you. Made love to you in my dreams."

She didn't question how he came to be here, or how he escaped the confines of death and crossed over from the other world. Maybe he had never really been in the land of the dead. Perhaps Samuel had not died, and he was shipped back East to survive his wound. He lay in a coma until finally, he woke up. Madrid kept them apart, as it had for so many years.

Damn the questions! Salia didn't care if he was a ghost or alive. All she knew was that Samuel was here. He had come back to her!

For the first time in years she felt truly alive. She let out a heartfelt cry, flinging her arms around his neck.

He hugged her, squeezing his eyes tightly. He dipped his head into her shoulder blade, inhaling the scent of her. "Peaches. You always smell of peaches. I have craved peaches for six long years. Let's not waste any more time. There's a train waiting for us."

He waved a white trench coat over the two of them. He placed an arm around her waist, and she snuggled into the warmth of his body. They walked to the station in Madrid and boarded a train for Albuquerque. Samuel wore a hat shoved low on his forehead, hiding his face.

Salia cocked a floppy hat over one side of her face, masking the other side of her face with her long hair. She giggled. They were like spies departing Madrid in the dead of night.

Dead? Don't even think that word! We are both alive. He is not a ghost. I can smell him, taste him. She was with Samuel. He had come back to her and was no longer angry. He still loved her?

She snuck a peek at the other passengers, wondering if they could, also, see Samuel.

For just a second, she felt panic because everyone was ignoring them.

"Everything okay?" he whispered in her ear.

"Yes," she said in a tiny voice.

———

29

Salia and Samuel were led to a private compartment. Keeping his head down so the conductor wouldn't see his face, he gave the conductor their tickets, along with a five dollar tip. "We don't want to be disturbed," he said in a muffled voice.

The conductor smiled, pocketing his money.

Samuel slammed the door to their compartment. He turned on his heel, glaring at her.

Salia crossed her legs and blinked. She nervously scratched her thumb with her index finger. *Why doesn't he say something?* Salia suddenly felt shy around him, like long ago.

He dropped to his knees, burying his head in her lap, rubbing his face on her legs and moaning.

Salia stroked his blonde head with trembling fingers, smiling at how his hair curled at the ends. She ran a finger down his cheek, stroking his long sideburn.

"I could ravish you right here on this train. I'm warning you. Touch me once more like that, and I won't be able to help myself," he growled. "The conductor will get one hell of a surprise when he opens the door in Albuquerque."

She swallowed.

Samuel twisted her hair in his hands and shoved her head against the back of the seat. "I can smell you, and it's driving me crazy."

He gave her a feathery kiss and cradled her in his arms, hugging her like he might never let her go.

Salia closed her eyes. She could stay in his arms forever.

They rode in silence the rest of the trip. It was a comforting silence, an *I've-finally-come-home* silence.

They arrived at the train station in Albuquerque, and Salia did not question how Samuel happened to have a key in his pocket for the best room at the Alvarado Hotel. Even in Albuquerque Samuel had to hide his face as best he could, since he had owned a chunk of the city.

He still owns a lot of businesses in Albuquerque, or at least his heir does. No, Samuel does. He is not a ghost. Samuel can tell me later what happened but right now...

Salia stood beside him in the elevator, holding hands. She looked at the floor, avoiding the elevator operator. She could have earlier turned back into Catalina or some other disguise, but she was with Samuel. With him, she needed to be herself. She had to be Salia because Samuel never knew she was a witch. The only magic he believed in was love.

Her heart pounded with fear because if Samuel should ever find out the truth about her, she would lose him once again. Only she wouldn't lose him to the graveyard this time, but to a living hell where he lived but didn't want her. He would find her disgusting and freakish. Worst of all, Samuel would doubt his feelings for her and wonder if he ever really loved her. He would believe she bewitched him with a powerful love spell, like the villagers warned him.

Perhaps I have placed a love spell on Samuel, in death. All those nights I slept on his grave, my love was so strong, that I reached beyond the grave and brought him back to life.

But the reason he returned was unimportant. Samuel was here. With her. And so alive. His body was not cold like a corpse but burning up with heat. Pulsing with need...

For her. And she felt like that teenage girl again, in awe that any man would ever love her.

Samuel flicked on the light and locked the room. He yanked her hard against him, kneading her skin.

She felt his heat through the silkiness of her clothing.

"I was barely able to contain myself on the train with you so close, but I had to keep my hands to myself and play the gentleman. I had to stop from throwing you across the seat and pounding into you, pouring my seed into you. Let's make another baby, Salia," he cruelly said.

"What?"

"Sh. It's alright. I won't force you."

Samuel slid his hand up her thigh and made her cry out, regardless of whom in the next room heard. He breathed heavily. "I want the whole damn world to know that you want me, you hear! Not some other man!"

"But I don't want any other man."

"That you crave me as I crave you. I need the world to know I can make you sing like a canary. Scream like a banshee. But I've had to bide my time, until..."

"Samuel, you're scaring me."

"I'm going to explode, if I don't have you soon and empty myself into you. I want to consume you. All of you. Heart. Body. Mind. And soul." He smashed his lips against her mouth and ran his hands down her hips. He grabbed at her shoulders, ripping her dress in two.

She was stunned by his savagery...

But it had been six years.

And her urgency matched his. She pushed herself into him, grinding her hips against his hard body and moaning. She scratched at his back, moaning out his name.

He swung her up in his arms and carried her over to the bed.

He tore off the rest of her clothes and scanned her nakedness with a lust that made her blush.

Salia opened her thighs.

Her erotic pose drove him wild, and he drove her insane with his lips and his tongue until she bucked her body and did cry out like a banshee.

Samuel laughed in triumph, ripping his clothes off.

He bounced on the bed beside her and held her legs down with his own, pinning her to the bed.

His tongue played with her senses. It was as if her bones were liquid and she could barely move. Her body tingled with a pleasant numbness that made her groan when he grabbed her wrists, yanking her arms above her head. "Say you love me," he demanded in a ragged voice. "Say it."

"I love you, S..."

He cursed and brought his mouth down on hers with such punishing force that she bit her cheek, tasting blood.

He pushed his tongue in her mouth and she almost choked.

But then he kissed her in a gentler manner and she bucked her hips, begging him, "Please..."

He reached his hand down and grabbed her, kneading and stroking her until she cried out.

He laughed.

"Say you love me," Salia countered in a raspy voice.

"Do you doubt it?" he growled.

Samuel was like a savage as he rammed himself into her like a man possessed, rocking his hips against hers. Pushing inside her. Shoving against her. Grabbing her hips and taking her on a wild ride. He made love to her hard, jabbing into her like a wild mustang into a mare in heat.

It was wild. It was passionate. It was something Salia never experienced before.

Odd, she didn't remember Samuel being this big.

And she threw back her head and screamed in pleasure, crying out in ecstasy. She groaned into his ear, "I love you. Love you. Love you."

Samuel closed his eyes and moaned, shuddering above her. He thrust once more and hollered loudly, groaning in pleasure and then collapsing on top of her, his body slick with sweat.

"Sweetheart," he whispered into her ear.

"I don't remember you making love, quite like that," she said, sighing with contentment.

Silence.

They lay there like two spoons.

And so they slept with sated pleasure, Salia with a peaceful smile on her lips. Her face looked radiantly happy, as if she dreamt the most pleasant of dreams.

She turned in her sleep and sighed, moaning as if he still made love to her in her dreams.

At least Salia slept. Beside her, Samuel lay with his eyes wide open. He blinked at the ceiling papered in an elaborate fashion to look like Michelangelo's Sistine Chapel. He cocked his head at visions of heaven and hell on the ceiling, wondering where exactly he was headed.

Salia was breathing evenly and was in a deep sleep where she wouldn't be easily disturbed.

Samuel reached for his pants and pulled from the pocket an ordinary-looking rock.

He clenched his piedra imán, and lifted his arm, running a hand over his face. He turned on his side very gently so he wouldn't awaken her. He watched her sleep with the look of a predator because it was no longer her husband, Samuel Stuwart. Her bedmate was Lucas Monterrey, head of the Las Cruces witches, the same man who killed Salia's half-brother, Jefe. Lucas was the man masquerading as Marshal Joseph Quill, who often visited Storm-Chaser—his main reason to befriend Salia's son, Dark-Shadow, the reincarnation of the great witch Montezuma.

Lucas Monterrey. Her natural enemy.

Enemies make strange bed fellows.

He lay with a sheet wrapped around the lower part of his naked body. His broad chest was no longer cream colored and slender like Samuel's but gleamed bronze. His chest was broader and more muscular. His hair was no longer blonde and cut short but was blue-black in color, hanging to his shoulders like the mane of a wild, black mustang. His eyes were no longer sky blue in color but green like a lime.

Moonlight shone in from the window, illuminating Salia's face. She appeared vulnerable with her eyes closed, her body relaxed, and mouth slightly open.

Lucas narrowed his eyes at her soft face, smiling to the side of his mouth—it was not a nice smile.

"I should just slit her throat. Take her power while she's sleeping—cold, heartless bitch. *I love you...I love you...Samuel,*" he mimicked in a tortured, high-pitched voice.

He turned on his side and kicked her.

Salia didn't stir.

She slept peacefully beside Lucas.

———

30

Salia stretched her arms above her head, smiling at bright sunlight streaming in through the window. It was going to be a wonderful day—Samuel was back!

She turned her head and smiled at the man sleeping beside her.

Her smile turned to horror and she screamed. She sat up, banging her heels against the mattress and scurrying to the corner of the bed. She yanked the sheet to cover her nakedness and swung her legs off the bed.

A hand came down and clamped her thigh.

Salia yanked at her leg, banging her head against the mahogany headboard.

Lucas opened one eye, chuckling at the look of fear in her eyes.

Oh my God—him! He's naked, she thought in rising panic. Not that Salia could possibly panic any more than she already did, nor feel any more confused than she already was. Not that she could possibly feel any more alone, even though the bed was dwarfed by the large, muscular, beautiful, utterly naked male, perfect specimen exposed before her and obviously still desiring her.

"What have you done with Samuel?" she cried.

"Why he's right here, darling. Not happy to see me, my dear?" he drawled in Samuel Stuwart's southern style voice.

"How dare you! How could you! You're just like Lord Tez, a seducer, a master of tricks!"

"Ah, so you think I'm as powerful and masculine as the dark knight."

She pounded his bare back with her fists. Lucas roared with laughter, holding his shaking stomach, tears squirting his eyes, flowing down his cheeks.

She screeched and kicked him with her other leg.

"Uh-uh," he said and grabbed at that wayward leg, dragging her towards him and settling Salia on his nakedness.

She pinched and bit and scratched.

"That's it. Fight me, you wild cat," he whispered in her ear, nibbling on her ear lobe.

Salia sheathed her cat claws.

They rolled around on the bed and wrestled, neither giving an inch. The only thing that gave was the sheet no longer covering her.

He lowered his head and suckled on her left breast.

She screamed and arched her back.

"Good! Make it easy for me."

"You goddamn bastard!"

And he rammed himself into her, burying his face in the skin of her neck, lapping her up with his tongue and devouring her.

Salia was shocked that she was all wet. Her body was excited while her mind and heart rebelled at his rape of her senses. He was driving her crazy, what his lips and tongue were doing against her neck and in the hollow of her shoulder.

Lucas forced her thighs open wider with his own hard thighs, leisurely circling his hips against her.

She groaned in half ecstasy and the other half self-condemnation. Her body was shaking with need again for this man. This damned Lucas Monterrey, whom she hated more than she hated anything. Had always hated from the moment she first laid eyes on him. "Arrogant. Conceited. Asshole. Son of a Las Cruces bitch!" Yet, her arms of their own volition encircled his neck, pulling him closer. "I hate you," she moaned into his ear.

For just a second, he quit moving against her.

But then his lust overcame his common sense. Lucas moved with force and unfulfilled need while reaching between her thighs, gently stroking her.

"I hate you," she groaned, then threw back her head, crying out with pleasure.

He laughed, but it was a hollow-sounding laugh.

And Lucas damned himself as he shot his seed into her.

She glared up at him. "Get off me, pig!"

He rolled from on top of her and sat on the edge of the bed with his head hanging between his elbows. Lucas shook his big head like a dog. He turned and grinned. "I can't help it if you intoxicate me. You've always intoxicated me. So much so that I..."

162

"Rape me," she said and threw a pillow at him. "That's the third time you've raped me Lucas." And she slapped her hand across his back. From beneath her fingernails sharp claws protruded and once again, she scratched him like a cat.

Blood ran down his back that now looked like it was cut to ribbons. He clutched his piedra imán and flexed his back, smoothly clearing his skin of blood and cuts. He scoffed and said, "I raped you? Believe what you want, little actress, but I know differently. You were wild and free. You surrendered completely, holding nothing back. You turn to jelly in my arms. You're still shaking inside, wobbling about like a contented bowl of Jell-O. You love me. Admit it." Lucas smiled at her, a slow sensuous smile.

"I hate myself that I take such pleasure in your rapes. Damn you to hell, Lucas. Damn my body! But my heart is filled with loathing for you. I have hated you since that first time."

"You know as well as I do, that the first time I did not rape you, as you claim. And just now you enjoyed it, you little hypocrite. Does it count as rape if you throw back your head and scream in ecstasy?"

Salia blushed and in a small, hurting voice said, "You cheated. You used a piedra imán against me and pretended to be Samuel. That's worse than rape. How can you and still live with yourself?"

"All's fair in making love and war, my sweet enemy. Your problem, Salia," he drawled, "is that you've never known what you really want."

"And you think I want you?"

"I just proved it, didn't I?"

"You may be able to make my body do what you wish, but you can't make me love you. I was raised to hate you. I hate you Lucas. Hate you."

He visibly flinched, as if she struck him.

"You've always been an egotistical womanizer who thinks he's god's gift to all women. Some stud meant to service all women with his big hard..."

Lucas slapped his hand hard against the mattress and she flinched.

Salia jumped on the mattress, breathing heavily with her hair a wild mess around her face. She dove under the covers, her body trembling beneath the sheet she wrapped around herself, as if she was a mummy.

"It's a bit late to hide your body from me, Salia."

"Lucas?"

He smiled at her and said in a husky voice, "What is it, my sweet?"

She frowned. "Why do you persist, even after all these years, in believing there is something between us?"

Lucas sighed and ran a hand through his hair. "You and I have a history, Salia, only I'm not dead and buried, like the unfortunate Samuel, but alive with my blood pounding for you," he said in a voice just as harsh as hers had been.

"Leave me alone! You bring back too many memories."

"Things you'd like to forget?" He swung his head back around, locking his eyes with hers. "Things you've so conveniently forgotten these last seven years?" he said in a flat voice.

She couldn't look away even if she wanted to. His gaze was too powerful and she was feeling that power now. Salia knew if he wanted to, Lucas could even kill her with his eyes. He was so much more powerful than she was. Had always been more powerful and grown more so over the years, whereas she stayed the same. Unlike her mother, Salia was never interested in harnessing power. All she wanted to do was act and sing upon the stage. She needed to become someone else, anyone but Salia Esperanza Stuwart, third generation witch, daughter of Felicita and granddaughter of La India.

Lucas let out a heartfelt sigh, his voice vibrating with passion. "I've searched for you all these years, Salia. I've waited for you, wanting you and aching with need. All these years, I knew you were alive. I would have felt it if you were dead. You and I are connected, whether you like it or not. I am your destiny as you are mine."

"I've never believed that!"

"I really do care for you," he mumbled.

A mask came over her face and she stared back like a cold, marble statue.

"Heartless, as always. You are like a cat," he growled, clenching his fists.

"Well, it seems Marcelina is not the only one who knows my secret. Why do you think I'm called Catalina?" she said, smiling at him. It was not a nice smile. More like a hiss.

"I knew it was you tonight at the opera. I could smell you—peaches. I should do to you what I did to your worthless brother." And he wrapped his hands around her throat.

164

"So you're the one who killed Jefe? You killed my brother and then have the nerve to make love to me?"

"You should thank me for getting rid of that vermin. The world's a better place without Jefe. Your brother had no love for you. He arranged for your death, didn't he?"

"I don't know for sure it was Jefe."

"Yes, you do. Jefe wanted you dead so he could have your piedra imán."

"Maybe it was you who killed Samuel," she said and shrank back from him in horror.

He paled. "Is that what you think of me...that I would...? No! No! I wanted you to come to me of your own free will. I never wanted his ghost between us. If I hadn't been far away that night, I would have saved you from that burning house. I would have found a way to break the Esperanza curse and taken you away from all of this."

"So you say. I don't buy your knight-in-shining-armor act. On the contrary, your armor looks mighty rusted," Salia said, her voice dripping like acid. "Kill me," she pleaded and grabbed his hands, wrapping them around her throat.

Even that little gesture excited him and a flush rose to his face.

"Kill me so that I might really be with Samuel for all eternity. So that I can join my love."

He jerked back his hands as if she burned him. Lucas bent at the waist, the pain severe in his gut. "Even in death you can't leave him, even now."

She sneered at him.

Lucas grabbed her by the shoulders and shook her.

Her teeth rattled but Salia still managed to proclaim in a vibrating voice, "I will always love Samuel."

"And in your small heart there's room for no one else, is there?"

"I hate you," she said and spit at him.

He reeled from her words, growling low in his throat and ripping the sheet from her body.

She clawed his chest. "Not again! I won't. Never again," she said.

Lucas ran a hand down his face and it was now Samuel she fought against. "Sugar, it's me, darling," he whispered in her ear.

Salia moaned, melting against him. He was Samuel. Her Samuel. Only it wasn't Samuel. He had never been so rough and savage, calling to her own wild nature. Yet, she looked into his turquoise eyes and knew that it was her own heart staring back at her. "Samuel, your eyes are swimming in tears because you miss me as much as I miss you. Love me as I love you. Ache for me like I ache for you."

And once again, Samuel made love to Salia. Only when she opened her legs to invite him in, Lucas thrust inside her, with his lime-green eyes glaring at her.

"I hate you," she screamed, trying to claw at his face.

"Still the sweet Salia I remember," he said, laughing. His laughter hurt his chest and Lucas thought his ribs might crack.

Once more, he brought Salia to an earth shattering orgasm, and she threw her arms around his neck, crying out. And she cried. And she cried, her tears threatening to drown him. "Sh," he whispered in a tender voice. "Surrender, Salia."

Like a wild cat she beat his chest with her fists and screamed.

He punished her with his own earth-shattering orgasm, shuddering on top of her, his body quivering and pulsing.

"Get off me," she yelled and brought up her fist to punch him in the chin.

Lucas jumped off her like she was a hot potato.

Salia swung at the air and missed.

His hands were shaking with anger as he yanked his denim jeans on, buttoning his shirt crookedly. The rugged pants were different than the refined white linen dress pants Lucas wore last night, but in his craziness it was Samuel's shirt he buttoned across his chest. The differences in sizes made the shirt bulge and pop a button.

Salia yanked the sheet up to her chin. "Now hear this once and for all. I love Samuel," she said in a regal voice. "I never would have been unfaithful to him nor deceived Samuel, but I had no choice. So it is written. So it shall be."

She vomited right there on the bed.

"Well it wasn't that bad was it?" he said in a dry voice.

Lucas drew a hand across his face and the shirt now fit him, though the pants were too large. He had become Samuel again. "Is this what it takes, Salia, to win you? Must I..."

She didn't let him finish. Salia put out a hand to him like he was the devil himself. "Stay away from me, Lucas."

"You want me to stay this way and pretend? We can both pretend then. I'll be Samuel and you can be Catalina. Perhaps she has a heart."

"Get out! Get out, you crazy bastard!"

"Very well," he said and turned back into Lucas Monterrey, popping another shirt button. "Damn it, Salia, this isn't a contest of our powers. I am simply a man who wants you." He touched her cheek. "You are a beautiful woman. It's as easy as that."

She bit his finger.

"Yipes!"

"You'll never take Samuel's place. How can you? My husband was an honorable man."

"Your husband was a cold, ruthless millionaire."

"Samuel was a gentleman. He was not a savage!"

"Oh, spare me the bullshit, Salia, that you're better than me. You and I are the same."

"I'm not like you, Lucas. You're a pig, just like Jefe. You can never fill Samuel's shoes."

"I could kill you for what you've just said. I've killed men for much less."

"So kill me then and be done with it! I'd rather be lying in the grave with Samuel than in your bed. That is what you have proven to me by your despicable masquerade. For me, there will never be any other man but Samuel."

"To hell with you then. I'll leave you alone, Salia, but get the hell out of my head."

"Whatever sex magic you've wrought..."

"Sex magic! I don't need to use sex magic on you! I'm not a bad guy—I'm not Jefe!"

He cuffed his ears with his hands, no longer willing to listen to anything she had to say, but Salia jumped from the bed, blocking his exit and poking his chest with her finger. "Your betrayal is more than I can bear, to have hope taken from me that the light will shine once more in my life. All I've found is the darkness and a black pit even wider than before because I betrayed Samuel again. And all because of you. How dare you masquerade as Samuel. How dare you! I hope you mean it when you say you're done with me," she said.

Lucas played with the door handle. Her words cut him like a knife. Salia insulted him and hurt him to the limit. He spun around, glaring at her.

She glared back at him with hatred.

He grinned. It was not a nice grin.

Lucas ran a hand down his face and once more turned into Samuel.

Her face softened with a yearning look in her eyes.

An anger rose in his chest and a hurt so great, his heart might explode from the pain and his chest crack open. He wanted to place his hands around her throat and choke her for good. How would she feel if her beloved Samuel killed her? If the last thing she saw when she took her last breath was hatred shining in Samuel's eyes?

Lucas dragged her back to the bed, his body stiff and erect. Only it was Samuel's body and Samuel's face that Salia stared up at expectantly with her mouth softly open and her tongue circling her moist lips.

He was oh so tempted...

He wanted to strike back at Salia, and hurt her the way he was aching so Lucas grabbed at the sheet, yanking it down to her ankles.

His eyes roamed her body from head to toe and he sneered. "Goodbye, Salia," he drawled in Samuel's voice. Revulsion shone from his turquoise eyes. His handsome face was twisted into an ugly mask of hatred. "I'll never forgive you, slut, for what you've done. I despise you, whore. You may be beautiful, but a harlot crawls beneath your skin. Madrid was right when they warned me you are trash. Damn coyote half-breed with a prickly cactus between your legs. You're just like your mother. You're not good enough to wipe my boots. Go back to the other side of the tracks where you belong, witch. I should have hung you when I had the chance. May the Penitentes catch you and kill you for what you are. I hope your neck snaps at the end of their rope. You're not a human being but a damned alley cat whining in heat. You betrayed me! Witch! Daughter of Felicita and granddaughter of La India—two of the most feared women in Madrid. Evil women, and their blood flows through you. You were never respectable, even with all my money. You are trash. Will always be garbage. A child of Witch Hill, and I hate your fucking guts!"

Salia dropped to her knees, wrapping her arms around her waist and rocking. She cried out in pain but her cries sounded more like the mews of a kitten flung into a dark well.

Salia lifted her head to his departing footsteps. She reached out a hand, moaning as she watched Samuel walk away from her.

Samuel did not look back. His shoulders were stiff with hatred.

It was Lucas who slammed the door.

He stormed down the hallway of the fashionable Alvarado Hotel, his shirt tail flying behind him. Stripes of blood stained the back of his shirt.

———————

31

His face was haggard and incredibly vulnerable. Lucas finally opened his heart to Salia, like a raw, open sore. He flinched—and Lucas thought Salia couldn't hurt him. He was in the throes of such pain he could hardly bear it.

He walked past a group of men selling their wares outside the Alvarado Hotel, alongside the railroad tracks. "Hey, Monterrey," a man called out.

He ignored them and the flamenco dancers with their brightly twirling skirts and flowing mantillas dancing outside the hotel for the luncheon crowd.

He walked, with his head down, cursing. There was no moving her. How could she be so unfeeling about everything? How could Salia make love to him like she was dying for him and yet act like he meant nothing to her?

Yesterday, he parked his truck behind the Alvarado. He now unlocked the glove compartment and grabbed a bottle of whiskey.

Lucas walked with long strides up Central Avenue.

He stopped when he reached Second Street and the Montezuma Saloon that had a big sign mounted on top that was faded but still readable. The sign read: Open 7 Days a Week, 24 Hours a Day. However, the saloon had been boarded up and closed during the Great Depression.

Lucas slid down the wall, plaster scraping against his wounds that Salia inflicted. *She's my curse*, he thought, flabbergasted that his heart still wanted her. He rubbed his chest, massaging his organ that was only tender where she was concerned.

Public drinking was against the law. Those moral church ladies decreed that liquor should be consumed in private. Liquor was the root of all evil.

Well, Lucas begged to differ—Salia Stuwart was the root of all evil.

"Bitch! Beautiful heartless bitch," he slurred into his bottle.

He took another swig of the strong whiskey. "Ah." The liquor burned his gut just like that witch Salia did.

The thought had repelled him of sleeping with his enemy all those years ago, but his father commanded him. Lucas had no choice but to obey, and he steeled his mind against her. As for his heart, Lucas always thought he had no heart. No use to shield an organ that didn't exist.

But then he saw Salia standing there for the second time looking vulnerable, breakable, and still so incredibly young. Her mother and grandmother were dead. And even though she was Samuel Stuwart's mistress, she was so innocent looking and beautiful. Salia. The elusive Salia. The untouchable Salia—his enemy.

And so he lost it then. His resolve against her and for the first time in his life, his steel armor melted and Lucas lost control. And like a man imprisoned for so long by his own stilted emotions, a damn burst within his heart, and Lucas learned he was as human as the next man. When he fell, Lucas tumbled into a chasm of his own making for he nurtured a hatred of the Esperanza witches and carried the grudge passed on down through the centuries...

A grudge begun in Spain when Francisco Monterrey, head of the Monterrey witches, was turned over to the Spanish Inquisition by the Esperanza witches. And so their feud began.

Only the authorities did not retrieve all of Francisco's magical possessions. They knew nothing of his piedra imán, the same magic stone Lucas possessed.

As fate would have it, the Esperanza family ended up in Madrid and the Monterreys in Las Cruces. Both landed in New Mexico about 150 years ago and carried on their feud. There was murder, mayhem and trickery on both sides.

Lucas entered the cursed liaison with Salia, fully expecting to hate her the way he hated all the Esperanzas. He even wanted to kill her, thinking he might. That he would leave her on the bed when he was finished, with her neck broken, her head hanging limp like a rag doll. Hanging just like his ancestor, the great Francisco.

What Lucas hadn't expected was to like Salia so much the second time he encountered her. Even though he once took her virginity and she was Samuel Stuwart's mistress, Salia appeared like a frightened virgin in her white dress with the sweet face of an angel and so soft, Lucas feared he might melt if he lay on top of her.

Lucas had been so enraged by his feelings that he ripped her clothes from her body, hoping her skinniness would turn him off...but she was even more exquisite than their first time together.

The fact that Salia locked her knees against him maddened him even further and so he shoved her knees apart, exposing her full nakedness to his glittering eyes filled with astonishment by her beauty. Lucas had been filled with self-loathing because of his feelings for her, and he wanted to destroy Salia for weakening him.

He should have killed her. Her murder would have saved him.

Instead, he made love to her, hoping the act would purge her from his system, would make him realize that beneath the sheets she was like every other woman. Clinging. Stupid. Clumsy.

Only Salia hadn't been like other women, nor had their lovemaking. Lucas hadn't expected to want her again so soon after the act was finished, or to need her with a desire that took his breath away.

He had been secretly pleased she fought him. That Salia wasn't so soft after all, and she wasn't so sweet.

Only this morning, in the present, Lucas wished Salia was sweet on him, and that she didn't hate him so much.

Lucas remembered how Salia ran away from him after their first coupling and good thing, too, since he secretly followed her and was all set to ravage her again and seduce her...and then...

He had watched her vomit, just like this morning.

Even now his own stomach turned at the thought of how much she hated him.

The fact that Salia wasn't chasing after him like all the others only made Lucas want her more. Made him respect her more and admire Salia.

When Lucas heard she married Samuel Stuwart, he really lost it. Lucas was never so confused in his life. He wanted to kill Samuel and murder Salia. He even came up with a plan to kidnap her. But Lucas never carried any of his plans out. He simply brooded; imagining, feeling, and believing that it was his pride that made him feel so many new things. Before Salia, Lucas didn't know he was capable of feeling jealousy nibbling at his mind and eating away at his insides. A rivalry that made him realize murder would solve nothing. Stealing the bride would only make him a thief. And what thief ever really owned what he stole?

None of his scheming dulled the pain in his chest that made Lucas wonder if he might die from wanting Salia because then, Lucas believed he could never love any woman. And he cursed Salia for making him feel so much.

If only Lucas could turn back the clock to a time when he had no heart.

Before her marriage, Lucas actually felt they might have a chance together.

After her marriage he still hoped.

But now, Stuwart had been dead for six years, long enough for any woman to mourn and get on with her life. To rejoin the living.

Lucas tilted his head back, swallowing some whiskey. Maybe he was pushing Salia too fast. Perhaps he should slow down and court her like a gentleman might. She preferred gentlemen. Salia could get to know him. Really know him. A little at a time. Let her see he wasn't that bad a guy.

Lucas slurred into his bottle, "I can play the gentlemen as well as he can."

And he hated, really loathed the man in the grave. Lucas couldn't compete with a ghost. No amount of magic would work for that. Nor did he want Salia by trickery. Lucas wanted her to come to him of her own free will and give her heart to him, the way she did to Stuwart.

Lucas wanted more than sex between them.

Only how to get close enough to Salia so that she could get to know him? Really know him. He wasn't a bad guy. Lucas wasn't the devil she painted him out to be. He was no Jefe.

"Damn drunk," a man said and kicked at his leg.

Lucas dropped his near-empty bottle, watching his last drops of liquor empty onto the boardwalk. "Mister, that's damn impolite to take the last drops of liquor from a thirsty man, when the state is so dry. From a desperate man," he slurred.

The man's buddy kicked him in the other leg.

Lucas looked with reddened eyes at the fat man. "You spilled my drink," he slurred, pointing to the empty bottle.

Yet a third man grabbed his black western style hat and threw it in the air. "Hey, wino, come and get it. Come and get your medicine," he said, holding his fists like a boxer.

Medicine? Hell. He needed a drink.

The fourth man pulled a knife from his pocket.

Now that form of communication Lucas understood, and he grinned at the knife. Lucas was in the mood to kick the shit out of someone. A good ass kicking was just the medicine he needed to put him in a better mood. Better even than the last drops in a whiskey bottle.

Lucas growled low in his throat like an animal and surprised the four men when he leaped to his feet in a movement so fast, they didn't even blink and he was on them.

Lucas punched one in the face—crunch went a nose smashed into a cheek bone. Man was ugly as sin anyway.

Lucas kicked out his leg, shoving his snakeskin boot at the stomach of another man who vomited his spleen.

Lucas then whirled on the man who had posed with his two fists and now turned to run. He grabbed the man's collar, shoving his head through the wall of the Montezuma.

The fourth man dropped his knife.

Lucas snapped his right fingers.

The snakeskin on his right boot came alive, unwrapping itself from his boot until a rattlesnake slithered towards the man, its tail shaking and rattling.

The man was so stunned to see the snake from his boot come to life that he didn't put up a fight when the snake opened its fangs and bit his neck.

The snake then slid down the man's body and slithered back to Lucas's boot, rewrapping itself and melding back into the leather.

"S'cuse me," Lucas said to the man who was holding a hand to his bit neck and crying out something about dying. He walked around the man, staggering down 2nd Street in a much better mood than before and with a more promising future. He even tried to whistle, but his numb lips wouldn't work.

"Tha's what I need to do. Court her slowly."

He poked a big fist into his jean pockets, searching for his truck keys, forgetting that he was still Lucas Monterrey and not Joseph Quill. The more successful man, Quill, owned a car. Monterrey did not. Lucas usually traveled as a white falcon, soaring through the air with the speed of the wind or as a mountain lion.

"Be patient," he mumbled to himself.

He cursed because he couldn't find his keys.

"Let her get to know me." He continued on down the street, lifting one snakeskin boot high in the air and then slamming it down to earth, not knowing where the hell he was headed. Damnation Lucas always figured, but who gives a crap. He never did, until now. Salia came back to New Mexico along with a rainbow. In the distance was a colorful arch of lights. Salia was the red gold at the end of the rainbow—always being chased but never found.

"I was forced on her and that can't be easy for any woman," he slurred, walking crookedly down the street.

"She likes Anglo men. I can even be rich. Rich bitch," he said, hiccupping.

Lucas stumbled on a curb, landing on his face in the mud. He just lay there shivering with the heebie jeebies.

He passed out, snoring loudly.

A police officer passed by and turned him around so his face was looking up instead of eating mud. Only it wasn't a drunken Spanish man who lay there but an Anglo passed out on the street. A U.S. Marshal for crying out loud. And drunk as a skunk.

The cop blew his whistle and called for a car.

Joseph Quill was lifted into the police car and thrown into a jail cell to sleep off the effects of Salia.

Several hours later, Lucas woke up on a flea-infested mattress. He sat up, hanging his aching head, snorting with disgust at himself.

He stood on shaky legs. Lucas had swallowed nearly a full bottle of whiskey and he was still drunk, though not plastered like before. He reached in his pants pocket, but his piedra imán was missing.

He lifted two fingers to his lips and whistled loudly.

In a trash can by a deserted desk, the ordinary-looking lodestone, lifted into the air and flew towards his open hand.

"Ouch! Not so hard." He petted the rock, cooing to it. "I know you don't like being thrown away like garbage, but it wasn't me who did it. No! We're not going to get revenge, just because you spent a few hours under a half-eaten egg sandwich. Here. I'll clean you off."

A line cracked against the rock because it broke into a smile.

Lucas gripped the rock tightly, spun, and transformed into a falcon with golden-colored eyes.

He hopped on the window sill and through the bars. Lucas flew above the Alvarado Hotel, circling the building, but there was no sign of Salia.

Lucas spread his wings wide, flying around Albuquerque like the bird of prey he was.

Ah, there she is.

Catalina was walking on Gold Avenue, towards the Opera House. The normally confident, famous opera singer was walking with her head bowed and her arms crossed, hugging her back. She appeared to have shrunk, moving her feet slowly, like she was in pain.

The falcon dived from the sky, clawing at her scalp.

She screamed, waving her hands on her head, but the bird was already soaring towards Santa Fe with a bit of hair in its beak.

Lucas flew crookedly, drunk on both the smell of Salia's scalp, the taste of her hair and the liquor he drank.

His truck was still parked at the Alvarado.

Mustn't drink and drive, he thought and hiccupped, spinning in the air and flying upside down.

A strong smell of whiskey permeated the air, evaporating into the clouds.

I should have crapped on her head.

32

Lucas had one hell of a hangover. He shuffled on bare feet around his small adobe house in Santa Fe. His head throbbed, but there was a determined glint to his eyes as he packed a black traveling bag, clearing out his things.

Sofia cleared her throat. "Where are you going, my love."

He turned and blinked his eyes at his long suffering mistress of three years. Sofia's black stringy hair covered one side of her face. She always looked unhappy and rarely smiled. Sofia was so damned depressing to be around. Like the darkness.

Bingo. He should have left sooner. Gotten out when the coast was clear so he wouldn't have to endure Sofia's wrath. Sofia was a Las Cruces witch convinced Lucas must love her. He stayed with her all these years, hadn't he?

In her view, Sofia was a goddess among women. With her voluptuous body and wild love making, she could bring a man to his knees but more often, Sofia was the one who balanced on her knees before his spread knees, using her magical tongue and lips to make him moan and groan and cry out. Only Lucas never once cried out Sofia's name. There were many, many times he made the mistake of crying out Salia's name—a hated name to Sofia, a despised name with the power to drive Sofia mad.

Sofia actually believed that the more powerful witch, the elusive Salia, placed a love spell on Lucas. He may close his eyes and see Salia when he rammed himself into Sofia, but he belonged to Sofia, or so she thought. Lucas may have other women but he always came back to his house in Santa Fe where Sofia waited, biting her nails, brushing her hair. Masturbating until he returned to her again. She claimed to be faithful to him and accused him of having a black heart. Oh how Lucas made her suffer. He often returned to Sofia with the stink of other women on his fingers, their odor on his shirt and their taste on his lips.

Sofia was the one who stalked him, practically raped him, and insisted she be his housekeeper, cook, and laundress. Sofia would like to be his jailer.

She was exceedingly good in bed though so Lucas allowed her to serve him in more ways than one. And she wasn't bad looking.

"Where are you going this time?" she asked, her black eyes flashing daggers. Sofia was never happy with his secretiveness and disappearances. His coming and going whenever he pleased. Lucas was away more often than not. He merely showed up occasionally to do some business in Santa Fe. He slept with Sofia and then was gone in the morning, sometimes before the sun rose. Even when he was in Santa Fe with Sofia waiting naked for him in bed, Lucas would come home smelling of the stink of other women and it was at these times that she really wanted to kill him. Murder him for the hell he put her through. For the holes he shot in her heart.

Lucas sighed deeply. The damn thing of it was, he didn't care, and it was ashamed because he really wished he loved Sofia, because then everything would be so easy since she loved him. Well, Sofia loving him was her misfortune. Lucas never promised her anything than what he was.

"Where are you going?" Sofia again asked and she tapped her toe on the wooden floor.

"None of your damned business," he snapped.

"When are you coming back?" she said in a surly voice.

"I said, none of your damned business! How many times have I told you, Sofia? Enough with the questioning," he growled. "Stay out of my life. What I do doesn't concern you."

"Stay out of your life? I have slaved for you and taken care of you. Look. I am turning into an old woman because of you." She held up her work-roughened hands.

"Well, I never asked you to take care of me. I don't need looking after."

"It's her, isn't it? I knew it as soon as I saw your face. Salia has come back," she screamed at him.

"Shut up! Don't even mention her name to me," he yelled.

"Well, you can't leave me. I'm pregnant. How can you leave the mother of your only child?"

"You're not pregnant, Sofia," he said and shoved his hat on his head. He loathed a clinging, scheming, lying woman. He especially hated being trapped by anyone. "I made sure I wouldn't make you pregnant. I don't want you to be the mother of my child."

She flinched.

"If you're having a baby, then it's some other man's child and I wish you well."

"I have never been unfaithful to you. Yet you sleep with other women. Dirty women. Filthy women. Whores all of them. I hope you catch a disease for your unfaithfulness." She spit on his boots.

"I have the right to sleep with whomever I choose. I never made any promises to you, Sofia, and you know that. We're not married," he reminded her. How many times had he said these words?

"So have you found her yet, your Salia?" She spit out the name. Sofia was foaming at the mouth, saliva dribbling down her chin.

He tightened his lips and clenched his fists, fighting the urge to slap her. He never hit a woman unless it was self-defense, but Sofia knew every button to push. He stayed with her far too long than was healthy.

She yanked her nightgown over her head and stood naked, her dark nipples erect and winking at him.

Without meaning to, he winked back.

She wrapped her muscular leg around his, humping her body against him and moaning.

She stroked the front of his pants, massaging him.

Again without meaning too, he could feel his arousal.

So could she. Sofia dipped her head, nibbling at the front of his pants, making his denim jeans wet with her mouth. She looked up at him with lustful eyes. "And does your Salia know how to do this like I do? Can she bring you to your knees like I can?"

Lucas shocked her when he reached a hand down and yanked Sofia by her hair, twisting her head towards the back of her neck. "I grow weary of your jealousies. It's time we ended this here and now. Why do you persist in believing there is something more between us?" How ironic he quoted nearly the same words Salia said to him, however, he didn't see the irony nor would he ever compare himself to Sofia. The woman was so pathetic, weak and stupid. So unattractive the way she clung to him.

"What's the matter? Has the Stuwart witch bested you yet again?" She poked his chest.

"Salia's dead, remember? Don't ever mention her name again." He lifted the handle of his black travel bag and turned towards the door.

Sofia threw herself on the floor, grabbing at his boot.

Lucas walked towards the door, dragging Sofia along the floor, sweeping the dust with her hair.

"Don't leave me! I'll kill myself if you go."

"So kill yourself. I'll even go to your funeral. See you get a proper burial."

Lucas gave one final kick of his leg and freed himself from her suffocating love.

"You're going to her, aren't you?" she screamed at his back.

"You can keep the house. I put it in your name." He threw the deed at her and slammed the door behind him.

Sofia stared at her name on the house deed. *Lucas is really leaving me. This time he won't be back.*

She had some sense of mind to throw her nightgown, backwards, over her head.

She ran out to the street, her long brown hair flying wildly behind her. Sofia was barefoot and the cobblestone walkway burned her feet but she paid no mind.

She spun in all directions, looking around the nearly deserted street.

"Lucas," she screamed. "Monterrey!"

There was no sign of him. Lucas had vanished into the very air.

The street was silent except for the clicking of a pair of cowboy boots on the cobblestone walkway. The boots were made of snakeskin.

Did she imagine it, or did a snake seem to slither across each boot as he walked?

She examined the man with the snakeskin boots. He was a U.S. Marshal carrying a worn travel bag.

He walked right by Sofia, lifted his dusty black western hat to her and smiled to the side of his mouth.

His golden-brown eyes didn't smile at her though. The man had the coldest eyes.

The tall, golden haired man in the tight western blue jeans, white shirt and ornamented vest walked towards the train station.

Sofia yearned to stop the marshal and ask him if he had seen a tall, handsome, Spanish man walk by and which direction he headed but instead, she spit on the sidewalk after the marshal passed her. Police and lawmen. Sofia hated them all. She wouldn't beg this one for any information. She would rather die first.

Sofia was dying inside. She slid down the wall of the adobe house, bending her knees to her chest. She lifted her toes and a slight breeze blew her nightgown around her hips, exposing her womanly parts for all of Santa Fe to see.

But it was only the U.S. Marshal who was within viewing range of her charms and he wasn't looking His mind seemed to be on other things.

When the U.S. Marshal turned to cross the street, the rays of the sun struck his badge and ricocheted into her eyes.

Sofia raised her arms to ward off the blinding light.

Joseph Quill just kept on walking towards the train station. He never even looked back at the woman who had been Lucas Monterrey's lover these last three years.

He bought a train ticket for Albuquerque.

Early this morning, Lucas flew into Santa Fe on the White Falcon Special.

Now, Quill was traveling to make his home in Albuquerque, and he rode on the Atchison Topeka Santa Fe Railroad.

He rode in the best compartment of the train.

That was Joseph Quill from this day forward, U.S. Marshal and gentleman. First class all the way.

———

Part Four

The House at the Bottom of Witch Hill

And so once again the house sprouted.
The walls of the house growing like poison ivy.
The wood alive like any plant.
Breathing in the black, coal dust of Madrid.

33

"Fetch my moccasins, Grandson. Come. The sun is just beginning to rise," Storm-Chaser said.

Dark-Shadow yanked on a pair of faded blue jeans that were too short for his growing legs. He slipped his feet into a pair of moccasins and followed him from the apartment.

The Pueblo was outlined by the rising sun, appearing pink in color rather than sandy-brown adobe. It rained yesterday and a smell of drying mud lingered—a musky odor intermixed with a smell of blood from smashed mosquitoes. Crickets chirped and frogs bellowed, accompanied by a variety of insects playing a symphony.

With wrinkled brow, Storm-Chaser walked with his head down.

Dark-shadow rubbed his eyes and yawned. A young man was climbing out a window from an apartment building on the seventh level. He was of medium height and so skinny, his ribs showed even from here. It was his cousin Flaco. Storm-Chaser tried to teach Flaco the way of the shaman, but Flaco was lazy. He was never interested in being a shaman, nor cared what happened to the ceremonial pipe given the people by the Thunder Spirit. Flaco only cared for himself.

Flaco scurried down the ladder and disappeared into the shadows.

Dark-Shadow was glad that Storm-Chaser did not notice Flaco. He hated it when his cousin and grandfather argued. Dark-Shadow dreaded to think what would happen if Grandfather discovered what Flaco was up to. Flaco bragged to Dark-Shadow that he had the ability to bewitch girls with magic. At night, he visited various girls of the Pueblo and without any of the girls awakening, he climbed into their beds.

Flaco taunted Dark-Shadow about his father, telling him that Wolfe was like a woman, preferring to live with his male lover rather than raise his son. Dark-Shadow had seen Wolfe only seven times, once for every year of his life. He was relieved when Flaco revealed the big family secret. At least now Dark-Shadow knew why his father didn't want him. Anyway, Dark-Shadow considered Storm-Chaser his father.

Storm-Chaser looked out over small man-made ditches snaking about a field to the east of their apartment. The irrigation ditches were dug to collect rainfall. Fruit trees, corn, tomatoes, lettuce and various other vegetables were planted next to the ditches.

Storm-Chaser raised his arms to the sky. "I pray to San Ysidro Labrado that our crops flourish, overflowing the land with food for the people. Bring us rain, oh San Ysidro."

Dark-Shadow bowed his head, as was expected. The saint they prayed to was the Patron Saint of Farming. Dark-Shadow witnessed his grandfather crack open the sky with the help of his supernatural helper, the Thunder Spirit. Grandfather must still be drunk to pray for rain from a Catholic saint.

Storm-Chaser looked up at the cloudless sky. "Well, perhaps tomorrow."

"This morning, you brought the rains to the Pueblo. Don't you remember, Grandfather? See. The ground is still moist. There is water yet in the ditches."

"That was last week. The land is moist from my tears for I am troubled. Take me to my sweat lodge, Grandson. We must pray together."

Dark-Shadow held him by the elbow and they walked around the apartment to the back.

Storm-Chaser lit a fire in front of the sweat lodge to boil water in a kettle which hung from a rod between two stakes. He then poured the water over the rocks that were in a small hole. He closed the small flap opening used to regulate the temperature. Storm-Chaser sat cross-legged.

Dark-Shadow knelt before him and bowed.

Storm-Chaser placed his hands on his head, a thumb against each temple. They breathed in the steam from the rocks engulfing the sweat lodge. They stayed in this silent manner—Storm-Chaser massaging Dark-Shadow's temples until sweat poured down his neck, dampening his hair.

"We, the Indian people of the Pueblos of New Mexico, are descended from the great cacique [chief] Montezuma," Storm-Chaser said.

He looked closely at Dark-Shadow, making him feel weird. Dark-Shadow heard this all before. The Pueblo regularly held special feasts and danced around a pole in honor of their hero, the legendary Montezuma.

Storm-Chaser chanted a prayer, calling on the spirits of his ancestors, and on the spirit of his mentor, the old shaman. His throat wobbled like a turkey's as he sang, "I ask that this boy not be led into darkness."

Dark-Shadow jerked his head, surprised at his grandfather's words.

"Do not give him the curse of death but the gift of life. Do not give him the black power of malevolence but the white magic of healing. Give this boy a pure heart and soul."

Storm-Chaser peered at Dark-Shadow. His grandfather's eye looked wild and bulged from his eye socket. "There are forces about who would use you, Grandson, for who you are."

There was something about the way Storm-Chaser was looking at him that made his heart beat faster.

"You must never go over to their side," Storm-Chaser said.

If it weren't for the fact that his grandfather looked at him with such a serious expression, Dark-Shadow would have thought he was still drunk. None of this made any sense to him. Led into darkness? Yet, he was aware of dark forces. Storm-Chaser taught him about the light and the dark. As an apprentice shaman, Dark-Shadow knew the healing arts involved not only antidotes for diseases from nature, but healing of witchcraft spells. To fight the darkness, a shaman must resort to sorcery sometimes. There was a fine line between a witch, a sorcerer, a wizard, and a shaman and sometimes, the lines crossed.

"Be on your guard," Storm-Chaser warned him.

"I will," Dark-Shadow solemnly said, not knowing what else to say. He had no idea what Grandfather was talking about.

"They will come at you while you're a child."

Hiss steamed against the rocks and Dark-Shadow jumped. He could hear his pounding heart and grandfather's hair rising from his scalp. Dark-Shadow never questioned his acute hearing, assuming everyone heard what he did.

Storm-Chaser yanked Dark-Shadow towards him, wrapping his arms around the little boy, hugging and squeezing him. "It has begun," Storm-Chaser said, and he pulled him tighter against his chest. "They have lain dormant all these years. I can feel the forces gathering," he whispered.

"I'm hungry," Dark-Shadow said, wincing.

"Let us go into the house and eat breakfast. I can smell the fresh tortillas."

They left the sweat lodge and made their way to the apartment, the old man leaning on the boy.

"Remember what I have always told you, Grandson. Never reveal to others what I tell you."

Dark-Shadow nodded his head. His life was cloaked in secrets he was sworn not to tell, and secrets that were kept from him. He wondered why powerful forces would be interested in a child. He did not confide to his grandfather that dark forces already invaded his dreams. Dark-Shadow was unsure what the horrible visions were that came to him at night when he was sleeping. The visions enticed, repelled, and confused him.

They entered the apartment and Spider-Woman tapped her bare foot, waiting for them. "The food is growing cold on the table," she said with a sour face.

Grandfather wolfed down his food while Spider-Woman hovered about Dark-Shadow. If given the chance, she would interrogate him like always. But even if she beat him with a rod, Dark-Shadow knew how to keep a secret and would never reveal what Storm-Chaser told him in the sweat lodge.

Dark-Shadow chewed his food and stared at the wall, ignoring Spider-Woman who jabbed her elbow into his side. There was the smooth skin of her face, and then the ragged wrinkles crossing her skin. Her fingertips touched softly, and her fingernails drew blood. The loose flesh of her arm, wobbled harmlessly like an old lady, while the bone of her elbow jabbed like the butt of a rifle into his rib. The only woman his grandfather ever chose to see was the soft one.

Spider-Woman reached beneath the table and pinched Dark-Shadow, scraping a fingernail across his bare stomach. He could feel blood seeping from his belly button that once tied him to his real mother. Around Dark-Shadow's neck hung a bag in the shape of an eagle containing his umbilical cord, the only tie to his dead, nameless mother. It was as if part of his heart still beat within that cord. His Aunt Weeping-Woman told Dark-Shadow that his mother died giving birth to him and that he killed her. Dark-Shadow was sad and guilt-ridden but relieved to find out Spider-Woman was not his real mother.

Spider-Woman left scars on his back, legs, and arms. She kicked, scratched and clawed him everywhere but his face and head. Storm-Chaser allowed her the right of a mother to discipline her son, but she knew where to draw the line so Dark-Shadow didn't think Spider-Woman would actually kill him. And Dark-Shadow knew how to keep his mouth shut and not tell Grandfather just how bad the abuse she inflicted on him.

One. Two. Three, Dark-Shadow counted, cringing from the pain of her fingernails. *Control. Control. Control.* He feared one day he would lose control and pinch the old woman back. Or worse, throw her across the room with just one look. This was why he closed his eyes. None knew that Dark-Shadow had the ability to move objects by just looking at them and when he shut his eyes, he could see his mother's body sliding down the wall like a rag doll, her bones broken and her head cracked in half. Deep down inside, Dark-Shadow was afraid of his own dark forces. He was frightened that when his grandfather spoke about dark forces gathering and coming for him, that it was himself he must fight against. He had, after all, killed his real mother. What sort of blackness lives within a monster capable of that?

Storm-Chaser looked over at him and winked. "The mescal is sweet, is it not?" he said, chewing noisily.

Dark-Shadow flicked open his eyes and smiled at his grandfather in such a way as to relate to him that life is sweet.

Yet, Storm-Chaser never saw the worried look in the little boy's eyes, or the guilt on his face making his hand shake when he lifted his spoon. Storm-Chaser did not hear his twisting stomach whenever Dark-Shadow thought of his real mother. The mother he secretly yearned for. The mother Dark-Shadow murdered. Guilt consumed him and pounded his head whenever he looked at his living mother, the mother he wanted to kill.

A man sees what he wants to see. Nothing more. Nothing less. Such is his reality. This is what allows him to cope. Not the real world but a fantasy.

34

At the beauty shop the bell above the door rang, and Carlotta ran to open it.

A beautiful red-headed woman stood at the threshold. "My name is Catalina. Is your mother here?"

"Are you Catalina, the opera singer?"

"Yes," she said, smiling warmly. "And you must be one of the twins."

"I'm Carlotta," she said shyly, in awe of the famous woman. "Did you travel all the way from Albuquerque to Santa Fe on the train just to get your hair done at *Eternal Beauty*?

Catalina didn't answer because Mama dropped her scissors and ran into Catalina's open arms. They kissed each other on the cheek.

Carlotta inched her broom closer, eavesdropping. Normally Mama yelled at her if she lingered about, but Mama was preoccupied with the singer. Carlotta was stunned that they were friends.

"I was wondering when you'd come to see me," Mama said.

"Oh, Marcy, it's been so difficult these nine days. I was in such a dark place," and Catalina wiped a tear from her eye, blowing her nose into a lace handkerchief.

"Ay, I know. Your poor baby son. Where did you bury the boy? Were you ever able to give him a proper burial?"

"Please...don't ever mention my baby again," she said sadly, wringing her hands in her lap.

Mama whispered, looking around the beauty shop, "Did your husband's ghost follow you from the cemetery the other night?"

Mama was always sensing dead people. And Carlotta moved her ear closer, chills running up her spine.

Catalina said in a dry voice, "You're a medium. Perhaps you conjured Samuel at his tombstone."

"Me? I did nothing," Mama squeaked.

"Let's have a séance one evening. Come to my house. I...I need to speak with Samuel and see if he's okay."

"Ah, my friend, it must be hard. You loved him so much."

"As you love Juan," Catalina said, dabbing at her eyes with her hand-kerchief. She held Mama's hand, squeezing her fingers. "Please, Marcy, we must never let anything or anyone come between us again."

Mama nodded, smiling softly.

Catalina and Mama acted like they were the only two in the room, reminiscing and giggling like school girls. Carlotta wondered, *where did Mama meet the singer from Spain? The woman is years younger. How can they possibly have so many memories together? And Marcy? Whoever calls Mama by that nickname? Mama looks thirty-eight and Catalina looks eighteen, young enough to be Mama's daughter.*

Carlotta was even more stunned when Catalina jumped from the chair and grabbed Mama, dancing the Charleston with her to a tune on the radio, as if they were school girls.

Both women gasped and stared at the open door with pale faces and fearful eyes, hair standing on end.

Carlotta turned her head to what they were staring at.

Who they were staring at.

Pacheco Sandoval twisted the door handle, gluing his eyes to Carlotta and her sister, both nearly seven. "Your daughters are very beautiful, Marcelina Martinez," he said.

"Rodriguez. My name is Rodriguez," she said in a small voice.

Quickly, she hurried to finish Catalina's hair, her hands working furiously.

Catalina stared with watery eyes, mesmerized at Pacheco's fancy boots that were too big for his feet.

He walked clumsily over to her, tilting his hat. "Miss Catalina, I would be honored to have your autograph."

Catalina swallowed like there was a frog in her throat. She coughed. "Yes. Of course."

Mama ran to the back room, huffing and puffing. Carlotta never saw her move so fast, returning and throwing a piece of paper and pen at the singer.

Catalina scribbled her name with a shaky hand, jumped from the chair and scurried out the door with Mama holding it open for her.

Catalina stumbled across the road. The singer looked at Pacheco's car and the vanity front license plate that had the name *Salia*. Her shoulders shook like she was crying.

What made Carlotta's jaw open even wider was the fact that Mama never asked Catalina to pay, and normally she charged rich clients double. Nor had *Eternal Beauty* ever offered a free haircut to a new customer. Another first was the fact that Mama didn't save Catalina's hair cuttings to make a client doll. Mama actually swept the hair into the dust bin herself and then went to the back room, pretending to rummage around the supply closet. Mama was really burning Catalina's hair cuttings.

Carlotta examined Pacheco, never having seen the head of the Penitentes up close before. His moustache looked more like a smear of black fur above his lip with a Hitler-like white stripe down the center of his moustache, beneath his nose. He looked like a bull and acted like a bull in a China shop, waving his head around, demanding a haircut and shave.

"Okidoki. The razor is sharp as a pistol," Mama said, smiling at Pacheco like she wanted to slice his head off instead of his whiskers.

———————

35

November 1st and 2nd was *Dia de los Muertos* or *Day of the Dead*, a yearly tradition to remember and pray for deceased family and friends. Most of the villagers had been at Bones Creek Cemetery since yesterday and were drunk. Some were dressed as skeletons. A guitarist was strumming a tune, and a bunch of old ladies were singing sad ballads for the dead. Others were sitting on the graves, playing cards or dancing by the tombstones—partying with deceased friends and relatives who were buried six feet under.

Dark-Shadow held the string of a giant kite with a skeleton on it. He stood at the edge of the graveyard, watching with a somber face the villagers building their Altars of the Dead for adults since today was *All Souls Day*. Yesterday, the first of November, was *Day of the Little Angles* when dead kids and babies were exalted. Earlier, there had been a parade and Dark-Shadow missed it this year, having to help his grandfather with a healing. Dark-Shadow wished he knew who his mother was and where she was buried so he could decorate her grave.

The hair raised on his neck. Someone was watching him.

Across the way his step-cousin, Two-Face, and her band of witches, the Bat and Dead-Man-Walking glared at him.

Dark-Shadow gave them a half-hearted wave, his knees knocking together with fright.

Of course, they didn't wave back.

Dark-Shadow sighed with relief that they quickly lost interest in him. Today was Friday, one of the days of the week that is a Witches Sabbath when their magic is most powerful. The raggedy trio roamed the cemetery, taking notes, asking questions.

Dark-Shadow had a special relationship with the wind, which had been his play friend ever since he could remember. *Mister Wind* carried their words across the cemetery to his ears—"has anyone ever returned from the dead on *Dia de los Muertos?*" the three witches asked.

And the wind brought him the random responses of the crowd.

"*Dia de los Muertos* is celebrated to create a portal for the souls of the dead to cross over and visit."

"To this purpose, we speak to the ghosts as if they are still alive, with us."

"We remember the past. It is as if we are having a wake for all who are buried here."

"We bring an extra glass of beer, set the glass next to the tombstone and drink together."

"Sometimes, the glass on the grave is drained."

"The dead are listening."

"Can you not hear them?"

"The spirits are coming. They have heard our prayers."

A woman wearing a white fur coat drove up in a fancy car. People swarmed her, begging for an autograph from the famous opera singer, Catalina. The beautician, Marcelina, who knew his grandfather, accompanied the star. He had never seen anyone famous before and was shy to approach her. Instead, Dark-Shadow cocked his head in their direction, listening in.

"But how do you know the dead Samuel Stuwart?" someone asked her.

"He and I are...were old friends. We met back East," she said.

It seemed Dark-Shadow was the only one who wondered if Catalina was lying. She had to have been a young girl when she met the dead tycoon. *Maybe she's his illegitimate daughter. Perhaps she's the true heir and not that nephew who inherited the coal mine. Boy, she's pretty*, he thought.

"Please. No more autographs. Please leave Catalina alone to build her altar. See to your own dead," Marcelina said, shooing everyone away.

Samuel Stuwart's tombstone had its own private corner. Marcelina stood guard with her muscular arms crossed while Catalina scrubbed the elaborate headstone. She blanketed the grave with marigolds, which are considered the *flower of the dead*.

Marcelina set up a table draped with sky-blue silk. Catalina set out sugar and chocolate skulls with Samuel Stuwart's name on them. The women placed dozens of candles around the life-size tomb, so Dark-Shadow assumed they meant to stay at the grave until the next day.

Catalina leaned a painting against the tomb. Dark-Shadow had never seen a picture of the millionaire before and cocked his head at the image of a blonde, arrogant man dressed in a white suit, who looked as if he owned the world.

Catalina placed a pipe, a plate of steak, and glass of red wine in a gold-rimmed glass next to the painting, to entice his spirit to rise from his grave and share a meal with her. She added a loaf of *bread of the dead*, which is sweet egg bread, shaped like a skull. There was, also, a rabbit decorated with frosting to look like twisted bones.

Catalina stared at the picture, raising her own glass of wine, and speaking to the dead man. Dark-Shadow felt embarrassed to be listening in on such a private, heartbreaking, one-sided conversation, but he was enthralled by the famous singer.

Catalina wasn't the only one talking to a ghost. Most everyone was reminiscing with their dearly departed.

Catalina kissed the tombstone and Marcelina took her place to speak to the grave.

Dark-Shadow remembered Grandfather saying that the beautician was a medium so could channel the dead. No wonder the singer brought her along.

"You didn't really know me, Mr. Stuwart, but you loved my friend Salia so I am forever your friend. Oh, but you might remember my husband, Juan, who used to play baseball for your team," Marcelina said.

Catalina draped a blanket on the tombstone. "So you won't be cold." She sniffed his pipe, squeezing her eyes tightly.

Marcelina placed an arm around her shoulders. "But what about your dead son?"

Catalina shrugged her shoulders and spoke in a broken voice, near to tears. "I don't know what happened to my baby's ashes. Why don't you go to your papa's grave while I speak privately to Samuel?"

Marcelina walked over to the opposite corner of the cemetery, carrying a *Day of the Dead* doll with her. The dolls represent babies who have died.

Catalina knelt on the grave. "All that nonsense with Lucas Monterrey was before we were married, darling. My mother made me go with him. I kept my clothing on and…and Lucas ripped my clothes off. His glittering eyes were filled with such hatred for me, I thought Lucas might kill me, rather than go through with the deed. It was then that I realized he was no happier than me about our coupling. That Lucas, too, had been forced. And knowing this, made the act easier for me. I had to, else face my mother. Please understand, Samuel. And the other times, well…he tricked me."

Dark-Shadow found her words curious. *Actors are weird*, he thought, shrugging his small shoulders.

"I believed Lucas was you the other night, Samuel. Please forgive me. His magic...he is so powerful. Lucas promised to leave me alone, so you mustn't worry," she gently said to the painting. "Samuel, I'm so sorry about Bradley. I know how you loved the boy, but believe me, our son is better off without me. I was suffocating in Madrid, after you were killed. I had to get out. Please, Samuel, you've got to understand..."

Dark-Shadow suddenly felt uncomfortable, like he was trespassing on her heart.

She seemed to sense his feelings and looked up, staring at Dark-Shadow with haunted eyes. She shifted her gaze to the bag around his neck, shaped like an eagle, the bag with the umbilical cord once connecting him to the woman who gave birth to him. The dried-up umbilical cord was his long-life charm.

Catalina looked tortured, and she tore her gaze from Dark-Shadow, staring at the grave with a pale face.

Dark-Shadow believed the connection he felt when Catalina looked at him, was his imagination. She was a famous opera singer, after all, and he a mere small, Native American boy. He was a budding shaman, yes, but unimportant to all but his own Pueblo.

Whistling, Dark-Shadow went on his way along the Turquoise Trail, towards the village. He sang a song:

"Hush, my darling, if you never say a word.

Mama's going to kill you a mocking bird.

Hush, my darling, if you never cry.

I promise you, you will never die."

The skeleton on his kite waved about, being pushed by his friend, *Mister Wind*.

36

The Turquoise Trail, a dirt road snaking between Madrid and Santa Fe, was once the trading route between the New World and Spain. Thus, the road is buffed from feet, horse's hooves, wagon wheels and car tires. New Mexico is called the *Land of Enchantment*. Even though the turquoise and silver long ago mined by the Indians is no more, sunrise and sunset hold a magical quality, causing the Turquoise Trail to sparkle with gems.

But...the attention of travelers is arrested by the house at the bottom of Witch Hill, rising three stories and zigzagging downward to the left, the stench of roasted flesh still on the burnt wood. The house appears to be leaning against Witch Hill, the hill supporting the still-standing walls and holding it up. The exterior walls left standing are blackened, not an unusual sight in Madrid since the village's mainstay is coal. Indeed, the entire village of Madrid looks as if it has been smoked.

The house sits back a ways from the Turquoise Trail, yet close enough so that eyes from the house can watch all who ride by. Can hear every breath. Time every heartbeat. Smell each body odor—the wax in ones' ears, a dab of perfume on the neck. At least, that's what it feels like to travelers passing the house. Of course that's when the house had six eyes watching. Three witches—Felicita, Salia and La India. Yet even though all three ladies and that word is used loosely are now dead, the house seems even more malevolent. Those passing get a chill rippling up their spines that three witches died here.

Nowadays, the house gives off an even stronger feeling that someone watches from the house.

Watching. Debating...

Whether to pounce.

Dark-Shadow was running alongside the Turquoise Trail back to the Pueblo.

Dark-Shadow, help us, the house whispered.

The boy was so stunned that his left foot slid on the loose dirt and he fell.

He glanced at a three story house towering below a hill. He shook his head. It must have been his imagination that the house spoke to him. Inanimate objects can't communicate.

Can they?

Come hither, Dark-Shadow and play with me. Run to the top of the hill and catch me, if you can.

He licked his lips. Now Dark-Shadow knew for certain the hill did not speak to him through his ears. The words penetrated his mind. Some unseen force seemed to be guiding him—to this place. Now. On the *Day of the Dead*.

Dark-Shadow felt a déjà vu moment, yet he had never before been in this part of Madrid, at the northern end of the Turquoise Trail. Grandfather always went the long way, avoiding this path. Dark-Shadow felt certain he had seen this house. He had run to the top of the hill and played in the weeds with the rattlesnakes. But there had been no house then. He would have remembered a house such as this one...

In his dreams.

The house leaned toward the hill, resting its weary walls.

Weary walls? Now why would he use that odd term to describe a house? Weary? As if the house lived. As though the house was tired of waiting...

But what was the house waiting for?

Of course it was his imagination the house spoke. It must have been his old friend, the enchanted wind, whistling in his ear as he ran. Pushing against his back. Moving him closer...

To the house at the bottom of Witch Hill.

Dark-Shadow rarely came to Madrid, maybe once a year with Grandfather. He headed this way today to run with his kite and because it was a nice, sunny *Day of the Dead*.

He whistled with admiration at the house that was spanking brand new. Unlike the rest of the buildings in Madrid, the walls were white shimmering wood. Not blackened adobe or boards. The symmetry of the construction was perfect. Arched windows. Large engraved mahogany door. Chimneys sweeping up from the roof. A round attic window centered beneath red gables with a woman staring out. Dark-Shadow blinked his eyes and she vanished.

202

If ever I could build a house, it would look like this one, he thought and shocked himself for even thinking such a thing. Grandfather taught him not to be envious of others.

Still, he admired the white picket fence and nice yard with a shady cottonwood tree rising crookedly in the middle of luscious grass—an odd site in November.

I think I'll just rest against the trunk of that tree.

He was in no hurry. Grandfather left yesterday morning for the Taos Pueblo. A group of Taos Indians had returned from the *Region of the Dead* in the lower Rio Grande in Mexico and brought back enough peyote for their own needs and that of many of the other pueblos Taos traded with. Grandfather not only needed peyote for his medical practice, but the Pueblo needed peyote for their secret religious services. All at the Pueblo were members of the *Native American Church*, also, known as the *Peyote Religion*.

The monks closed Dark-Shadow's boarding school for a few days due to the heaters breaking. He returned home a couple hours after Grandfather left.

There is a friend in this house, he thought and was taken aback as to why he would think this. Dark-Shadow had no idea but felt oddly drawn to the house.

The picket gate creaked a *hello* in welcome, which he didn't find odd since *Mister Wind* often blew open doors for him.

Dark-Shadow settled his back against a tree trunk in the middle of the yard, closing his eyes. He concentrated on the house across from him, listening for any story the boards of the house might have to tell. He didn't think the house could communicate but if encouraged, these walls might speak, and so Dark-Shadow tried to draw the house out. He believed, like most Native Americans, that anything made from nature, such as boards that were once part of a tree, could speak and tell their history, if only one were willing to listen.

If this house could talk...

Dark-Shadow, help us.

He flicked open his eyes and stared at the *Help Wanted* sign hanging from the front door. Odd, he swore no sign was there before but then Dark-Shadow barely glanced at the door when he sat down. He was normally a stickler for details and normally nothing escaped his eagle-eye vision.

But there was something about this house. It was impossible to take in all the detail of such a grand house.

Earlier, the construction appeared perfect, the yard well manicured, but the house now looked like it could use a handy man. Mow the lawn. Trim the branches of the tree. Paint the trim of the wrap-around porch. The grass was wild. Everywhere else in Madrid the grass was winter-dead lawn, but this green lawn needed a mowing. The wealthy owners must still be watering the lawn to keep it green and growing.

But the curtains were drawn, the house appearing deserted, as if no one lived there in a very long time. Dusty cobwebs criss-crossed the heavy drapery. Oops. There were no drapes on the windows, merely cobwebs covering the panes, preventing an outsider from peeping through a window.

However, the cobwebs didn't mean someone couldn't peep out and spy. Even though the house seemed deserted, Dark-Shadow felt someone watching him from the house.

Over there. From the northwest window on the third floor.

There. Where the dust was cleared and a clean streak in the window made.

Whoever was watching him jumped back from the window.

A sigh came from the boards of the house. The boards must have moved, swelling from last night's rain. Considering how dry New Mexico is, the crusty mold between the boards of the house was odd. No other homes became moldy.

Where the heck did this house get so much moisture from so that the wood is moldy?

A creaking noise squeaked from the house.

He dismissed the sound as simple wood breathing.

And then Dark-Shadow heard another creak.

And another.

A continuous creaking, making his pulse beat faster.

He tiptoed around the house, to the back where the creaking noise was coming from from—an old lady moving in a rocking chair. The skinniest old lady he ever saw. She was skin and bones and sat with a shawl around her shoulders. She wore a skirt with wide, horizontal, rainbow-colored stripes. A bright yellow shawl made her grayish-brown complexion appear even pastier. Two long, white braids hung down the front of her shawl that she clasped together, holding the lace so tightly he could see the bones of her fingers. A two-headed snake was wrapped around her wrist but was a bracelet of such artisan that the snake appeared life-like, unlike the woman. Her eyes were red and irritated. She never blinked as she rocked, simply staring straight ahead, not once turning her head to Dark-Shadow.

She's Native American. Must be a servant, he thought.

He spoke to her in his native tongue but the woman didn't answer. She just kept rocking.

Staring straight ahead.

Rocking.

Staring straight ahead.

Rocking.

"Ma'am?" he said in slightly choppy English.

Perhaps she's deaf.

He was afraid to reach out a finger and poke her, for fear her bones would break.

The woman coughed, a dry hacking cough, and it looked like dust flew from her mouth.

Dark-Shadow stepped to the front of the rocker so that she might see him.

She looked right through him with glassy red, staring eyes.

Dark-Shadow knelt so she would be forced to see him—if she could see. "Would you like a glass of water?" he said.

She was not only blind but deaf, too.

She scratched at her chin. "We have been expecting you," was all she said, but more like spit the words from her mouth. Saliva dribbled down her chin making a mud-colored streak across her skin.

The hair rose at the nape of his neck, but then he dismissed his eerie feelings as silly. She was an old lady, crazy maybe.

"As you can see, the house is falling down around us," she said and began to whine.

She exaggerated. The house was not in that bad a shape, looking like it only needed a few minor repairs.

"You must rebuild the house," she said, slapping her hands against the chair arms, like it was all settled.

Dark-Shadow was looking to earn some money before heading back to school. He wanted to keep it a secret and use the money to purchase a gift for Grandfather's birthday. But a seven year-old boy rebuild this house? "I can paint and clean up the yard," he said.

The money she offered was good.

"Daughter," she yelled, surprising him with the force of her lungs.

The back door was flung open. A middle-aged woman with black hair and very white skin smiled at him affectionately. He guessed she carried a parasol to protect her complexion from the sun. She was tall. Regal. Dressed in the fashion of the last century. She was elaborately dressed in a feminine gown with lace all the way up to her ears. Her gown was blood red which was not a color normally seen in daytime. The blood red ruffles seemed to glide as she moved. Her dress matched the red lipstick on her wide lips.

The woman stood rather manly with her fists on her hips. She was more handsome than pretty with a hawkish nose. She devoured him with her hazel-colored eyes—even Spider-Woman never looked at Dark-Shadow like she wanted to eat him for dinner.

He took a step back, remembering his dreams of these women and their names—*Felicita and La India*.

His retreat seemed to amuse Felicita. Her eyes darted about like a lizard, yet Dark-Shadow knew that as her eyeballs rolled around, she was scanning him.

"You may call me Miss Felicita," she told him in a voice scratchy like fingernails against a chalk board. Felicita spoke in a tone telling him that all she was willing to share with him was her name. In fact, she seemed eager for him to know her name. She stood with her chin proudly thrust out.

This middle-aged woman fascinated him. The veins of her face were like a road map of a journey not yet finished.

The best feature Miss Felicita possessed was a mass of dark hair piled atop her head from which a single black rose seemed to anchor her hair to her head. Her big hair made her face look out of proportion. Her head seemed to teeter upon her neck. Indeed, her neck was wrapped with lace and linen and gave the appearance that the wrapping was used simply to anchor her head to her neck. When she moved, her head bobbed.

She was richly dressed in meticulous fashion that was at odds with a dirty piece of cloth wrapped around her neck. The linen had smudges of fingerprints, as if she tried to remove the wrapping. It appeared like her bobbing head was bandaged to her neck.

I hope she doesn't ask me to remove the linen. Dark-Shadow opened his eyes wide as he remembered a dream he had of Felicita. She had begged him to remove the wrapping and when Dark-Shadow did, her head rolled down her shoulders, laughing and bouncing on the floor.

"Do you believe in fate, young Man? How destinies are woven together? How the future is revealed in dreams?" Felicita said.

He nodded his head that yes, of course, he believed. He was a shaman. Well, he would one day be a shaman and dreams and visions were at the core of the shamanic life.

"Well, you are a salvation, my boy, as my mother-in-law here has said. We are two old women in need of a pair of strong arms."

"You're not so old, and I'm really not that strong yet. But when I grow up…"

"Already you have won my heart, boy. I will cut out my heart from my chest and feed you my heart for dinner," Felicita offered, smiling like she meant it.

"Don't do that!"

"Ah, you have a soft heart, which can be useful."

"I just need to earn some money to purchase Storm-Chaser a gift for his birthday."

"You coming to Witch Hill will be our little secret then," she said, chuckling and wringing her hands with pleasure.

"I can only work for you this week though. I'm not in school because the heaters broke down," he said.

"Ah, you're a big strong school boy of nearly seven. I'm sure you can handle any work. Open the door and go into the house then."

Felicita peered at his hand, as if willing him to reach for the door handle. It seemed Dark-Shadow must open the door to the house. The choice must be his.

He yanked open the door and she sighed contentedly.

"Isn't she coming into the house?" he said, pointing to the old lady in the rocking chair with the sun shining in her eyes. It was a wonder she didn't scratch her dry eyeballs out.

"No. She rocks."

"She rocks?"

"That is what she does. She rocks and guards the house."

"Like a dog?"

"No. Like a snake. You are much too soft for your own good," Felicita said, sounding impatient. "Go on inside the house. There is much work to be done."

For just a moment, he thought about Storm-Chaser warning him about dark forces. He snorted—these were two harmless old ladies in need of his help. Thus, Dark-Shadow slammed the door behind them, trapping himself in Felicita's kitchen and the house at the bottom of Witch Hill.

On the porch, the chair began to rock again, creaking, sounding like a rattlesnake's tail.

The porch boards made a noise like a hiss.

The chair was now empty, rocking by itself.

———

37

Felicita pointed out to Dark-Shadow the work needed around the house and the yard. He did a few little jobs and then returned the next day, and the day after that.

It was his last day and she led him up the stairs, to the second floor, to a small bedroom. The room was not elaborately furnished like the rest of the house. It had only a small bed and dresser, looking more like a jail cell than bedroom. Indeed. There was a depressive air about the room, as if someone was once imprisoned here.

"My daughter's room. I always wanted a son but all I got was a worthless, heartless, disobedient girl. I would like you to board this room up," she said in a flat voice.

He pounded some boards across the door, sealing the room shut from any intruders. As if anyone would intrude upon Miss Felicita. She was a cold fish, that one. Try as she might to make him feel at ease by being friendly, Dark-Shadow couldn't help but feel she was judging him. Her haughtiness, her display of superiority made it seem like any smile or attention she lavished upon him should make Dark-Shadow feel lucky. And the way she treated her mother-in-law. He was raised to respect his elders and to be kind and giving, even to Spider-Woman. Miss Felicita had no manners. She was rude and even cruel to her mother-in-law.

Like she did every day, Miss Felicita invited him into the kitchen for lunch. And like every day, he ate while she devoured him with her eyes, twirling her finger inside an empty cup.

And just like every day, he sipped his tea and grew sleepy.

Each day he seemed to be sleepier than the day before.

Today, Dark-Shadow was so sleepy after drinking his tea that his head fell and hit the table.

Felicita grabbed a handful of her grandson's hair and yanked Dark-Shadow's head up.

His eyes stared back at her, unseeing.

Dark-Shadow wasn't dead. The tea she had been giving him, stronger and stronger each day, acted as a tranquilizer and helped build up his system so he could tolerate a strong dosage—anyone else would be dead from the amount he drank.

"I will not make the same mistake with you as I did with Storm-Chaser. I offered him power, but he refused. You I do not leave a choice," she hissed.

Felicita released Dark-Shadow so that his forehead hit the table with a thump.

"Be right back," she told him, winking.

He lay there, paralyzed, his head on the table.

Felicita left Dark-Shadow in her kitchen and went outside. She skipped over to two large trees that had a rope tied between the trunks. She held a pink parasol over her head and jumped the rope while it magically turned. She sang:

"Hush, my darling, if you never say a word.

Grandma's going to kill you a mocking bird.

Hush, my Boy, if you never cry.

I promise you, you will never die."

Felicita skipped to her apple orchard, humming.

Row after row of dead apple trees lined up behind the house, their branches dry and brittle.

Dead center in the middle of the orchard grew a tree with roots sticking up from the ground like snakes. This tree's branches and trunk were black in color with spindly branches reaching out. A rotting apple hung from one branch, the only apple in the orchard.

Felicita picked the last apple from her orchard. "I have been saving you, my darling, for something special," she told the apple, kissing the fruit of temptation.

Felicita rubbed the fruit against the red lace of her mantilla which cascaded from her head and was held in place by a black rose. After she finished rubbing the apple, the fruit was shiny red and luscious looking.

Humming softly, she skipped back to the house, singing, "The snake seduced the first woman, Eve, with an apple. And was not Eve the first witch, because she bewitched the first man, Adam? Wasn't this why man and woman were thrown out of the Garden of Eden because God has no tolerance for witches?"

"Bah! What need have we for God?"

Dark-Shadow still lay in the kitchen with his head upon the butcher table.

Humming, she shoved a miniature black rose in the core of the apple.

"It is destiny that you will never be a great shaman, Grandson. The Reincarnation did not return to lead the Pueblo people. You have returned to lead the elite. You are the reincarnation of Montezuma, who was no shaman but an Aztec and a great witch. And the Esperanza line began with the reincarnation of the Aztec goddess, Tonantzin, fallen sister of Tezcatlipoca. Tonantzin drugged and seduced her brother. She became pregnant and her baby stillborn. In revenge, Tezcatlipoca stole their dead baby, and hid the corpse from his sister."

"Like a thief in the night, Tonantzin then stole other babies from their sleep, leaving a sacrificial knife in their cradles. She wept all night for the children she stole because none of the babies were her own dead child. In the morning, Tonantzin walked into the river and was not seen again until the moon rose in mid-sky. In the dead of night, she leaves her watery grave to steal more babies and again weep for the missing children."

"Tonantzin wept for the children of Tezcatlipoca, just as her reincarnation, La Llorona, mother of the *Sisterhood of the Black Rose*, still weeps."

"Well, weep no more! Emperor Montezuma has returned to us!"

And Felicita threw up her arms in triumph and let out a war cry.

"Mother," she yelled at the porch, "I need your help. The boy is big."

La India lifted her weary bones from the rocking chair, rattling over to the kitchen.

They each took an arm and a leg, carrying Dark-Shadow out of the house and placing him beneath the large cottonwood tree.

"You still smell like a corpse, my dear. All the toilet water hasn't helped," Felicita told La India.

She ran to her rocking chair, her bones rattling.

Felicita gently patted Dark-Shadow's face.

The boy was stubborn, refusing to wake up.

She pulled her arm back and slapped him hard across the cheek.

He flicked open his eyes. Dark-Shadow didn't seem to feel the slap.

"You have been dreaming," she said in a hypnotic voice.

He blinked his eyes.

"It's alright. A big boy like you needs his rest. You have not finished growing," Felicita cooed.

He rubbed his stomach. "I feel such emptiness inside."

Felicita held out to Dark-Shadow the most appetizing-looking apple.

He licked his lips and took the fruit.

It was his choice. His.

With eyes glittering with excitement, she watched her grandson take bite after bite of the apple from her orchard.

Before he could spit out something choking him, she slapped his back, causing him to swallow the black rose.

"I'm so stuffed I can't possibly take another bite," he said.

"Yes, you are stuffed with the thing kings are made of."

"Thank you."

"My pleasure and you are so welcome," Felicita added, displaying her own rare manners. She laughed and gloated. She did it! Felicita finally beat that old bastard Storm-Chaser, her arch enemy. Her great love and great hate. He had been her Adam and she his Eve. Only it did not turn out well for either of them.

"What a damned week, but all things must come to an end," she said, slapping her thighs and offering him some cash.

Dark-Shadow pocketed his money.

"You are like the grandson we never had," they both cooed at him.

La India removed the snake bracelet from her arm, kissing the two heads of the cobras. She sighed deeply, handing the bracelet to him. "I want you to have this, my boy."

"Wow! My grandfather has rattlers but no cobras. You don't find cobras in these parts."

"You must never show the bracelet to your grandfather," Felicita said.

"Keep the bracelet hidden else Spider-Woman will claim the bracelet as her own," La India said.

"You're right. Thanks."

"You are a good boy. Use the bracelet wisely," they both said.

He placed the snake bracelet around his wrist, and a power surged through his body. Dark-Shadow smiled at the heads of the cobras that appeared to be sleeping. "It seems like the snake is real."

"Yes, cobras are deadly."

He stroked the twin heads of the cobras and they purred at his touch.

Felicita removed a black ring from her index finger. "I know this ring cannot compete with the majesty of a King Cobra, but this ring has been in my family for generations. It would touch me deeply if you would take the ring."

She placed the ring upon his finger, lowered her head and kissed his hand, touching her forehead to the base of his fingers.

There was a red skull on the ring. The skull appeared to be a ruby, but the color in the stone circulated.

He bounded down the steps of the porch. Dark-Shadow continued up the Turquoise trail, never looking back at the house at the bottom of Witch Hill.

Behind him, the house faded and in its place stood, not the architectural dream he discovered when he stumbled upon the house, but a house no longer shimmering white in color but blackened from fire. The east side of the house had all three stories still intact, but the west side of the house was jagged with large chunks of the house burned to ashes. The roof was now smoked. Only a few of the gables of the roof were intact. The rest of the house was open at the top, the chimneys crumbling to dust.

And on the porch two empty chairs rocked, fading and then appearing.

Fading then appearing...

The chairs stopped rocking.

All was as before.

Merely silence from the house at Witch Hill.

But from the third story, east corner window, a smudge appeared in the cobwebs covering the glass.

And so the house at the bottom of Witch Hill watched and waited.

Watching.

Waiting.

The house was patient. Look how long Witch Hill waited for the Reincarnation.

Centuries...

Watching.

Waiting.

———

38

A dusty truck barreled along the windy Turquoise Trail, dirt flying around screeching, balding tires. The back of the pickup was filled to capacity with a bit of clothing and a potpourri of items used in magic.

Two-Face drove the truck which rolled towards Santa Fe and I-25.

Dead-Man-Walking wore ultra-dark sunglasses to shield his reddish albino eyes from the sun. He rode shotgun.

The tiny Bat, whose head barely touched the handle of a grocery cart, bounced in the middle of the dead man and Two-Face. He could see at night like a bat, but in daylight he, too, couldn't see very well. In his lap was the *Day of the Dead* notes the Bat scribbled a few days ago at the cemetery.

The trio were headed to Columbus, New Mexico and the border of Mexico, to the *Region of the Dead*—Nopala, a supernatural place, teetering in the mountains of Mexico. It is said that in Nopala is a gateway to the sacred place where Tezcatlipoca, Patron of the Witches, lives. In a lot of ways, the trio felt like Christopher Columbus embarking on a journey to discover the New World. Their intent—resurrect Jefe and bring him back to Santo Domingo Pueblo.

Two-Face normally wasn't so feminine but she dusted off her black rose which now lay on her head, rather flat. She was a long-standing member of the *Black Enchanting Rose*, one of the thirteen covens of the *Sisterhood of the Black Rose*. La Llorona, mother of the *Sisterhood of the Black Rose* is, also, found in the *Region of the Dead*.

Lastly, in the *Region of the Dead* lives a powerful witch called the Oraculo, who is a soothsayer. The trio hoped the Oraculo could tell them who the Reincarnation was and where he lived.

And so the truck wobbled on the Turquoise Trail with Two-Face honking at cars and screaming at drivers to "Get out of our fucking way!"

Dead-Man-Walking yelled, "Hey, Two-Face, isn't that your little step-cousin?"

She slammed on the brakes and jumped from the truck.

"Hey, you! I'm talking to you, scumbag!" Two-Face screamed.

Dark-Shadow stood frozen, staring at her with scared eyes.

She shoved him.

He fell on the ground, looking up at the three witches.

"Oh, look at the baby," Two-Face cooed, kicking dirt in his face.

"Why aren't you in school, boy?" Dead-Man-Walking asked.

He shrugged his shoulders.

"Can't you talk, dummy? Let's use some magic on him," the Bat said, laughing. "Do a supernatural removal of his testicles."

"What balls? Come on, boy, get up and fight like a man instead of the pussy you are," Two-Face snarled.

Dead-Man-Walking grabbed him by the arm pits, forcing Dark-Shadow to his feet.

"Ouch, you're hurting me," the little boy said.

Dead-Man-Walking shoved Dark-Shadow, and he fell to his knees.

Two-Face slapped him, cutting his lip with her turquoise ring.

The Bat danced like a boxer, excited by the blood and Dark-Shadow crying.

Dead-Man-Walking moved to the shade and stood with his arms crossed, yawning.

Two-Face raised a fist to strike Dark-Shadow again and quick as lightning, the boy grabbed her wrist, twisting her arm behind her back until she cried out. He let her go, kicking her in the knee.

The Bat took out a knife from his moccasins.

Dark-Shadow glared at him, struck his head back like a cobra, and hissed.

The Bat held out his knife, stabbing at Dark-Shadow who dodged the sharp blade.

Dark-Shadow narrowed his eyes at the knife handle.

Dead-Man-Walking moved from the tree watching with his mouth hanging open at the knife shaking in the Bat's hand.

Dark-Shadow turned the knife with his eyes, so that the blade was pointing at the Bat.

The Bat backed away, trying to shake the knife loose from his hand.

The tip of the knife touched the Bat's stomach, and the knife hung suspended in mid-air.

"Enough!" Dead-Man-Walking yelled.

Dark-Shadow removed his gaze from the knife, and the blade clattered to the ground.

The Bat touched his bleeding stomach, crying out in pain.

Two-Face examined the Bat. "Just a flesh wound she mumbled," and darted her eyes at Dark-Shadow who appeared confused.

"I'm sorry. I don't know what happened," Dark-Shadow said, and he was trembling.

"Where do you suppose the kid learned that trick with the knife?" Two-Face said.

"I don't think it was a trick. I believe the boy's confusion, but he is being tutored as a shaman," Dead-Man-Walking said.

"Maybe he's learning more magic on his own. Or Spider-Woman is teaching him," the Bat said.

"The shaman has taught you well, Dark-Shadow. What other tricks do you know?" Dead-Man-Walking said.

"I swear I didn't do anything!"

"Maybe it was you, Dark-Shadow, who made my father vanish," Two-Face growled.

Dead-Man-Walking punched her arm. "Don't be stupid, Two-Face. He was a baby. Want a ride, Dark-Shadow?" he said with hooded eyes.

"You aren't headed towards Santo Domingo," Dark-Shadow said.

"So what? Come and hang out with us. See what it's like to be with real men," he said and winked at Two-Face who blew cigar smoke in Dark-Shadow's face.

"I must get home before my grandfather misses me," he said.

"That bastard killed my..."

Dead-Man-Walking slammed a hand over her mouth. "Go, Dark-Shadow. We can play another day."

"Yeah. Go home to Grandpa before I kick your ass," the Bat said, puffing his chest out.

Dark-Shadow spun on his heels and took off running on the Turquoise Trail.

"The brat's got a long walk ahead of him," the Bat said, laughing.

"Forget about the kid," Two-Face said, yanking the truck door open. "We must be on our way to Mexico."

Belinda Vasquez Garcia

Dark-Shadow turned where the road winded, disappearing from view. At about the same time he vanished, an eagle soared in the sky, flying in the direction of the Pueblo.

———————

Sneak Peek at
RISE OF THE BLACK ROSE
(Land Of Enchantment Book 3)

Part One

LOVE MAKES FOOLS OUT OF EVERY MAN

Chapter One

November 30, 1940
Albuquerque, New Mexico

A red-haired, brown-eyed, freckled policeman paced in front of the Albuquerque national bank. It was midnight and a lone car rolled up Central Avenue, headed east towards the mountains dimly lit by a crescent moon. The street was now deserted, and the policeman clenched in his hand what looked like an ordinary-looking rock. He ran a hand over his face. His head vanished, followed by his neck until slowly, the policeman evaporated into fog.

His fog swirled up the arched windows of the first and second stories of the bank, waving across the roof like smoke.

His fog danced across the roof tiles, wrapping around the center air conditioner and, whoosh, vanishing between the coils.

His fog traveled through the air conditioner ducts like a snake, seeping through an air vent in the bank.

His fog hissed through the vent like steam, swirling in the bank lobby, traveling in the air, up to a vent which provided fresh air in the vault.

The fog spun like a small tornado. A pair of boots formed in the fog, followed by pants, a shirt, neck and head, until the policeman stood in full

218

uniform, rocking dizzily. He gripped in his hand his plain-looking rock which was actually magnetic. The policeman grinned at the stacks of money in the vault.

He filled a huge bag with cash.

With bulging muscles, he turned the large, circular handle of the vault door and strolled into the bank lobby, whistling.

The policeman walked up to a corner and smiled at a security camera. He flipped a bird with his middle finger while mouthing the "F..." word. He took his time towards the exit, swinging the bag of cash.

He swaggered out of the bank with the alarms screaming behind him from the open doors.

Three police cars roared up Central Avenue.

The red-headed policeman ran, laughing, and dodging a couple of bullets.

He darted into an alley and clutched his shape-shifting rock, a rare piedra imán whose magic has been known since roman times. He spun until he transformed into a white falcon.

A police car screeched into the alley and the falcon soared over the car roof, shaking its beak like the bird was chuckling.

The flacon flew downtown to the Franciscan hotel and circled the American flag flying from the pueblo-style building. The falcon landed on its claws behind the hotel and hopped in a circle. When the bird stopped spinning, a black-haired man wobbled. He was taller than the red-haired policeman had been. The bird had turned into a much more handsome man with a five-o'clock shadow, a steely look in his lime-green eyes and a chiseled jaw.

The man shook his dizzy head and walked around to the entrance of the hotel, swinging the bag of hundred dollar bills in his hand.

"Good evening, Mr. Monterrey," the hotel clerk said.

"Evening," Lucas answered.

"May I help with your bag?"

"Nope. It's just laundry."

"More laundry?"

"That was my dirty laundry last night. This is the clean laundry," Lucas said and strolled into the bar.

He set his bag on the floor and straddled a stool. "Whiskey," he told the bartender. "A bottle."

Lucas carried the bottle, along with his "laundry" to his room. He dumped the cash on the bedspread and lay on his side, bouncing on the mattress. To most people, he was a traveling salesman. To some Lucas considered special friends; he was the head of the Las Cruces witches. His enemies knew all too well that he was a warlock most didn't want to mess with. The few who had been foolish enough to try, well, they didn't live to tell the tale.

Lucas wasn't as power hungry as some witches, but if forced to kill another witch he, naturally, took their power at the moment of death. Thus, he was one of the few elite who could shape-shift into inanimate objects, such as smoke and fog. Of course, he, also, needed the magnetic magic of his piedra imán for any transformations.

Lucas screwed open the bottle and took a few swallows. He leaned against the headboard, frowning at the loose money. Hell, loose was a meaningful way to term the stolen cash on his bed. He felt like a loose man, a whore thief. Lucas couldn't believe he was using his magic to become a bank robber, just to get the cash to impress a cold-hearted woman. Okay, so he had to admit the charade was fun, along with the bank robbing, and making fools of the police. Lucas had been extremely bored until Eva la Catalina trampled on his heart.

Lucas shook his big head like a dog and snorted with disgust—robbing banks for love of a woman who hated his guts!

He nicknamed her *Cat*—her claws ripped his heart to ribbons.

She called him *bastard*.

Lucas whispered *sweetheart* into her ear.

She screamed *creep* at him.

He called her *darling*.

Cat yelled at him that he was an *asshole*.

They both hissed at each other "enemy", their families feuding for centuries, starting in Spain and spilling over to New Mexico. Cat was, also, descended from a long line of witches.

Lucas took out a picture from his wallet that Cat didn't know he possessed. He had snapped a camera when she lay sleeping peacefully beside him. Not only was her body naked, but so was her face, revealing the woman Cat really was.

She was naked on her stomach with her reddish curls sweeping her rising buttocks. Her sensuous lips smiled with satisfaction. Her long, feathery lashes brushed her pink cheeks. She had perfectly arched eyebrows above a small, slightly turned-up nose. Her iridescent skin glowed with a peachy sheen. She had beautiful cheekbones and a kissable cleft on her chin.

Lucas frowned at a black rose in the picture that was on the nightstand on Cat's side of the bed. He had not meant to include the rose in the photograph. Cat was a member of the *Black Enchanting Rose*, one of 13 covens of the *Sisterhood of the Black Rose*. Lucas belonged to the *Castle de Luna Negra* [Castle of the Dark Moon], one of 13 covens of the *Brotherhood of the Castle*. In most cases, there was bad blood between the *Brotherhood* and the *Sisterhood*.

Lucas lightly flicked the photo with his finger and smiled, knowing that wherever Cat was, she felt a slight pounding on her forehead. He chuckled, waiting a moment, in case she ran for an aspirin for her "headache".

He eyed her buttocks rising from beneath her reddish curls, feeling aroused.

Many times, Cat accused him of using sex magic against her. Hell, he might as well since she believed him guilty. Lucas put the picture to his tongue and caressed the buttocks, licking where her legs met, imagining Cat writhing on the bed, moaning.

Suddenly, he remembered and dropped the picture like it burned him. Cat was most likely thinking of another man while she writhed on the bed, screaming in passion, regardless of the headache he had given her by knocking her picture in the head.

Damn her to hell! She gave him more than a pounding head. His groin pounded so hard, he thought he might explode.

Lucas groaned and slammed his head against the headboard, breathing deeply, his chest rising painfully. There was a lot of harm he could do with Cat's image, and Lucas had been tempted many times. Perhaps, only Cat's death would free him from the misery of wanting her.

"Well, my sweet love, any magic is fair in love and war," he said to the picture and then spit on her beautiful face.

His heart squeezed in his chest that his spit dampened Cat's cheeks, which she probably thought were her tears—tears for another man!

"I should just rip the picture in two, right where her heart is and finally be done with her!"

But Lucas couldn't imagine a world without Cat. Quick, he cleaned off the photo so he wouldn't damage her picture.

He sighed deeply, setting her photo on the pillow next to him.

He kicked off his boots, and yawned.

Lucas still had a hell of a lot of banks to rob so he could get the cash to buy a house, a fancy car, and plenty of money in the bank.

It took a lot of bills to compete with a dead man.

Lucas took another swallow of whiskey to help him sleep.

He lay on his side, his head resting on a pillow.

Lucas stared at the picture on the pillow beside him.

"Goodnight, my darling," he softly said. "Bitch."

ABOUT THE AUTHOR

Belinda Vasquez Garcia is a former Software Engineer and Web Developer. She holds a Bachelor's degree in Applied Mathematics from the University of New Mexico. She is a native of California and splits her time between New Mexico and Florida. She lives with her husband Bobby, dog Toby, and cat Shakespeare.

The first book in the *Land of Enchantment*, THE WITCH NARRATIVES REINCARNATION, is 2013 Best Fantasy INTERNATIONAL LATINO BOOK AWARDS Finalist and was 2012 Best Fantasy New Mexico / Arizona Book Awards Finalist. Her book, RETURN OF THE BONES, was a finalist for the Santa Fe Writers Project Literary Awards.

If you wish to know more about Belinda, please visit her website at
http://www.belindavasquezgarcia.com.

Belinda, also, has a blog at:
http://belindavasquezgarcia.com/blog.

If you wish to keep up with Belinda and her books, join her fan page on Facebook by liking *Belinda Vasquez Garcia*.
http://facebook.com/AuthorBelinda

She would be thrilled if you followed her on Twitter:
Belinda V. Garcia@magicprose
http://twitter.com/MagicProse

Lastly, she would like to thank you for purchasing *Ghosts of the Black Rose*.

Printed in Great Britain
by Amazon.co.uk, Ltd.,
Marston Gate.